Suburban Guerrillas

Suburban
Guerrillas

A Novel by Joseph Freda

W. W. NORTON & COMPANY
NEW YORK ■ LONDON

Printed in the United States of America
First Edition

The text of this book is composed in Goudy with the display
set in Eurostile Bold Extended and Modula Tall. Composed and
manufactured by the Maple-Vail Book Manufacturing Group.
Book design by Beth Tondreau Design / Robin Bentz.

Library of Congress Cataloging-in-Publication Data
Freda, Joseph, 1951–
Suburban guerrillas : a novel / Joseph Freda.
p.   cm.
I. Title.
PS3556.R366S8   1995
813'.54—dc20   94-36705

ISBN 0-393-03768-1

W.W. Norton & Company, Inc., 500 Fifth Avenue, New York, N.Y. 10110
W.W. Norton & Company Ltd., 10 Coptic Street, London WC1A 1PC

1 2 3 4 5 6 7 8 9 0

for Elise

CONTENTS

Suburban Guerrillas

King of the Straight and Narrow

Thursday afternoon and Ed Jacques had his big Mack running a straight seventy along the Mass Pike. The trailer was empty. He had just dropped a load of copier paper at General Electric in Albany, and now he was headed home. With the trailer empty, he could roll along no sweat, make the hills without down-shifting.

It was a beautiful afternoon in late May. The leaves had been out for two weeks; the western Massachusetts hillsides were a fresh green. The sun was shining. A breeze coming in the win-dow, country tunes on the radio. Straight and steady. No curves, no swerves. Ed kept the left front wheel twelve inches off the white line. Exactly twelve inches. Or eight, or six. What-ever. He had marked a gauge on his side mirror, and on these long runs he practiced holding the eighteen-wheel tractor and trailer on a steady course. With the white stripes peeling away under the twelve-inch mark, he could hold it this way for miles.

He had to. It was part of his training. Saturday was the annual Blessing of the Lawn Mower Fleet, and Ed had a title to defend. He was the reigning King of the Straight and Narrow, and he intended to hang on to his crown. Hurley, New Hampshire, had begun the festival in the early eighties as a civic-pride event and a fund-raiser for local nursing homes and day-care centers. Taking their lead from the Blessing of the Fishing Fleet in Gloucester, Massachusetts, the planners of the event scheduled a parade of lawn mowers, cutting competitions, garden tractor pulls, and, of course, the Blessing of the Fleet. They had clinics on Briggs & Stratton tune-ups and blade sharpening. They held a beauty contest, where the Turf Queen was crowned. But Ed's specialty was the Straight-Line Race, in which each contestant cut a straight swath across the middle of the town common. He had won the event for five years running, and he attributed his success to constant training, determination, and single-mindedness.

So on his daily run to Albany or Poughkeepsie or Augusta, Maine, where he delivered bulk paper to GE and Union Carbide and Digital, he'd practice for the race by keeping his big Mack a given distance from the white line: fifteen inches, twelve, or on empty stretches of road, six.

He dropped the semi at the terminal and drove home in his own pickup. He took his lunch pail inside and shouted halloo to Thelma. Her muffled "Hi!" came up from the laundry room. Ed went out to cut the front yard. He liked to get the front done on Thursday evenings, because it was easy to do, and it was mostly what the neighbors saw. Then he'd do the backyard on Friday, and he'd be all set for the weekend. The residents of Monadnock Street took pride in their properties, keeping their houses painted, the yards trimmed, the driveways freshly sealed. No broken pickets went unfixed, no car unwashed, no fallen leaves unraked. And of

all the well-kept properties on the street, the most well-kept property belonged to Ed. He took great pride in it. He did not have one
of the great Victorians or stately four-squares. His cape, though,
was nicely set off with hemlocks and lilacs, flower beds and rock
gardens. But the *pièce de résistance* was his lawn. Ed had the green-
est, thickest lawn on the street, the result of a rigid schedule of
fertilizing and seeding and thatching, of aerating and mowing and
raking. He watered it in the summer, limed it in the fall. He
dreamed about it all the long New Hampshire winter, pictured it
dormant under its covering of snow, each individual grass plant
building up its energy for the green tumult of spring.

When he finished the front yard, Ed went in for dinner. Thelma
was just setting out a pot roast.

"Good run today?" she asked.

"Ye-ah, good run. Clear sailing out there on the pike." He anticipated her next question. "Easy day tomorrow. Pick up a trailer in
Boston, run it down to Hartford."

"That's good," she said, and joined him at the table. "I thought
we might have the kids over after the festivities on Saturday. Maybe
a weenie roast."

"Sure," Ed said. "That'd be fun." They'd been doing it for years,
ever since Ed had been running in the race, so why stop now?

"I'll pick up some stuff, then." She ladled gravy over her meat
and potatoes. "Gert Bartolomeo says Minnie Stark is putting her
property out back up for sale."

"Oh, I don't believe that," he said. "Fred would never have let
that go."

"That's what Gert says."

"Aaah—you listen to those hens long enough, you'll believe
any foolishness."

The hen party—that's what Ed called Thelma's group of friends.
Gert Bartolomeo, Minnie Stark, Mrs. Bain. Get together and cluck
about this neighbor, cackle over that town bigwig. No thanks.

Next morning, he left for work just as he did every day: at four
o'clock, parking lights on, engine off, rolling out of his driveway

and down Monadnock Street. The street ran downhill, and he always rolled without his engine because he did not want to wake his neighbors. Ed Jacques was a considerate man, and he respected his neighbors' peace. Each morning he passed their houses—the Vanns, the Rosens, the Bains—and he thought of them sleeping.

To him sleep seemed like a pool into which they all slipped at night. Their heartbeats slowed; their souls commingled. Dreams were the proof. In the community of sleep, he and his neighbors shared visions, entwined emotions. They could be happy together or sad, angry or afraid, but they were in sleep as they were in their waking lives: a community. Toward morning they began to rise to the surface of the sleep pool, like dream trout rising to the new day, until one by one they broke through.

He happened to break through first every day. And he knew who was second. He had seen her, or at least her shadow, behind her shade.

Mrs. Stevens lived in one of the big Victorian houses halfway down the street. One morning, as he rolled along in darkness, he had noticed the light in a second-story room. He saw a shadow move behind the shade. It turned sideways: a woman. She bent, raised a leg, and in a motion that was both efficient and languid, she pulled on her hose.

And then he was past. He had never seen a woman other than his wife perform that motion, and even though he didn't really see Mrs. Stevens, only her shadow, it had left him giddy. Wow. Mrs. Stevens should move that lamp.

He always thought of her as Mrs. Stevens, even though he knew her name: Susie. The other neighbors, those who knew the Stevenses, called her Susie. Susie and Bob. The nice young couple in the white Victorian. No kids. Bob was a marketing hotshot at Digital. Susie worked for the airlines. Flew out of Logan. That's why she was the second person awake on the street. She drew early flights, and it was an hour's drive to Boston.

She was Hawaiian or half Chinese or some mix he could not decipher. Her face was full and round, with Asian eyes and high cheekbones, framed by thick, black hair cut bluntly at the neck. For some reason he could not explain, her face reminded him of a night in Korea. After a day of being sniped at from across a frozen field, the moon came up over the snow, full and beaming, drawing a silver road out to the horizon. That was almost forty years ago.

On his way home from Hartford, running the long, open stretch of I-84 in northern Connecticut, he held the Mack six inches off the white line for two straight miles, two and a half. He was approaching the third mile when "Your Cheating Heart" came over the radio. He couldn't help it, he thought of Mrs. Stevens. Her face, round and moonlike, drifted into his thoughts, and for a moment he imagined her beside him in the cab, the wind blowing her hair, the sun slanting in on her shoulder. She'd enjoy the ride, the music. She'd look shyly over at him, smile a quiet Asian smile. And at the next rest area—he reached out and embraced the air above the steering wheel, pulled a phantom Mrs. Stevens to him.

The truck wobbled. He straightened it out. Jesus! Damned fool! Grabbing at the air like a lovesick boy. What would his buddies at the terminal think? What would Thelma think?

When he got home, he cut the backyard. Then he sprayed the little tractor with the hose, rubbed the dried grass off the blade housing, scrubbed the film of grease off the engine. Thelma came out with a beer and a sandwich, and he ate while he worked. He wanted his tractor in tip-top shape for the parade tomorrow. He polished the baby-moon wheel covers, waxed the yellow hood and fenders. He affixed a pair of CB antennas to the tractor, and finally gave it his special touch: he bolted a chrome Mack bulldog—the hood ornament off his big rig—to the front of the mower.

After he had showered and pulled on a pair of loose shorts, Ed went out to the yard. The grass was damp and prickly. He flexed his toes in it. When they were younger, he and Thelma used to drag a blanket outside at night and make love in the freshly cut grass. Thelma was always convinced that their oldest girl had been conceived under the crab apple tree, so she had insisted that her name be Eve. He wondered what Thelma would do if he tried to drag her out to the apple tree now. Probably go along, probably go along. He imagined cutting through his neighbors' backyards to Mrs. Stevens's house, standing in the shadows and watching for movement behind her shades.

He forced his thoughts away from her. He flexed his toes in the grass, felt the cool, pure energy of the earth entering through the soles of his feet. So much to be thankful for, such a good life. He had never thought he deserved much. When his father died, Ed had had to drop out of school. Ninth grade. He worked in the quarry and took care of his mother and brothers. Then came Korea, and he learned to drive trucks in the army. Ever since, trucking had been good to him. He'd earned a good wage, had seen some countryside. He was the traveler in the marriage, the adventurer. Thelma didn't like to stray far from home. She walked all over town every day, but even when she drove, she got no farther than Nashua or Manchester. To her, his daily travels made him seem seasoned and world-wise. The cities he saw: Albany, Burlington, Bangor! And the great arteries of commerce: the New York State Thruway, the Mass Pike, I-95! No man knew these cities and highways like her husband. He had heard the pride in her voice when she repeated his road stories to her friends.

But, he thought, it's not so much. After thirty-five years of running the roads, you get to know what's over the next hill. Mrs. Stevens, now, *she's* got some horizons! In one day she could cover as many miles as he could in a week. Every day she jetted off to places he'd only heard about or seen on television: Kansas City, Albuquerque, Salt Lake. Seattle, maybe. He pictured her in the air-conditioned comfort of an airliner, smiling graciously and passing out cool drinks to the passengers. He tried to picture her horizons: the clouds, the curve of the earth, the mysterious darkness of the stratosphere.

Although he knew he should go inside, Ed slipped on his moccasins and headed down the street. In the gathering twilight, house lights began to snap on. He could hear his neighbors settling into their evenings: dishes clinking at the Vanns', a piano scale tinkling at the Rosens', a television droning at the Bains'. How he loved this street! He loved the older houses and the big maple trees, the bikes strewn across lawns, the quiet rain of sprinklers. He loved meeting his neighbors on these walks, greeting them and making small talk. He felt safe on this street. He felt at home.

As he neared the big Victorians down the way, he noticed a couple approaching. In the waning light, he couldn't quite make them out, but then his heart kicked as he identified her graceful figure. Mrs. Stevens and her husband, Bob, out for an evening stroll.

"Evening," he said.

"Hello," Bob Stevens said.

"Nice night," he said, and would have passed on, since he didn't know them, really, except to say hello. But some impulse stopped him—a glimpse of her face, almost luminous in the afterglow of sunset.

"You folks going down to the festivities tomorrow?"

They looked at each other, and Mrs. Stevens asked, "What festivities?"

Her voice was surprisingly girlish.

"The Blessing of the Fleet," he said.

"The Blessing of the Fleet?" Bob Stevens asked.

"The lawn mower fleet. Oh, it's quite the shindig. They have—"

"The Blessing of the *Lawn Mower Fleet?*" Bob Stevens cut him off, laughing.

"That's wild!" Mrs. Stevens said. She laughed a high, girlish laugh.

"It's quite the shindig," Ed said. Boy, they'd lived here, what—two years, and didn't know about the Blessing of the Fleet? "There's a parade of lawn mowers, and—"

"A parade of *lawn mowers?*" Bob Stevens asked.

Mrs. Stevens laughed again. Ed risked a look at her.

"There's a parade, and tractor pulls, and the whole town turns out. You folks—" his glance included them both, so Bob Stevens wouldn't suspect anything—"you folks ought to come down."

Bob Stevens laughed. "I'll be in Chicago tomorrow. Sorry I'll have to miss this grand event."

This was the most Ed had even spoken with the Stevenses. He decided he didn't like Bob.

"Well, just thought I'd let you know," he said, and began to edge past.

The Stevenses began to move too.

"Thank you," Mrs. Stevens said. And after a step, "What time does it start?"

"Twelve noon," Ed said, and they parted ways. But he carried with him that last image, the way she had turned her head over her shoulder to look at him. It was as languid as the motion he had seen in her window that morning, and it left his heart at a fast idle.

Exactly at eleven-thirty, the King of the Straight and Narrow rolled out of his driveway. He didn't want to raise dust all over his polished machine, so he rolled under gravity power just as he did with his truck every morning.

Ahead of him, several neighbors were beginning to stroll towards town. They hailed him as he approached.

"Hey, Ed!" hollered old Mr. Bain. "Keep it on the straight and narrow!"

"You bet!" he replied.

"No broken eggs, Ed," called Marisse Vann.

"No broken eggs," he promised.

The object of the Straight-Line Race was to get from one side of the town common to the other in the shortest time with the straightest line. And stay as close as possible to a row of brown hen's eggs, one row of eggs per competitor. Of course, if you came too close, or deviated from your path, you'd break an egg. Failure would be clearly marked.

Ed had not broken an egg in five years, and each year he had tried to run closer and faster. The straight part he had down cold. Due to his practice in the big rig, and his ability to concentrate, his run across the town common was always the straightest. Last year they had shot it with a transit, and his swath, a mere two inches off the eggs, didn't deviate more than an inch from one end to the other. His goal this year was to come within an inch of the eggs.

When he passed the Stevenses' house he kept his eyes straight ahead and forced himself not to glance at the upstairs window. The place seemed pretty quiet. Maybe Mrs. Stevens was flying.

Downtown the crowd was gathering. People were driving their lawn mowers, pushing them, hauling them in the backs of pickups. There were lawn mowers everywhere. Toros, Snappers, Lawn-Boys. Wheel Horses, Fords, Arienses. When they were started, they coughed out little clouds of blue smoke. Fifty American flags lined the perimeter of the common, and by the parade marshal's podium hung a banner: "God Bless Those Who Bless Their Lawns."

Ed maneuvered through the crowd to an area reserved for riding mowers and garden tractors. He was happy that he could start from his favorite spot, just under the big oak tree on the east side. He had hung out on this corner when he was a kid, smoking cigarettes and chewing gum with his buddies. Later, after he'd met Thelma, they'd pulled under the tree on Friday nights and waited for their pals to show. And even now, when they walked down for Sunday breakfast, they'd meet their lifelong friends on the bench under this tree.

He nodded to the other people around him, waved at friends. He complimented one fellow on his Toro self-propelled, as well as a man and his daughter on their lustrous new John Deere garden tractor. New people in town. Those little Deeres don't come cheap.

At last the parade marshal cranked the PA system to life, asked for everybody's attention, and began his speech. "Welcome, ladies and gentlemen, boys and girls, to the Seventh Annual Blessing of the Lawn Mower Fleet! What a day we have in store! We have races, a beauty contest, clinics sponsored by . . ."

Ed tuned him out and let his eye run over the crowd. Thelma sat on a lawn chair in the doorway of the video store with the rest of the hen party. Ed liked her permed hair and sunglasses. Not bad for sixty. She'd kept her lean figure, even after all the kids.

She's really the hub, he thought. She's what keeps the family wheel turning. They all thought of him throwing yard parties and barbecues, plowing their driveways. On Christmas mornings, taking the kids for rides in the back of his pickup. But Thelma deserved the real credit. It was she who performed the constant, everyday acts of goodness that tended to get overlooked: baby-sitting the grandkids, shopping for them, shuttling them to school, swimming lessons, Scouts. He might get the glory of a perfect charbroiled steak; she deserved the credit for buying the right cut of meat.

The parade marshal was into the prayer part of his speech. Ed tuned back in.

". . . and keep us from aphids and cutworms and other crawling things, and shelter us from the downpours this spring so the grass seed doesn't get washed away, but send us enough rain in July and August so the lawns don't all dry up and turn brown. And protect us from machinery-related incidents. Let us have no sprained backs from balky starter cords, no leg burns from brushes with the muffler, and no cut-off toes from slipping into the blade. Lord, protect us and bless our lawns, and please don't let the Arabs raise the price of oil again, Amen!"

Amen, said the crowd.

"And now, the Blessing of the Lawn Mower Fleet!"

A cheer went up from the crowd.

"The first category is Two-Legged Pushers!"

The first group began pushing their old-fashioned, engineless mowers past the reviewing stand, and the parade marshal read off their names: Carl's Cutter, Mow 'Em Down, Saturday Morn. The owners pushed past in relative quiet, waving and smiling, looking quaint. Old ladies and hobbyists, Ed thought. If you can't raise a racket and turn the air blue, leave the thing in the garage.

Next came the Power Pushers, the largest group. A hundred mowers, starting in even rows of red and green and yellow, with clouds of blue smoke rising. The parade marshal called them all:

Lucy B, Chlorophyll Clyde, Toad's Terror. As they passed the reviewing stand, the Power Pushers made sure to maintain their even rows; they didn't want to push their running mowers into the heels of the guy in front of them. Clip Job, Fast Freddy, Miller Time.

It took twenty minutes for the Power Pushers to get past the reviewing stand, and then the parade marshal called for Ed's group: Riders and Garden Tractors. Best group in the parade, Ed thought. The serious yard men. Oh sure, they all had power pushers at home, but they entered their main machines in the parade. Ed started his engine, and when the row in front of him pulled forward, he eased out the clutch.

As he circled the common, he could get a full view of the crowd. Bigger than ever before. People lined the sidewalk and shop doorways. When he spotted friends or neighbors, he waved. They called to him: "Good luck, Ed!" and "Give 'em hell, Ed!" His children and grandchildren were positioned in knots around the common— "Go Dad!"—and it made him feel so proud to know he had put five families into this community, and that they all had turned out respectable. Ernie, still at home, was a heller in a car, but he'd be getting married soon enough, probably, and then he'd settle down. The rest of them had. Ed Junior with his own delivery truck and two young sons. And the three girls—Eve, Elizabeth, and Edie— all married with kids. "Gram-pa!" called little Kirsten.

When the parade marshal called Ed's mower—"Little Mack!"— Thelma stood and applauded, as did the rest of the hen party. He smiled broadly and waved. After the Blessing of the Fleet, Ed parked under the oak tree and set out to see the other events. He paused at a tune-up clinic, caught a mulching demonstration. He got a kick out of the oil-change competition, with the contestants getting sloppy and black. One of his favorite events was the garden tractor pull. The little tractors were paired up by horsepower and linked with a chain. At the drop of the flag, their engines roared, the chain snapped taut, and they snorted and strained to pull each other across a chalk line on the pavement. Tires slipped and smoked, clutches heated up, engines conked out. Nuts, Ed thought. What's the sense in spending good money on a tractor and then straining its guts out over some foolishness?

He stopped in front of the video store to see Thelma, and was greeted by the hens. "Hey, Ed!" "Gonna drive it straight, Ed?" They all cackled. "Oh, we know he drives it straight!" He just grinned and shook his head. Good thing they were on his side.

He walked over to the common. It was cordoned off with bright orange pylons and tape. The course had been laid out for the Straight-Line Race, with row upon row of evenly spaced eggs. The eggs were donated by Fallon's Egg Farm, and those that weren't broken in the race would be gathered up and made into omelets over big cinder-block grills. Every contestant got a free omelet.

The parade marshal spoke over the PA system: "Ladies and gentlemen, boys and girls, we're gonna start getting ready for the biggest event of the day—the Straight-Line Race! Contestants please approach the reviewing stand for your numbers."

As the reigning king, Ed received the numeral 1 to stick to the front of his mower and the back of his shirt. An official directed him to his starting position. He would cut the centermost swath on the common. The high-ranking contestants from last year were positioned to his right and left, and the rest of the pack flanked out from there. He liked the idea of the fastest contestants cutting across the center of the common, with everybody else spread back—a flying wedge of grass clippings. In this way the town common would be mowed, and the season of the yard officially kicked off.

Ed felt real pride as he looked at the mowers being lined up on either side of him, thirty in all. Anton Circelli was to his left and a guy named Hodges to his right. They had finished in second and third place last year. He shook hands with them both and wished them luck. These were the real yard men. This was the event that really proved what you could do. Who cared about how quick a guy could change his oil or whether one tractor could outsnort another one? When you got down to it, the mark of a good yard man, and, in Ed's view, a good citizen, was how well you cut your grass. It was simple: your rows had to be straight, and you had to get it done quickly. A neat, quick job. Take care of your lawn that way, and your lawn would take care of you. He knew this to be so; all his friends and neighbors admired his lawn, and hence, him. For all they knew, he beat his wife and kicked his dog, but as long as all they saw was his neat, trim lawn, they'd think he was a fine fellow.

When everybody was in position, the parade marshal called for quiet. All the engines were cut. The crowd gathered around the edge of the common. Ed's family was almost directly across from him. Thelma, Eddie and his family, the girls and their kids. This was Ed's favorite moment. He could hear the murmur of the crowd, the flapping of the American flags in the breeze. In the distance, the whining of a diesel rig out on the highway.

The parade marshal began naming the contestants from each end of the common. There was scattered applause and encouragement, increasing as he got closer to the center. As the parade marshal called out the names of the top-ranked contestants and finally Ed, the whole crowd cheered and whistled. But Ed paid no attention. He didn't so much as nod when his name was called. He needed his concentration to run the race, and he was focusing inward and on the line of eggs just off his left wheel.

Two inches, he was thinking. Two inches off the eggs until you get up to full throttle. Just focus on the eggs. Cut on the dotted line. A cinch.

"Ladies and gentlemen, start your lawn mowers!"

Thirty mowers burst into life. A great roar thundered across the common, a blue cloud rose and then dissipated in the breeze. Ed brought Little Mack up to half throttle. Too fast a takeoff could jerk you sideways. A lot of guys made that mistake and lost the race at the start.

The parade marshal held up a green flag. Ed kept his eye where he could see the flag but was focused on the eggs. He allowed a quick glance at his family, and then back to the eggs.

The flag dropped. Ed popped the clutch and Little Mack shot forward. A good start—didn't swerve, didn't spin the tires. Anton and Hodges started well, too, with Anton slightly in the lead. Ed was right where he wanted to be—two inches off the eggs. Little Mack felt good—steady and solid and eager for more. He thumbed the throttle up to three-quarters, and Little Mack roared and drew even with Anton. Hodges lagged slightly behind. Two inches, mind the two inches. Little Mack was faster than Anton's mower, Ed knew. When he had gained full momentum at three-quarters throttle, Ed thumbed the lever all the way down. Little Mack roared and jumped forward. Ed was out in front.

Two inches. He was right there. Cutting a straight, fast swath across the common. Halfway now. He allowed a peripheral glance: on both sides, mowers streamed back in his wake. He pictured a rooster tail of finely cut grass spraying up in back of him. Eat clippings, slowpokes!

Only Anton was close, but Ed knew that if he just held a straight course, he could stay ahead. The only other way to gain points, and to improve his own performance, was to cut closer to the eggs. Ever so slightly, he nudged the wheel. Nobody else even noticed. But he was a half inch closer to the eggs. They flew past his left front tire; Little Mack felt as solid as his big rig on the turnpike. He nudged it again. An inch! An inch off the eggs—five blades of grass! Measure that with your rulers, by Jesus, and know that Ed Jacques is one grass-cutting son of a bitch!

He was ten yards from the finish line when it happened. He knew he had the race locked up. Anton was a full length behind him. Little Mack felt good under his hand. He could chance a smile at his family—they were right there, after all. So as he dragged his eye away from the line of eggs, intending to look at Thelma and wink— she'd like that, she and her friends would talk about it for summers to come, how Ed was running ahead of the pack, one inch off the eggs, and he looked over and winked at his wife—as he swept his eye toward her, expecting to encounter her dark shades, his eye snagged on something else. It was both dark and light at the same time: the full-moon face of Mrs. Stevens. She was there, not three feet from Thelma, her black hair glistening in the sun, staring right at him.

He was aware of three things at once: her calm, beautiful stare, the spasm in his arms, and the mighty "Ooohhh!" from the crowd as he veered left and ran over three straight eggs. As he swerved back into his lane, Anton caught him. Before he straightened out, Anton passed him and crossed the finish line.

He cut the throttle and braked to a stop. His head was steamy with embarrassment. *She knew, she saw!* He was a fool! He picked Anton's grass clippings out of his collar. Eddie and his kids clustered round, as did the girls and theirs.

"Tough break, Pop," Eddie said.

"Grandpa—you broke the eggs!" scolded little Kirsten. He picked her up and bounced her, pulled the others close. It made him want to weep.

Only his wife hung back. She had seen. She had to. So had her friends. She stood alone now, just beyond the orange tape. As he watched, his heart beating its apology, she slipped under the tape and passed around the little family grouping. She walked with the same tentative, ginger step she used on his own freshly cut lawn, as if paying respect to his work. She stepped back down the swath, and began gathering up the broken eggshells.

TWO

Sunday at the Human Being Factory

Ed Jacques finished raking the dead branches out of the hedge along the edge of his property and loaded them into the wheelbarrow. Through the hedge he could hear the sloshing and spraying of his neighbor, Ray Vann, as Ray washed his cars.

Ed poked his head over the hedge.

"Gonna scrub the paint right off them ca-a-ahs," he said.

Ray laughed. "My offering to the rain gods, Ed. Clean cars on Sunday, rain on Monday. Works every time."

"Ye-ah," Ed said. "Be pouring by midnight if you threw a coat of wax on 'em."

Ed wheeled his barrow past the pool. He called to Scott and Lee, the two oldest grandchildren: "I'm taking this brush across the street.

You keep an eye on those younger kids and keep 'em out of the deep end." Scott and Lee were playing Marco Polo, and the younger kids clung to the edge or floated in the shallow end. Ed made a quick count as he wheeled away: seven—yes, seven. Besides Scott and Lee, there were Eve's twins, Elizabeth's little boy Wally, and Edie's two girls Krystal and Kirsten. Seven.

Ed dumped the branches down the bank onto his brush pile. He owned the little patch of hillside across the street from his house— it ran twenty yards down to the neighbor's fence—and he kept his brush pile here, a mulch pile, too, with the dead leaves and weedings from the garden, and a few rows of tomatoes, peppers, and squash. What he liked most about this little scrap of land, though, was the view. Years ago he had built a granite bench here, as the view from this spot was probably the best in all of Hurley. Monadnock Street sat up high anyway, and from the bench you could look out over the whole town: the peaked roofs of the houses sticking up through the trees—white clapboard houses, mostly, colonials and capes with roofs of black or green or brick-red shingles. Three streets down the hill to his left, the stone mill sat quietly amid its stacks of red, black, and gray granite. They didn't cut as much down there as they used to—curbstones and veneers mostly. Putnam's was the last quarry in Hurley, once the highest-producing granite town in the Granite State. When Ed was a kid there had been twenty-nine quarries in Hurley, and everybody worked for them. Now, the fine old Victorian houses of the quarry owners were occupied by relocated Massachusetts yuppies, and instead of a hundred trucks a day leaving town to haul granite to Boston and New York and D.C., there were a scant half-dozen.

Ed sat on his granite bench, and the voices of his grandchildren came to him; their shouts, splashes, and squeals washed up against his tired back like a balm. He had gotten a lot of work done today: washed the cars, cleaned the pool for the kids, touched up the mortar on the front walk, and raked out that hedge. He liked to take a few minutes after a day's work to rest on the bench. The view just stretched away over the town and across the Souhegan River valley to the Monadnocks. He could see part of Wilton off to the west, and on the far hillside, Lyndeborough. In the distance, Pack Monadnock, and to its left, Mount Monadnock itself. It was a great view—a million-dollar view, he and Thelma always said—and apparently other people agreed, for in the mornings and especially in the evenings, people from the neighboring streets would walk up Monadnock Street to this spot, to sit on the bench and look out over the town and the valley. It placed you, he thought. The view reminded you that you were where you were supposed to be, that the world was still the same as when you last checked.

A small cloud passed in front of the sun, and Ed shivered in his sweat. He flicked bits of bark off his forearms. When the quarries gave out, the furniture mills did okay, and when that moved elsewhere—down South or offshore—along came the Bud plant in Merrimack and Coca-Cola in Nashua and Raytheon building radar systems in Manchester, and then in the seventies and eighties, Digital and Sanders and Nashua Corporation, all making computers or disks or paper. Plenty of jobs for everybody, and Hurley had prospered along with the rest of southern New Hampshire. But now, the summer of 1989, everybody was talking recession. Ed believed it. Computers were slowing down. The military contracts were drying up. He was still delivering plenty of printer paper to the big companies around New England, but some of the younger drivers had started to worry about layoffs.

A blast of air like a truck's brakes jolted him. He looked up and spotted the hot-air balloon floating alongside the sun. It had not been a cloud at all, a moment ago, but Ted Stearn's green-and-purple *Wild Goose* passing before the sun on a late-afternoon flight.

"Balloon!" the kids yelled from the pool. "Hey, Grandpa! Look at the balloon!"

He shaded his eyes with a hand. The balloon was going to pass to the south, not overhead as they frequently did. Hurley had become, for some reason, a center for hot-air balloonists. Most weekends, morning and evening flights left a clutch of these bright eggs hanging in the valley. As big as houses, made of colorful fabric, the balloons always brought people out into the street to watch. They took off from an open field on the west end of town, and the prevailing breezes often carried them right up over Monadnock Street. Sometimes they passed so close you could talk to the people in the basket.

Ray Vann heard the balloon and looked up from drying off his car. He had just washed Marisse's Subaru wagon and was now finishing up his Honda, and when he heard the blast of propane he looked to the sky. He couldn't see anything from his driveway, but he noticed Ed out on his bench, so he took a final swipe at the Honda's trunk lid and walked over, shaking out his towel.

"Hey, Ed," he said. "Which one is it?"

"Ted Stearn."

"Wow—nice."

"You ever go up?"

"Nope, you?"

"Never," Ed said, shaking his head. "I'd sure like to, though."

Both men shaded their eyes and watched the balloon. They saw a long flame flash up from the basket; a second later they heard the propane blast.

Ed nodded up the street, toward the dead end. "He's got to gain a little altitude to clear this ridge," he said. "Must be a nice view from up there."

"You bet," Ray said. "Be nice to take a ride sometime, but I've heard you've got to book 'em way in advance."

"They ain't cheap either," Ed said. "Couple hundred bucks a shot."

Ray flicked his towel at his toe. Neither he nor Ed was the kind of man who would spend two hundred bucks on a balloon ride, even though they could both afford it. Two hundred bucks would buy a new pair of snow tires or pay for a delivery of fuel oil.

"Got your buggies all washed up?" Ed asked.

"Yeah, pain in the neck," Ray said, although it was an obligatory response. He actually liked washing the cars—the friendly sound of water spraying on sheet metal and the steady, monotonous motion of the sponge put him in an almost meditative state. But he and Ed held their various projects and chores as a source of wry complaint, as if washing the car or cutting the grass or painting the trim was keeping them from some other, preferable activity, when, truth be told, they'd both rather do nothing more than dub around on exactly these things.

"Pain is right," Ed said. "I just washed both of mine this morning."

Actually, Ray knew, Ed had not only washed both of his own cars, but two of his daughters' as well. Sunday morning was when Ed washed his cars, so his various family usually found time to drop by with doughnuts and the paper. Sometimes Ed would have as many as three or four cars backed up. Ed's kids all drove nice cars; although Ed was strictly a Chevy man—he drove a Chevy pickup and his wife a Celebrity wagon—his kids all had expensive foreign jobs. Ray didn't understand how they could afford them. Eddie Junior delivered bread to the local supermarkets, and he had a Peugeot wagon with leather interior. Eve cut hair, and she had a Mazda sports car. Edie didn't do anything, as far as Ray could tell, and her husband worked in the stone mill—hell, even they had a nice Acura. It came, Ray imagined, from some salt-of-the-earth understanding of the way things worked; Ed had simply passed on his native money-management skills to his kids. Ed had worked all his life, he had the best-kept place on the street, owned an apartment house across town, and always had plenty of reserve for improvements: reline the swimming pool—no problem, a crew shows up Monday morning; foundation leaking—the excavation team digs it out, reseals it, puts in footer drains, and then the landscapers come in and fix it all up nice. New roof, new vinyl siding, central air—whatever the place needed, Ed always had the dough.

Ray admired his neighbor tremendously, and wished he had his knack. Here *he* was in his late thirties, with two college degrees and a good job in high-tech, a mid-fifties salary and stock options, and his wife, Marisse, with a steady, modest-paying graphic design job down at the newspaper, and by the time they paid the mortgage and the taxes and the car payments, the insurance and the utilities and the charge cards, there was enough to go out to eat on once a week and to keep a little back for emergencies, but there wasn't enough to start building up a bankroll, let alone buy investment property or a new car every couple of years. Ray couldn't figure it, and he didn't waste much time trying. It was all he could do to commute off to his job five, and sometimes six, days a week, have a little peaceful time in the evening to read the paper, and catch up on home and car maintenance on the weekends. It was the same with everybody he knew.

"Always something," Ed said, and glanced over his shoulder at the pool. The kids were splashing and shouting, and there came a bright "Marco!" followed by a muffled "Polo!" Ed hollered in his deep baritone: "Scott! You keeping an eye on those kids?"

Scott hollered back in the affirmative.

"Sounds like a kid factory back there, Ed."

"That's about the size of it. Big cookout tonight—the twins' birthday."

Ray said it sounded like fun.

"Hey, Ray," Ed said. "You hear anything about the property out back?"

"No—what?"

"Thelma heard Minnie Stark sold it."

"No way."

"That's what she heard. I hope to God it ain't true."

"Me too," although Ray was already trying to get his mind around it—what it would mean if the woods out back was sold. "How much property is it?"

"About five acres, her piece. Runs right in back of all these houses: me, you, Rosens, Bains."

"Gram-pa-a-ah!" came a long shriek from the pool. "Scott's letting the air out of Mickey!"

"Scott!" Ed yelled back. "She needs that to swim with—cut it out!" Ed turned to Ray: "It took me fifteen minutes to blow the goddamn thing up, and those kids'll have it down to nothing in about ten seconds!" He turned back toward the pool. "Do I have to come up there, Scott?"

Scott answered in the negative.

"See what you have to look forward to, kid?" Ed asked a little ruefully.

"Ha," Ray laughed, but didn't want to take the conversation in this direction. When he told people he and Marisse weren't having kids, he got such mixed reactions that he'd rather not get into it. Especially with a patriarch like Ed.

Ray was about to excuse himself and go on home when there came a *ding-a-ling!* from down the street. *Ding-a-ling!* Leonard Walker's white Good Humor truck made its slow way up the hill.

The kids heard it, too. "The ice cream man!" they yelled. "Grandpa, can we have ice cream? Please, Grandpa?"

Ray grinned at Ed, and Ed reached for his wallet. "What's Grandpa for?" he said.

As they waited for the Good Humor truck, Ray thought about what it must be like to have such a family as Ed had. Children and grandchildren who gathered at his place for pool parties. Guys like Ed worked all their lives and made families. Their families made families. That was the whole point of life: to perpetuate. To keep the human being factory going. That's why you wrestled eighteen-wheelers all over New England all week, as Ed did: to keep your genetic production line moving. That's why it was such an uneasy subject. And not just with Ed, either, but with plenty of people Ray's own age. They were probably even worse. His own generation had always been so obsessed with the cult of the self that when they began having children, the replication of their selves was seen as yet another Wonderful Thing, like looking into an infinity of mirrors. It became, like everything else, the fashionable thing to do. No wonder when Ray or Marisse shrugged or said "No time soon," the response was a look of compassion—*Oh, you don't know what you're missing!*—or of encouragement—*Come on, you guys would make great parents!*—or even of silent reproach—*Selfish bastards!* But

whatever the outward response, there was always a doubtful lingering of the eyes. Not making more humans? It was subversiveness of
the highest order.

The kids swarmed down from the pool—"The ice cream man! The
ice cream man!"—and Ed was counting: one, two, three, four. Five
bucks in his wallet. That ought to do it for . . . how many—seven
kids? One, two, three . . . oughta buy Ray something too. One,
two, three, four . . .

The truck pulled up, and not only his own crew swarmed it but
also the two Rosen girls and the Marcoux kids and there was a
general hubbub of deciding on flavors "I want a cherry popsicle!" "I
want grape!" or fudgesicles over chocolate ice milk or sno-cones,
and it was important for him to count, he kept trying to count but
they were all milling around, and he heard Ray greet the driver,
Leonard Walker. They were friends, a couple of high-tech guys.
Leonard worked for Digital and coached Little League and had
restored this old GMC Good Humor truck and dinked around with
it on weekends. Got a kick out of the kids. One, two . . . "How's
Tina and the kids?" he heard Ray ask, and Leonard replied: "Great.
Marcie comes home from college next week," hard to believe a
young guy like Leonard had an eighteen-year-old daughter, but
then again he and Thelma had had Eddie Junior pretty young, too,
"and I've got Seth painting the house." "Ha! Send him up my way
when he gets done," Ray said. Three, four, five . . . "Order me a
bomb-pop, Grandpa!" "One bomb-pop here, Leonard—who else?
Scott? Lee? Ray—better grab something while Grandpa's buying."

There was a buzzing from down the street and it got louder and
louder and they turned to look: a kid on a moped cut his engine
and coasted up to the truck. The kid had blue hair. It was aqua
blue, the color of a goddamn sno-cone, and shaved all around the
ears in little patterns. Jesus, the things kids do. And riding that
bike in a pair of shorts and rubber shower thongs, walking it into
the crowd of kids, who got suddenly quiet but Scott and Lee interested in the bike, the bike aqua blue the same color as the kid's

hair, and Ed was trying to count in this moment of silence, sorting the Rosen girls aside and the Marcoux kids aside, and it's one, two, three, four, Scott and Lee and the twins—already got their cones somehow while he wasn't looking—and Wally, that's five, and little Kirsten, and the kids giggling and twittering about the other kid's aqua hair, and then Leonard going on about his kids again "and Amy's working at the pool this summer" and it was that word that did it, that one short syllable that always summoned up a mixture of emotion in him, it was such a pleasure to hear the kids splashing on a hot summer day, but it was a lot of work keeping a pool in New England, such a short season: that one short syllable had a lot of reverberation, like ripples moving across the surface, and seven, *goddammit there are supposed to be seven*, ScottLeethe TwinsWallyKirsten. He heard himself breaking free from them and getting his bulk moving toward the pool: "Krystal! Where's Krystal? Goddammit, Scott, where's Krystal?" pounding his way up the driveway as everybody turned to stare, she was only four for Christ's sake and he was supposed to be watching her, "Krystal!" and then he was aware of somebody right behind him as he cut through the gate but he had his eye on the pool he had just vacuumed out that morning, his ear on his own footsteps pounding and the others yelling "Krystal!" but somebody else's feet pounding as well, and there, floating in the deep end just a few feet below the surface, he saw it: the black shape of a father's nightmares. And then Ray was past him, a neat lifeguard's dive under the surface, and Ed couldn't stop, didn't even try but went belly first with a tremendous splash and felt the familiar envelope of water close over his head, opened his eyes to bubbles and blue, and Ray's kicking shape hauling something up toward the surface. It was wrong, the shape was wrong, and Ed felt the bottom under his feet and launched himself toward the light with all his strength, began bellowing even before he broke through so that when he finally did, and his voice rang out into air instead of water, he didn't hear Ray at first, but took a second to clear his ears, and then he caught it: "It's okay, Ed," and he felt Ray's arm dragging him toward the wall. "It's only Mickey Mouse. The Mickey Mouse raft. It's okay. She's not in here."

She was down the bank. Halfway between the granite bench and the brush pile, licking a fudgesicle and idly gazing up at the sky, looking for balloons.

Ray hung to the back of the crowd that followed Ed. The women had rushed out of the house at the commotion, and when they found out what had happened they started giving everybody hell—Ed and the two older boys and even Krystal. They managed to ignore Ray. Well, almost. Only Edie, Krystal's mother and Ed's cutest daughter—Ray always thought she had a thing for him—only Edie came up to him and plucked at his wet sleeve and thanked him. Then she winked and said, "Heck, Ray, you wanna go swimming, put on a bathing suit. At least we'd get to see your legs."

As everybody clustered on the bank, Ray oozed on over to his place. His shoes were soggy and his insides weak. He paused in his driveway, coiled the hose, and emptied his wash bucket. In the street the scene began to dissolve: the kid with the blue hair walked his moped back downhill with the older Rosen girl, Leonard eased his truck away. A little excitement, was all. Edie and Eve and Ed's wife, Thelma, waited in their driveway with the kids milling around.

Ray felt something hanging within him, something as yet unnamed. It strained, as he had in his brief suspension between earth and water, to touch something solid and familiar yet desperately not wanting to. Ed came up the bank with Krystal, looked up and saw him, gave him a palms-up shrug and a little wave. They all turned to look at him, the grandparents and the daughters and the grandsons and granddaughters, and it began to break upon him, slowly at first and then faster, like rushing water, the many, many experiences that would not be his.

THREE

Condophobia

On his way home from work, Ray stopped at the quick-serve Texaco station on Main Street. He pulled up to the pumps, shut off his engine, and rolled down his window to be ready for the attendant. From inside the gas station, loud rock music blasted across the tarmac, and the smell of gasoline and lilacs wafted in on the early-evening air, but no attendant appeared. Ray peered in through the doorway, could see the guy lounging against the cement-block wall, talking on the phone and smoking a cigarette. The guy looked right at him but didn't budge. He was a kid—nineteen or so—with scraggly hair and a bad complexion; he laughed a loud horse laugh into the phone, took a long drag on his cigarette, and turned away from the door.

God, it was irritating, Ray thought as he got out to pump his gas. They used to call these places *service* stations. You used to get your tank filled, your oil checked, and your windshield washed. Now, hell, nobody ever offered to wash your windshield, you wouldn't dare let one of these dipshits near your hood, and, like tonight, you were lucky if you even got somebody out to pump your gas. When he went in to pay, the guy was just getting off the phone. The music was painfully loud.

"Nine eighty-eight, unleaded," Ray said, handing over his credit card.

"Nine eighty-*eight?*" the guy asked. "Couldn't spring for the extra few cents?"

The music pounded Ray's head. Christ, it was such an assault, and it wasn't even good rock. It was no way to keep customers. Ray wondered what the station owner would think if he drove up and heard this.

"Think you could turn it up a little?" he asked. "I don't think they can quite hear it in the next county."

The guy stubbed out his cigarette. "Hey, you listen to your music the way you like, I'll listen to mine."

"Sure. But I imagine the station manager wouldn't like your music driving away customers."

"I *am* the station manager, dude. Nights, anyway."

Typical, Ray thought as he drove away. Just typical of what life had become. He remembered as a kid in the 1950s when you truly got service—at the Sinclair station where his father got gas, the attendants had always been polite and called his father sir, and they gave him, Ray, a plastic dinosaur with each fill-up. Now, hell— they call you dude and give you a headache.

It was that evening, as he drove up Monadnock Street, that he discovered the survey crew taking transit shots down his lot line. "Nothing to do with your lot," the surveyor said. "It's the lot out back." He nodded toward the woods in back of Ray's house. "It's just been sold, and we're surveying it for the bank."

Sold! The word made Ray's heart sink. So it was true. The woods out back was his refuge—he'd walk back there in the evenings to release the pressures of the day. He loved the old quarry roads, the deep fragrance of the pines. He liked to take off his shoes and move as quietly as an animal. He liked to pause against the smooth bark of a beech tree and rub his face against it. If somebody built back there, that would be the end of his solitary walks.

He went inside and found Marisse. She was doing sit-ups in the back room.

"That's what I was afraid of," she said. She looked up from her exercise mat, unhooked her feet from under the couch, and propped herself back on her elbows. "When I saw those guys out there, I just got this bad feeling."

Ray went over and hugged her.

"Oh, there's plenty of woods back there," he said. "Even if they put in a house or two, there'll be plenty of trees between us and them."

Marisse stretched her leg out and bent to touch her toes. In her mid-thirties she was as limber as a young ballet dancer.

"I hope you're right," she said. "I just want to keep my privacy."

Ray rubbed her back. The backyard was their own little patch of earth, where Marisse could sunbathe in private and he could putter about as he pleased.

"I'm going out back for a little walk," he said.

"Don't be long," she said. "I'm starving, and it's your turn to cook."

He slipped into the woods at the back of his lot. The surveyors had already been there, and a bright orange ribbon winked at him from the trunk of a birch tree. He was tempted to move it ten feet deeper into the woods, but instead he edged himself in, ducking under branches, sidestepping brush piles, until he was far enough in that he couldn't see the daylight from his or his neighbors' backyards.

One day, when he was insulating the attic, he had come across an old photograph tacked to one of the rafters. It was in a dark corner and had obviously been there for years. He had hollered for

Marisse and brought it downstairs. It was a wide, panoramic shot of Hurley taken around the turn of the century and shot from Monadnock Hill. He could recognize the Rosens' old farmhouse and the Stevenses' Victorian. A dirt track, the rough predecessor of Monadnock Street, ran downhill toward the town, and there, in the middle distance, were the town hall and the Congregational church and a cluster of mill buildings. Those landmarks Ray and Marisse could recognize. But the very odd thing about the old photo was the landscape: there were no trees. The whole countryside, from Monadnock Hill down to Hurley, out along the whole Souhegan River valley, across to Wilton and Lyndeborough and Amherst, was barren. The hillsides were as smooth as farmland, which in fact they were. Oh, a few trees leaned over the farmhouses, and an orchard blossomed here and there, but there were no standing forests like the one Ray now walked through. All these tall pines and oaks were new growth. At the most, they were eighty or ninety years old.

In the foreground of the photo was an amazing sight: a small steam locomotive pulling a flatcar of granite. Marisse had squealed and pointed at it—"Imagine! A little railroad up here on the hill!"—but when Ray saw it he knew exactly where the photo had been taken. The woods behind his house had been riddled with quarries once, crisscrossed with old dirt roads and narrow-gauge rail. He knew this because when he walked in the woods he found these things. He walked in the old roadbeds; today they were open tunnels through the trees. They led to the quarries, the more accessible of which—Tamarack Quarry, Granite State Quarry—were now the favorite swimming holes and partying spots of Hurley's teenagers. But Ray sought out the more remote sites, those that couldn't be reached by four-wheel-drives or dirt bikes. He would take topographical maps and find the flattened strips of the old railbeds and follow them through the second-growth woods until they led to a heap of waste stone or a water-filled excavation. He had found a beautiful little quarry no more than twenty-five yards long by ten yards wide—an elongated triangle with the top squared off, almost the exact shape of the state. He named this the New Hampshire Quarry. Another one, a series of steppes down to the power line, he called the Power Line Quarry. But his favorite quarry, deep in the woods, was the Steam Engine Quarry, and it was, he knew, the site of the old photo. He had come across it one fall day as he followed an old railbed. The railbed rose steadily through the woods and crested a knoll, and there he found things he couldn't believe. Not only slabs of granite—great chunks of many tons—but also semifinished work: broken columns, a gargoyle peering out from under a rockslide, a base to what must have been a huge statue intended for a memorial in some distant city. So there had been not only a quarry, but also a milling operation.

The thing that attracted him most, though, was the old steam engine—obviously the same one in the photograph—sitting listed to one side where the ties had rotted away and the rail had sunk into the earth. The engine was now a hulk, its boiler a latticework of rust, every moving part seized solid. Even the wooden handles were rotted down to a few splinters. But Ray would climb gingerly into the cab and look out over the barrel-shaped snout, hang one arm out the open window, and imagine he was living during an earlier, simpler time, when all he did was haul granite from the quarry to the mill and from the mill to the main rail line in Hurley. He'd stop, chat with the other workingmen for a few minutes, and then, his load delivered, he'd chug his little engine back up the hill.

Ray tried to imagine what it must have been like to live in Hurley when there was no computer industry, no big defense buildup, none of the attendant support services. He had despised the development boom that had swept New Hampshire in the 1980s, and now it was at his back door. The cheap houses, the condo developments, the strip malls, the gas station attendants with shitty attitudes—it was all tied into the same lousy bundle. It was, Ray believed, the ruination of the state, of society in general. He had watched it happen on his daily commute. In the seventies, Route 101 had been a two-lane country road between Hurley and Nashua. He had enjoyed the drive through the pine woods and a few farms. But then the developers had come in like sharks to a kill, and now it was a four-lane, nine-mile strip of American kitsch. The developers had built six major shopping plazas, twenty-five strip malls, thirty-two office complexes, and hundreds and hundreds of condominium units. Not to mention the fast-food restaurants, drive-up banks, quick-serve gas stations, and mini-marts. To handle the increased traffic, they had put in twenty-one traffic lights. Driving 101 was like being caught in a telegram: Green Frog Car Wash, Dunkin' Donuts, Ridgewood Shopping Plaza, *STOP!* Ponderosa Steak House, Cinema Eight, Stop 'n Shop *STOP!* Jiffy Lube, Pier One Imports, Blockbuster Video, *STOP!*

New Jersey, Ray called it. Going to Nashua by way of New Jersey.

What really killed Ray was, people liked this. They called it efficient. They called it convenient. Getting stuck in traffic just to get to the hardware store wasn't what Ray called efficient. He'd drive five miles out of his way to avoid that kind of convenience. But the people who lived in the condos and the slapdash housing developments didn't seem to mind this. Seemed to like it, in fact. On Saturdays he'd see them out and about, driving from strip mall to discount store to supermarket, consuming, doing their bit to fuel the economic engine. When they needed groceries, they went to the huge supermarkets: Shop 'n Save, Purity Supreme, Shop-Rite. Ray preferred the little A&P right in Hurley, where they still ground your coffee at the checkout line and you'd leave with the smell of it on your shirt. When the condo-dwellers needed hardware or household goods, they went to the big discount department stores: Rich's, Ames, Wal-Mart, each with the same prepackaged junk. They'd drive from store to store, looking for the best prices.

Condomericans, he called them.

"Condomericans," he'd say to Marisse, as they sat at a stoplight while mall traffic emptied onto the road. He'd shake his head. "Frigging Condomericans."

Ray moved deeper into the woods until he came to a familiar knoll. At the top was a little granite outcropping with a perfect

Ray-sized ledge. He sat here, as he had many times. He watched the light turn bronze, listened to the leaves shift. The woods gradually transformed from a place he had entered to a place that had entered him. It was as if the permeable membrane of his skin allowed the light and temperature and essence of the woods to seep into him, and when he was saturated he felt at peace, as much a part of the woods as the granite on which he leaned. He tried, without moving a muscle, to feel where his fingers stopped and the ledge began, but he could discern no distinct edges. For some time he sat as still and without thought as stone, and then some subterranean vein shifted and he felt the gravitational pull of home and mate. He was baking haddock tonight.

Ray and Marisse had moved to New Hampshire in their twenties, had finished up college at UNH. In the 1970s, New Hampshire had seemed like such a cool place, after their remote hometown in New York State. You could live in the country but have easy access to Boston, a nice, clean city compared to New York. And there was a high level of consciousness—people kept up their properties, respected their natural surroundings, drove fuel-efficient cars. Ray had gotten a good job in high-tech—first at Digital, writing technical manuals, and later at Gentry Systems, a small start-up company that made publishing software. He and Marisse had moved to Hurley when he took the Digital job in nearby Merrimack, and they liked the town. Marisse found work as a graphic designer at the newspaper, and after four years of living in an apartment and saving hard, they bought their big old four-square on Monadnock Street.

When Ray and Marisse first moved to town, life was centered around the common, a grassy rectangle in the center of town with a gazebo, a war memorial, and tall trees. Around it were the essential businesses of the town: two churches, three diners, two barbershops, a great brick town hall with a real Paul Revere bell, the police station, a shoe-repair shop, Woolworth's, two gas stations, the newspaper office in the old brick school, the A&P, the hardware store. Everything a townsperson needed was clustered around the common, with the residential neighborhoods radiating out from this point. And Hurley had character. In summer there were band concerts and art shows on the common; in autumn, the Pumpkin Festival. After a long winter, the Blessing of the Lawn Mower Fleet brought people out into the fresh, spring air like woodchucks. People walked to town for Sunday breakfast or church. They met their neighbors and spoke to them. It was a good place to live.

But in the 1980s the boom began. Digital built several big plants in the area to make computers and software. Raytheon and Sanders expanded like crazy, growing fat on Ronald Reagan's defense contracts. The roads between towns got developed; outlying strip malls and new shopping plazas started pulling businesses out of the center of town. Ray began counting the new traffic lights on 101, began adding up the extra minutes to his commute. He and Marisse felt lucky to be living on Monadnock Street, for the neighborhood was nicely secluded from the development that began at the edges of the town. The other neighbors felt this way, too, and often said so when they'd meet on walks along the street or at Ed Jacques's granite bench overlooking the Souhegan River valley. They had it good. They had it better than most folks.

Two weeks after the survey crew left their bright orange ribbons in the trees, Ray and Marisse and many of their neighbors got a registered letter from the Hurley planning board notifying them of a public meeting on the property abutting them to the rear.

It was worse than they thought.

It was condos.

Ray and Marisse walked down to the meeting with Leonard and Tina Walker, and by the time they got to the town hall most of their neighbors were already there. Ed and Thelma Jacques, Nicolo and Gert Bartolomeo, Mr. and Mrs. Bain. Susie Stevens. Bob Marcoux in his plumber's overalls. The Rosens, Marty still in his suit from work, Cynthia passing a plate of cookies around. Amid the general hubbub, Ray pulled up four chairs on the other side of Ed Jacques.

"Thirty-six condos! How they going to fit thirty-six condos back there?"

"Ain't enough room in them woods for thirty-six condos."

"Ain't gonna be enough room in them condos for any woods."

"My, these are good cookies, Cynthia. Can I get the recipe?"

"What'll they do for a road? Do you suppose they'll send all those cars up Monadnock Street?

"Where else they gonna go?"

"Cars, trucks, tractors—anygoddamthing they want. If you're a contractor in this town, you can do anygoddamthing you want. Screwing the little guy, that's what this town's come to—screwing the little guy."

Amid this mutual enlightenment, Ray scanned the planning board. The moderator, John Boylston, was flanked by six other aspiring local politicos. Ray didn't really know them. His only other encounter with the planning board had been when he had gone before them to get clearance to build a deck on the back of his house. They were the usual bunch of well-meaning bumblers who used the planning board as a step toward becoming a selectman or a legislator to the State House in Concord. To Ray, the Hurley planning board was a contradiction in terms: just drive down Main Street and you'd pass a nice old Victorian home next to a Kentucky Fried Chicken next to a steel prefab auto body shop next to a condo complex. Some planning. The board was a rubber-stamp committee. Hell, here they were at a meeting to stick a frigging condo complex in one of the town's nicest neighborhoods, and the building inspector didn't even show up. The board's usual charade was to grumble among themselves, request the developer to do right by the community, and then roll back with their legs spread.

John Boylston called the meeting to order. "We have a plan submitted by Barr Construction to build a condominium complex off Monadnock Street," he said. "Tonight's meeting is for the abutters to view the plan and voice any concerns they have. No decision of any kind will be made tonight. This is purely an informational session. Does everybody understand the terms of tonight's meeting?"

Everybody mumbled and stirred for a minute, and Ed Jacques leaned over and assured Ray and Leonard that the plan was "already approved. Don't worry, it's already approved. This is just a formality, so they can get on with screwing the little guy."

The developer, Bill Barr, and his engineer and lawyer sat in the front row. They kept their backs to the neighbors, although from his angle Ray could see Barr's hawklike nose and overbite, one dull eye like a glass marble, and a toothpick that shifted from side to side. At a nod from the moderator, the engineer got up, unfurled the site plan, and tacked it to a corkboard on the wall. He was a young guy with a too-large sport coat and an eager but nervous look on his face, as though he was proud of his plan but wasn't sure what to expect from the abutters. The lawyer didn't inspire any greater trust. He was a short, middle-aged man, a bit too dapper in his tweed coat and vest, with his waxed and twirled mustache. He got up before the room and shook out a pair of half-lensed reading glasses.

"Good evening, folks," he said, smiling around. "Thank you for coming out to hear our plan to join you as neighbors." The people muttered and shifted. "As I'm sure you're aware, condominium living has become a popular lifestyle choice in recent years. These are well-kept, well-maintained residences that attract an upscale, professional buyer, and they prove to be good neighbors." The lawyer touched together the fingertips of both hands and looked at the neighbors over his half-lenses. "Our plan is to provide such a mutually beneficial arrangement for all the Monadnock Street resid—"

"Beneficial to whom?" Nicolo Bartolomeo interrupted. "How exactly is thirty-six condos with all that traffic beneficial to those of us who already live there?"

The lawyer raised his index finger. "By spreading out the tax base. By concentrating a number of dwellings in a small area, you get the best bang for the buck. And these people are—"

"Thirty-six condos," Nicolo continued, "means at least seventy-two more cars a day on that street. Seventy-two more cars going around that big curve, and the kids walking to school and playing.

How are you going to guarantee the safety of the kids who play up there?"

"Our plan calls for sidewalks leading into the complex," the lawyer said, "and widening the sidewalks on Monadnock Street."

Nicolo had the demeanor of a bulldog; his jowls actually shook as he spoke. "But with all that traffic—we don't see that much traffic in a week. That's what I'm concerned about, the safety of the kids."

The lawyer shook off Nicolo. "Surely the gentleman isn't suggesting that if parents encourage their kids to play in the street, the rest of the town should have to pay more than its share of the taxes?" He turned to the plan.

A muttering swept through the crowd. What did this guy mean? He was making it sound, somehow, like it was their fault. Or at least their responsibility.

"Now," the lawyer continued, "if we look at the plan—"

"Hold on just a second," Bob Marcoux spoke up. "You're making this out to be—"

"Kids are kids!" stated Gert Bartolomeo.

"Safety's the thing—"

"The issue isn't about tax base," said Marty Rosen. "It's about greed."

"It's about screwing the little guy, I tell you. It's about—"

John Boylston rapped on the table and called for order.

"Please, one person at a time!" he said. "You'll all have your chance to be heard. Right now Mr. Senfelder has the floor—why don't we let him present his plan and then we'll all discuss it."

Attorney Senfelder pulled out a telescoping pointer and began going over the plan. Thirty-six units divided among six townhouses, all facing on a new street that would empty onto Monadnock Street across from the Bartolomeo's driveway. The new street would run in back of seven existing Monadnock Street properties: Marcoux, Stevens, Walker, Bain, Rosen, ending in a parking lot behind Vann and Jacques. Attorney Senfelder explained how the street was designed to be a buffer between the existing properties and the condominiums.

"That's one hell of a buffer," Ed Jacques said. "Me and the Vanns here'll have cars pulling in behind us at all hours of the night. Their headlights'll shine right into our back doors."

John Boylston turned to the lawyer, who turned to the engineer. The engineer jumped to his plan and pointed out how a line of concrete barriers—"Jersey barriers, they call 'em"—could be placed at the edge of the parking lot to block the headlights. This caused more murmuring in the audience, and the weight of the development began to settle in on Ray. The vision of all those headlights hitting his house made him feel a little sick. A wall of ugly concrete barriers. Condomericans observing everything he did. Ray remembered the apartment complexes in which he and Marisse had lived: people changing their oil right out in the parking lot, tire tools clanging against the pavement, hoods slamming and engines revving. No, this condo development was not the thing for Monadnock Street. They would have to stop it somehow.

The neighbors were getting restless again, talking among themselves about their loss of privacy, about the beauty of the woods, about the greed of developers. Throughout this, Ray noticed, Barr sat half slouched in his chair, did not turn to face them, did not speak to the lawyer or the engineer or the planning board. His eye moved from board member to site plan, to other objects in the room: the open window, the American flag in the corner. His toothpick flicked back and forth, and he seemed almost bored, as if this were a distraction to get through so he could get on with bulldozing the woods. Ray imagined Barr and the lawyer before the meeting: *Let me do the talking,* the lawyer says. *There's always a few irate neighbors, but the board always goes for these developments. More money for the town.* Barr says, *Right, you do the talking. That's what I'm paying you for.* The lawyer, hating to kowtow to this redneck son of a bitch but appreciating the value of his contract, smiles and says, *Don't worry, it'll be a breeze. A cakewalk.*

"Where's all the water going to run off of this new street?" Nicolo wanted to know.

"And the snow? Where they gonna put all the snow when they clear that parking lot?"

"Right in your backyard, don't worry."

"Our backyards'll be their front yards."

"Why's that street got to be so close to the properties? Why can't they set it back?"

"Ain't enough room back they-ah. Have to cut out a building or two, cost 'em half a million in profits. Can't have that."

John Boylston pounded again for order. "Ladies and gentlemen, please! We must discuss this in an organized manner. One person at a time, and respect the floor. Nicolo, go ahead."

The crowd settled down again. Ed Jacques leaned over to Ray and whispered, "Planning board's a goddamned joke."

Nicolo wound up his most eloquent ex-selectman, ex-school-board, ex-library-committee manner. "I'm concerned that the infrastructure isn't there to support this kind of development. I'm not trying to keep anybody from earning a living—if I had some spare land I'd probably develop it too. But I'm concerned about the traffic impact and the water and sewerage impact. The water pressure's already low up there, and our cellars are wet as it is. This new development would draw more water than the whole street put together, and the new street's going to funnel all the runoff our way. There's a general upgrade's got to occur, and that's going to be expensive. Who's going to pay for all this?"

The lawyer assured them that a full impact survey had been done, and that Barr Construction was willing to undertake a reasonable share of the work, such as the aforementioned sidewalks. As for upgrading the town utilities, well, that was the town's responsibility. "You've just said that the water supply is substandard now. It's the town's job to fix that."

A general muttering among the people. This guy really knew how to twist your words around on you.

Tina Walker stood up, a little flushed. "I'm concerned about the safety of the kids," she said. "That's a lot of traffic to be dumping onto our street, and I don't care what you say, trying to keep kids out of the street is like trying to keep the sun from coming up in the morning."

Yeah, the crowd muttered. Right. You couldn't keep kids out of the street.

Something had been gnawing at Ray, and he finally got up. "I'm concerned about something else. This development has a severe impact on the character of the neighborhood. Monadnock Street is an established residential neighborhood, has been for many years. I have a question for the planning board: What is the zoning up there, and is this kind of land use permitted under the current zoning?"

John Boylston began to answer. "We were getting to that point, I believe—"

"An excellent point!" The lawyer cut him off. "Excellent point, and I'm glad you raised it. The zoning up there is currently for single-family use, and we are asking for a variance in this case, since multifamily use would not, in our opinion, have an adverse impact but in fact a positive one when you consider the tax advantages to existing residents."

"So you're saying," Ray said, "that under current town zoning laws, this development can't be built."

"Well," John Boylston said, "under the current—"

"The purpose of the variance," the lawyer said, "is to allow improvements when the building codes seem shortsighted. And there is legal precedent in Hurley to support a variance."

A wave of concern passed through the crowd.

"What do you mean by that?" Leonard Walker asked.

"I mean that Hurley has seen the wisdom of allowing multifamily developments in neighborhoods zoned single-family, and that to target an individual businessman now, and prevent him from providing affordable housing for people, well, that may have ramifications."

"You mean that since Hurley allowed developers to screw up other neighborhoods," Leonard said, "it shouldn't be allowed to stop you."

"That's not quite—"

"And what do you mean by ramifications?" Ray asked. "You're saying that if this board doesn't grant you a variance, you'll sue the town?"

"It's not clear that—"

"Sue the town, like hell!" Nicolo roared and jumped to his feet. "We've had enough of these developers running roughshod over us, and I say it's time to draw the line!"

Ed Jacques stood up, shoulder to shoulder with Nicolo. "I say it's time we kicked the sons of bitches out!"

"It's our town, not theirs!" said Gert Bartolomeo.

"Right!"

"Yeah!"

"Sue this, you bastards!" Bob Marcoux shook his fist.

Everybody stood, milled, scraped chairs. Only Barr remained seated, although he was now sitting up straight. No cakewalk, this.

John Boylston rapped everybody quiet.

"Mr. Barr, we have yet to hear from you. Is there anything you'd like to say to your neighbors to perhaps assuage their fears?"

Barr flicked his toothpick and shifted his eye from the moderator to his lawyer. The lawyer nodded, ever so slightly.

"Gonna build some good, affordable housing in there," Barr said, nodding. "Gonna do a good job."

He flicked his toothpick again, nodded, and settled back into his chair. End of speech.

John Boylston announced that the residents were free to study the site plan and ask the developers any questions they had. There would be another meeting in two weeks to make a decision on the variance and to propose any formal alterations to the plan.

Ray, Leonard, Ed, and Nicolo looked over the plan and then stood off to the side, muttering among themselves. Out of the corner of his eye Ray saw Susie Stevens making her way over to them.

She was wearing a simple white cotton dress, and her tanned arms and dark hair looked good. Smiling, and with Asian grace, she eased in between Ray and Leonard.

"We should do something in the next two weeks," she said. "We should make a strong statement, so the board won't grant the variance."

The men were silent for a moment, rendered into schoolboys by her attention. Then Nicolo spoke. "We can get up a petition," he said. "When I was a selectman, that was the sure way of getting everybody's attention. Get you a petition with a couple hundred signatures, they got to take notice."

"That's a good thing to do," Susie said. "I think there are others as well. Why don't we all get together to plan it? How about my place tomorrow evening?"

The men looked down for a moment, pausing to see if they had plans, or maybe just hesitant to take Susie Stevens up on such an offer without consulting their wives, but then Leonard said, "That's a good idea. We can figure out a plan of attack."

The others nodded and agreed to meet at Susie's at seven.

"Spread the word," she said.

Nearly everybody came to the meeting. Susie's husband, Bob, was away on business, Gert Bartolomeo and Thelma Jacques begged off, and Bob Marcoux had an emergency water leak down at the high school, but most everybody else showed up. Susie served coffee and tea. They talked, they listened, they drew up plans. They would oppose the development on three main points: the safety of the children, the cost to the town, and the damage to the character of the neighborhood. These were the three points with which other people in town could empathize: everybody wanted kids to be safe, everybody wanted lower taxes, and everybody wanted to protect the quality of life.

That week, Nicolo and the Bains went around from street to street collecting signatures on a petition that urged the planning board not to allow the variance on Monadnock Street. It stated furthermore that Hurley residents had had enough of developers encroaching on their neighborhoods, and the planning board should look on such proposals with a skeptical eye. Most people signed eagerly. "Too many condos already," they said. Or, "Let 'em build the condos in Nashua. Already botched it o-vah they-ah."

By the weekend, the petition had over six hundred signatures. Ray wrote a series of letters to the editor, signed by by various neighbors, urging Hurley residents to come to the next meeting to protest the condos. Susie Stevens and Leonard Walker set up several photographs on the big curve at the foot of Monadnock Street. They showed kids walking with books and swimming gear, and several cars bearing down on them. Another photo showed Leonard and his Good Humor truck, with a crowd of kids gathered around. Marisse and Tina Walker got these photos placed in the paper under a headline that read, "Hazardous Duty," and with captions that explained how the increased traffic would endanger their kids. Marisse designed a small poster to look like an old-time wood-type handbill. Under the title "Hurley Residents vs. Big Developers" it enumerated the three reasons why the condominium development should not be built, and urged Hurley residents to show their support at the meeting. Marisse and Ray posted these handbills in storefronts, on telephone poles, on supermarket bulletin boards. They worked shifts at the dump on Saturday, leafleting everybody who drove up with the week's trash. By the middle of the second week, Nicolo's petition had over a thousand names, and more letters and photos were printed in the paper.

Two hundred people showed up for the planning board meeting. The mob was so big it couldn't fit into the town hall meeting room, so a flustered John Boylston switched the venue to the gymnasium upstairs, abruptly ending a Cub Scout basketball game. Ray, Leonard, Ed, and Marty Rosen set up a chair-unfolding brigade, and amid the general shuffling and scraping, kidding and joking, everyone was seated. Spirits ran high.

"Looks like we got the numbers," Ray said to Ed, passing him a chair.

"Yeah, well," Ed contended, "I wouldn't put anything past those clowns on the board."

Barr and his entourage came in late. When they saw the size of the crowd, they consulted briefly. The lawyer smiled and made his way toward the front. The engineer followed, keeping his eyes on the lawyer's heels. Barr hung back. He leaned against the door-jamb, arms folded, toothpick jittering.

John Boylston called the meeting to order.

"We note there has been quite a bit of community action in the last two weeks," he said, "and the size of this crowd indicates that there's more than passing interest in the development up on Monadnock Street. We've got a couple of other items to cover tonight, but let's deal with Monadnock Street first, so you folks can get on to doing whatever you'd prefer to be doing on a Thursday night."

Laughter passed through the crowd. But tonight, instead of the tittering of a few neighbors, it was a deep rumble. The power of it gave Ray a thrill. It felt as if he and Leonard and Ed were at the controls of a powerful machine, and if they just operated it correctly, they'd make that deep rumble work for them.

"Tonight we're considering a request from Barr Construction for a variance in order to construct a thirty-six-unit condominium complex off Monadnock Street," John Boylston said.

The audience hissed, a sound like sudden wind. Ray caught Marisse's eye. She gave him a wide-eyed look like, *Wow! What have we started?*

Boylston turned toward Attorney Senfelder. "Do you have the application for variance?"

The lawyer handed over a manila folder. Boylston flipped through it and passed it on to the other board members. He looked out at the crowd.

"Do the abutters or anyone else have a statement to make before the board makes its decision?"

They had appointed Nicolo as their spokesperson, since he knew a lot of people in town, since he could speak well in situations like this, and since his son-in-law happened to be sitting on the board.

"I'm speaking for the abutters," Nicolo said. "For the past two weeks we've spoken to a lot of people in town, and everybody feels the same way: we're all fed up with the overdevelopment in Hurley, and it's time to say so."

The crowd rumbled its approval. The sound came to Ray not only through his ears, but also through his feet, as the floorboards of the gymnasium vibrated with it. Nicolo let the noise subside, and then handed a thick sheaf of paper to the moderator.

"Here's a petition to the planning board asking you not to grant the variance for this development. It's signed by twelve hundred people."

The rumble broke into a roar. *Twelve hundred people!* You couldn't get twelve hundred people in Hurley to agree on who should be President, let alone come together on something that didn't directly affect them. A nerve had obviously been touched. Ray felt the vibration right through to his stomach.

"We oppose the development on three points," Nicolo said, and as he listed them, Ray looked around the room. Most of the people were watching Nicolo with rapt attention, proud that one of their own was representing them against powers they previously felt were beyond their control. Barr, however, was not looking at Nicolo. When Ray's gaze worked around to the back of the hall, Barr locked onto it. The man was staring right at him. It wasn't a mean look, it wasn't threatening. It was a worse, in a way. Barr's face was void of expression, his eyes were dead—again Ray was reminded of a dull glass marble—as if Ray were just another object in the room, as if the roomful of people were just another object in the world. It was a dangerous look, because someone who could gaze upon this gathering, in the midst of this emotion, and still be dead inside— well, that was a dangerous man. Ray held his stare as long as he could, and then he turned back to Nicolo.

"Finally, I'd like to thank all the people who turned out tonight.

This development is planned for our backyards, but those of us who live on Monadnock Street would like to thank you for treating our backyards like your own. This has always been a town of good neighbors, and you've proved it tonight."

The room erupted in applause, people smiling and clearly happy that they were working together on something important to them all and to their town. Ray felt an odd fluttering in his chest, and he put his arm around Marisse.

"Thank you, Nicolo," John Boylston said. "Very well spoken, as usual. As this is an issue of some sensitivity, I want to make sure the board is fully aware of the town's sentiment. Understand that the board will make the decision on its own, and will consider all factors before it. But we do represent the town's interests, and just so the board is clear on how the town residents feel, I'd like to ask now for a voice—not a voice *vote*, because it's not a voting matter—but a *voiced expression*, shall we say, on this issue. All those in favor of granting a variance, so the development can be built, say 'Aye.' "

The two ayes—from the lawyer and the engineer—sounded weak in the big hall.

"Those opposed to granting a variance, say—"

"NAAAY!" roared the audience.

"Thank you," John Boylston said. "Does any member of the board have any questions or statements to make?"

None of them had any, at least none they'd make public. They conferred among themselves for a few minutes, flipped through the variance, tapped the thick petition. Finally, the moderator broke from the huddle.

"The planning board has reached a decision. Mr. Barr, Mr. Senfelder, it is the opinion of this town that a multifamily development in the Monadnock Street neighborhood would have such an adverse impact that we cannot grant a variance—"

The crowd erupted again, drowning him out. Ray hugged Marisse close, and he himself was pounded on the back, jostled, shoved, as the crowd cheered, applauded, stomped, and otherwise expressed their approval. When Ray finally extracted himself, he looked toward the back door. Barr was gone.

The neighbors and the townspeople stood around for a while, congratulating each other, shaking hands, striking up conversations with people they'd never met. They'd shown those son-of-a-bitching developers. Just let 'em try to mess with the little guy! Finally John Boylston kicked them all out so the planning board could get on with other business, and Ray and Marisse walked home. They were excited and happy. They held hands, touched. In the shadow of their big maple tree, they kissed.

"We should commemorate this night," Marisse said, teasing.

"Okay," Ray said. "But it has to be appropriate."

"Whatever you say."

"Wait here."

Ray went inside and got the double sleeping bag they used on camping trips. He took Marisse by the hand and led her into the backyard. The sky was the electric blue of twilight, with a big moon just coming up over the treetops. The woods surrounding the yard was deep and black. He eased Marisse into the woods, treading lightly so as not to snap twigs or rustle leaves. Off to their left a chorus of peepers shut down, their silence announcing the human presence. Ray and Marisse crept in deeper, feeling for branches in front of them, until the lights from their windows were no longer visible. Ray's eyes adjusted to the deeper dark, and he could make out tree trunks and the fine pattern of leaves and branches against the sky. He paused by a white birch tree, felt the waxy surface of its bark and its rough scars, smelled the dusty smell that birch trees have as their bark peels.

He found the old railbed with no problem and led Marisse along. They whispered, so as not to disturb the night woods. By the time they began the climb to the Steam Engine Quarry, the moon was beaming in through the treetops. They could see their own shadows on the forest floor. It was hard to believe that a spinning rock out in space could reflect so much distant sunlight that their shadows walked beside them though the woods.

When Marisse saw the steam engine, she gasped. "From the old picture?"

"The same," Ray said.

While Marisse walked around the old locomotive, touching it here and there, Ray spread out the sleeping bag on a slab of granite overlooking the quarry. The moon reflected in the still water, and Marisse came over and joined him.

"It's beautiful," she said.

Ray removed Marisse's clothes, a familiar and always poignant act. Then his own. As he settled into the sleeping bag with her, he caught a glimpse of the old steam engine—man-made artifact of an earlier time—and of the moon's reflection in the quarry. How many nights had the moon reflected just so, in the water, with no one there to see it? He adjusted himself to Marisse's quiet moves, fitted himself to her, and he was aware of the great cycles of life, greater than the recognizable cycles of breathing in and breathing out, of lovemaking and sleeping and waking, greater even than living and dying. There were larger cycles—biological and ecological—at work, and as he moved with Marisse he struggled like a half-blind man to see them. But he saw only the clues: the rusted, chipped shards of the past, the smooth, shining surface of the present. He saw Marisse's closed eyes, her smile of beatitude for which he would be eternally grateful. There in the ruins where other men once toiled and perhaps even prospered, he thought of the folly of human endeavor. Such a grand and futile scratching upon the earth!

Deeper in the woods, an owl hooted. The moon rippled the surface of the quarry. Ray began to grow calm. Already, the evening dew glistened in Marisse's hair.

FOUR

Teaser Ponies

When Tina Walker's daughter Marcie came home from her freshman year, she brought with her these things: T-shirts with the college logo for Tina and Leonard, neon sunglasses for the two younger kids, a slight Southern drawl, and a hickey the size of a quarter on her neck.

"Going-away present," was all she said.

Oh God, Tina thought. She's going to be too cool to talk to us. Tina and Marcie had always been open about things, so it seemed weird that Marcie was holding back. Leonard took it with his usual equanimity, gave Tina the raised-eyebrow shrug that said, *So we'll put up with it.*

After a few days of being back with the family, the two younger kids had kidded her enough—

"Good morning, slut puppy," fourteen-year old

Amy would say, as twelve-year-old Seth imitated Dracula: "I vant to suck your throat!"—so that Marcie soon settled back into the family rhythms. The hickey faded after a few days, although the drawl came and went with Marcie's mood.

Around the dinner table, Marcie regaled them with stories of life at the small Southern college: tailgate parties and encounters with redneck townies, long drives out into the mountains. She made them all laugh with her exaggerated accent and her spoofing of small-town Southern boys. Amy and Seth would crack up and then look at their older sister, the first of them to venture beyond New Hampshire, with shining admiration. Their favorite story was of Marcie's visit to a racehorse-breeding farm in Kentucky.

"Teaser ponies," Amy would say. "Let's hear about the teaser ponies!"

"Aw-w-w, c'mon, Mar-cie," Seth would say in an excellent Mr. Ed imitation, stamping a hoof under the table. "Tell us about the Tea-ser Po-nies!"

Teaser ponies were used in breeding racehorses, Marcie said. When a mare came into heat, she'd be put in a special breeding pen. Before the stud could come in, though, they'd bring in a teaser pony. At this point Seth always nickered and stamped his hoof.

"It's this cute little male pony," Marcie said, "and of course he can tell like, the mare's in heat? So he gets all excited"—nicker, nicker, went Mr. Ed, stomp, stomp—"but he can't do anything because they've got his, like, you know, *penis*, held back by this little leather, like, apron?"

STOMP, STOMP, went Mr. Ed under the table. "Aw, gosh, Mar-cie. Whips and chains. Whips and chains."

"So the teaser pony gets real excited, and he's hitting on the mare left and right, and she gets excited too and starts to get into it. So the pony tries to mount her"—STOMP!—"but he can't really because he's too little and of course they've got him all strapped down. He's going wild and so is she, and then they lead him out and let in the stud, and it's like, fade to the bedroom window, bring up the music. Next scene, they're like, smoking cigarettes."

"Aw shucks, Mar-cie," STOMP, STOMP, "I think I felt the earth move."

Tina told the story to Marisse at work, and they cracked up.

"Just what every woman needs," Marisse joked. "A teaser pony to get her worked up before her husband comes home."

"Ha!" Tina said. "As long as he keeps that little apron on."

"God, the poor pony," Marisse said. "He must go wild when they turn him out of that pen."

They had a good laugh, but Tina kept thinking about it afterward. Jason, she was thinking. Jason of the cute ponytail.

Jason was a twenty-year-old guy she knew at the health club. They often wound up riding stationary bikes next to each other. He was slender, taut as a tennis racquet, clean-shaven. He wore his dark hair pulled back in a short ponytail. Tina thought he timed his workout so he'd be on the bike the same time as she. They liked each other—she liked him because he was quiet and polite and had an offbeat sense of humor. He was a bit of a rebel, and she liked that he did not express it in the usual obnoxious teenage ways. They'd talk and joke as they rode their bikes, rolling their eyes at their more narcissistic compatriots: "Mr. Testosterone," they'd dubbed one bulked-up guy who worked out only in front of the mirror, and "Ms. Lycra Lingerie," who wore the skimpiest workout suits in the place. Jason had not gone to college right out of high school; he'd not known what he wanted to study, so he was taking some time off. He worked at the video store and lived with his parents.

He liked her, she could tell. She knew that at thirty-eight, she was an attractive woman, and she worked to stay that way. She exercised at the club three times a week, went skiing and hiking with Leonard and the kids. She could wear Marcie's and Amy's dresses, and she knew she looked good in her workout shorts and T-shirt. But it was more than that. Jason picked up on *her* rebellious side and kidded her about it, asked her what life was like "in the sixties." He seemed fascinated by that time, and she was curious about this. Marcie and her friends, too, were big on the sixties.

Tie-dye, peace signs. Even the music—she'd come home and Marcie would have Jimi Hendrix or The Doors blasting on the stereo.

"It's like we missed something really big," Jason said. "I picture
people your age, my parents' age, back then—it's like it was one
big party. Good music, drugs that didn't kill you, road trips. And
you had all these big societal things going on: Vietnam, peace
marches, all that. We don't have anything, my generation. You
guys had the big party, and the kids just before us are all stockbro-
kers and bond salesmen, and what do we have? Our sex and drugs
will kill you, and our rock and roll sucks."

Life's a bitch, Tina thought, and then felt ashamed for not having more compassion. She'd had it good: grown up well—if a little
fast; married a good guy; raised a nice family. Through the filter of
memory, she hadn't had to contend with problems that kids today
had to. No wonder they looked back to the sixties as a golden time.
She pedaled the bike and offered up a small prayer: Please don't let
them catch anything bad, and please, please, please don't let bell-
bottoms come back into style.

She saw Jason at the video store, too. Friday or Saturday nights
she or Leonard, or sometimes both, would stop in for an evening's
video. She'd kid Jason about it. "This is what the big party has
come to, kid. A wild Saturday night with Eddie Murphy."

He'd recommend movies, and she found that he had good taste.
Artsy thrillers, like *Diva* and *Stormy Monday.* He even had his own
copy of Nicolas Roeg's *Bad Timing,* which he let her borrow.

"If you're gonna spend Saturday night in front of the tube," he
said, "you might as well make it worthwhile."

She returned the tape on Monday at the health club.

"How'd you like it?" he asked.

"Great," she said, getting onto the exercise bike. "Fast cars,
soundtrack by The Who, kinky sex. Just what every mother needs
when her kids are out on the town."

"Ever have wine spilled on you like Theresa Russell did?"

Her foot slipped off the pedal. Pretty bold of Jason. "No," she
said, recovering her rhythm. "But I can't imagine it *burning.*" What

the hell, she thought. He started it. "It's probably more just like having your period."

"I wouldn't know," Jason mused, and held her eye.

She smiled broadly back at him, and he went off to the rowing machine.

It felt good, this light sexual banter with a young, attractive man. Oh, she and Leonard had plenty of it—banter, that is. They touched, teased, flirted. They made love not infrequently, but it did seem that their lives had gotten so busy in the last few years that they didn't make as much time for intimacy as they'd like. They both worked—she as a pasteup artist at the town newspaper, he as an engineer for Digital—and that took up a chunk of the day, and then after work Seth would have to be picked up from band practice, or Leonard would be off coaching Amy's basketball team or Little League, or there was food shopping, or Leonard had to work late, or there was a PTA meeting, or the dog had to go to the vet. And even when they both were home, the kids were always around, plus their friends.

Tina and Leonard looked forward to evenings alone with great anticipation, but even then events seemed to conspire against them. Just last Friday, Marcie was at a concert in Providence, Amy was spending the night with a friend, and Seth was at a Red Sox game with the Little League. She and Leonard realized they had the night to themselves, so they'd make it romantic, spend some time together. They had drinks. She made a candlelight dinner. They drank a bottle of wine. It was nice. Tina went upstairs to take a bath, and Leonard thought he'd take the family's black lab, Elvis, out for a quick walk so he wouldn't bug them later. Well, Elvis tangled with a skunk and got sprayed—*sprayed!*—and Leonard too, and they both came back stinking like she couldn't believe. Tomato juice was supposed to take out skunk, but she had used the last of the tomato juice in the Bloody Marys before dinner. There was still a bowl of spaghetti sauce on the counter, so she grabbed that and ordered Leonard and Elvis into the tub, and that's where they all were until midnight, scrubbing themselves off with red clam sauce. By the time she got Elvis and Leonard and the bathroom cleaned up, it was after one, and all she could do was flop onto the bed, her fingers smelling of garlic and wet dog.

Marcie started staying out late. Her car, Tina's old hand-me-down station wagon, would crunch the driveway gravel and Leonard would be instantly awake, aware of the intrusion. He'd look at the clock: 1:45, 2:15. Marcie would slip into the house quietly, waking no one else. Leonard was relieved that she had gotten home safely, but annoyed that it was so late. He lay in bed listening to Tina's breathing and the flow of water through the house as Marcie washed up. He had replumbed the kids' bathroom, when? Three, no four, years ago. Shouldn't need attention for a while.

Listening to the water coursing through the pipes, Leonard remembered when he and Tina were Marcie's age, going out to bars or cruising to the beach and partying all night. He knew it was good that she was doing these things, that she had a great spirit, but still, he worried about who she was hanging out with. He could see her with a bunch of young construction workers or landscapers—day laborers and his little girl! When he dreamed of Marcie, she was always twelve years old; her thin, yet-to-be-filled-out face and body and her innocent look always caused a pang in his heart. On these nights when he tried to return to sleep, he would flash little dream snatches of his daughter removed in time, poignantly teetering on the verge of womanhood.

One night he woke suddenly. No car in the driveway, no sudden noise; 2:40 on the clock. He felt the sudden dread that Marcie was in trouble, told himself that was superstitious, countered that she was, after all, of his flesh and blood and consciousness, and thereby privy to some psychic link, and finally he got up, pulled on his running shorts, and went downstairs for some ice cream.

He was leaning against the open refrigerator door when the headlights bounced off the wall and the gravel crunched.

"Frozen yogurt?" he offered when Marcie came in. "It's Bavarian
chocolate chip."

"Only if you feed me," she said, kicking off her sandals.

It was their old conspiracy: when the two other kids were babies,
waking everybody up at night, he would comfort Marcie by sneak-
ing her down to the kitchen for a little treat of ice cream. Looking
at her now, in her makeup and tank top, smelling of a smoky bar,
he loved how she took delight in the yogurt, how her eyes filled
with girlish delight as she licked the spoon.

"God, thanks," she said. "This feels good on my throat."

"What's happening at the Stone House?"

"An R&B band. Pretty good. You'd like them."

"Who was there?"

"Oh, a few friends from high school. The usual gang."

He could picture them sitting around the dark booths in the
Stone House, a converted mill on the east end of town. They'd be
pretty much like kids of any decade, drinking and smoking and
enjoying this time when they were no longer children but not quite
adults. He asked if she was seeing anybody.

"Nobody in particular."

He'd noticed she hadn't been sporting any new neck ornaments,
but he didn't mention this. He fed her some yogurt.

"Nobody catching your eye?"

"Not really." She seemed to muse on her yogurt.

"Nobody?"

She shook her head. "Not really. There's this guy, he doesn't
notice me and I don't know if he's all that cool anyway."

"Well, who is he?"

"Forget it, really. I shouldn't have mentioned it."

"You're not going to tell me? I can't believe you're not going to
tell me."

"Forget it, I said. And quit hogging all the yogurt."

Oh, man. When she got like this there was no moving her. She got that stubborn streak from Tina. He fed her another spoonful of yogurt.

"Okay, okay. I'm not hassling you, I just want to know who's keeping company with my baby."

"Come on, Dad. I'm a big girl. I can take care of myself. How do you think I manage at school without you?"

"I know you *think* you can take care of yourself, and you know I trust you, but I know young guys—"

"I've been on the pill since September, you know."

He knew, but Tina had sworn him to secrecy. He gave Marcie her moment of silent effect.

"Well, I'm glad you are," he said. "It takes that and then some, these days."

She sighed. "I know. I know. You can't protect me forever, you know."

He put his arm around her. His heart filled as she tucked in naturally under his bicep.

"I know, sweets. It's just that you've never been the father of a beautiful girl."

She rubbed his chest.

"I'm not really that attracted to him," she said. "He's just kind of cute."

He buried his nose in her hair. God, he hated the smell of cigarette smoke. All the late nights and smoky bars she would encounter in the next few years, and the guys who would look kind of cute. He wished her a silent blessing.

"Let's get some sleep," he said.

"Might as well," she said. "We sure pigged all the yogurt."

Jason asked Tina to lunch. He was only a little embarrassed and did it with a minimum of hemming and hawing. She accepted. Nothing wrong with a little lunch. They met at the diner in the center of town, and she took a booth near the windows. Outside, the noon tide of pickups and vans was beginning to roll in, as Hurley's tradesmen took their lunch break. Local businessmen, too, in dress shirts with their ties loosened; shop girls and secretaries, lighting up cigarettes; the elderly, walking over from the old folks' home for some bread pudding or pie. Tina loved the diner. She ordered a seafood salad and a club soda with lime. Jason had a cheeseburger, fries, and a Coke.

He was wearing a braided bracelet: black strands woven together with bright blue and hot pink. It looked nice against his tan.

"Let me see your bracelet," Tina said.

"It's a wristband."

"Nice. What's it for?"

"It's not *for* anything," he said. He looked away. "It's just there."

"Did a girl give it to you?" she asked, teasing.

"I wish." He met her eye briefly and then looked away again. he had a handsome, open face. Tina could tell that he thought a lot by the way he paused sometimes before answering, looked out the window at something distant. Sometimes, though, a cloud seemed to pass over his face, and he wouldn't meet her eye.

"How come you and Marcie never got to know each other in high school?" Tina asked. He was only two years ahead of Marcie; she could see them together.

"She was a little younger, for one thing. And we traveled in different circles. She always hung out with the jocks."

True. Marcie had always liked the basketball and football players, gangling or overbulked young men who shifted and stammered in Tina's presence and who seemed uncomfortable with their hands. Hands in their pockets, hands on their hips, hands propping them up against a doorjamb, hands cracking knuckles, hands clasped in front of their privates. Their hands, their natural tools on the court or field, became in her kitchen as uncontrollable as cats.

"And you were no jock," she said.

"Ha. No jock. I like working out, but playing games seems kind of silly. Like kids who never grow up."

She nodded. Marcie's boyfriends had been much like that. "But

Marcie's grown up a lot this year at school—or at least she's trying to."

"Yeah, that's true."

"You see Marcie?"

"Sometimes at the Stone House. She's usually with her old buddies, but I can tell she's bored. She's outgrown them. Some nights everybody grabs a six-pack and heads up to the top of Pack Monadnock. I see her up there, too."

"Oh? What do you do up there?"

"Hang out and shoot the shit. Crank up the music and drink some beers. They won't let you build a fire, but we light lanterns. You can climb up the ranger station and see Boston."

She imagined the scene: the kids' car windows open, the music thumping out. Beers passed around. She pictured Marcie up on the ranger station with Jason, gazing at the lights of Boston, and wondered what it would be like to stand close to him in the summer night and share such a view.

He seemed to be reading her thoughts. He grinned, rattled the ice in his Coke.

"You've got to realize something," he said. "Marcie's a bit of a babe."

"A babe?"

"A babe. A doll. Her makeup is always just so. Her hair always looks good. She's always dressed to kill, or at least to inflict serious bodily damage. She's a babe. Like you."

She held his eye for a moment and then turned to her salad.

"I'm not sure how to take that," she said.

"You're a babe." The grin spread across his face. "Look around you. You're the hottest thing in this place. Look around town. I see a lot of older women—not that you're *older* older, I mean, you know—I see a lot of women, mothers, come into the video store, and they don't look like you: funky hair, big earrings, lipstick that says, 'Let me smear up your face, big boy.' "

"Oh, get real, Jason." Jesus!

"I am for real. Okay, you tell me: what does the neckline of that blouse say?"

"It says, 'Why don't you mind your own business?' " God, the nerve! "Just because I don't go around looking like I just fell out of the L.L. Bean catalog is no reason to—"

"Exactly my point! Most of the other good ladies in town are playing out their roles as Mother. You're not. You're proof that you can be a good mother and still look like your basic hot number."

"Oh God, I can't believe this."

But she knew it was true. In part, anyway. What the hell—she liked clothes. She had her own sense of style, and if it was a little colorful for Hurley, whose business was it but hers? She liked to look nice, and it wasn't her fault if men found her attractive. Leonard was a tolerant man, allowed her her space. Besides, she liked the way she looked.

"Jason," she said, "there are some things you learn as you get older. Not being judgmental is one of them."

"Okay, Mom." He grinned.

"Learning to look beneath the surface is another."

He craned his head toward her neckline. She felt herself flush.

"Developing your own style shows a person's inner strength." She knew she was beginning to lecture, but the kid needed to be taught. "It shows you're not going along with somebody else's idea of what you're supposed to look like. I no more want to look like a house mouse than you want to look like a jock."

"Hey, take it easy. I think you look great—Marcie, too. Marcie's lucky." He paused, grinning, nodding his head toward her conspiratorially. "Not every kid has a babe for a mom."

Of course, she told Leonard. And of course, Leonard was nonplussed. Lunch? No big deal. He went out to lunch with women all the time.

"But that's business," she said. "That's different. This was more of a social call."

"Well." He looked up from the garbage disposal he was repairing.

Amy had ground up a racquetball, and the thing was all jammed up. "Social, business. It's okay by me if it's okay by you."

She came around the table and rumpled his hair.

"Let's make more time for each other," she said.

"Sure," he said. "Keep the dog away from skunks and the kids away from anything with moving parts."

"That's the problem with guys like Leonard and Ray," Marisse said. "They learned too well. Sometimes you want a little possessiveness, a little jealousy."

"I don't know," Tina said. They were at work. Marisse was pasting up the real estate page, and Tina was designing an ad for the Hillside Fruit Farm. The photo showed an old geezer popping an enormous strawberry into his mouth: *Pick Yer Own!*

"It's like, if there weren't a bit of the illicit about you and Jason, would you still be attracted to him?"

"I'm not attracted to him," Tina said. "I mean, not seriously. It's just fun. Which typeface do you like for the fruit farm: Benguiat or Windsor?"

"Benguiat. It looks like strawberry vines. I think you are attracted to him . . . a little."

"Well, maybe a little. He is cute as a button." She paused and looked up from her work. "But get real, Marisse. I'm old enough to be his mother. I'm happy with Leonard."

"I know you are," Marisse said, rubbing down an ad. "But are you *getting* enough?"

"Ha!" Tina laughed, without looking up from her computer. "Forty-eight-point head, or thirty-six?"

"Forty-eight," Marisse said. "Help the old guy sell some strawberries. It sounds like you and Leonard need to break out a bit—split for the islands for a week, go to Manhattan for some nightlife."

"Easy for you to say," Tina said. "I've got three kids to keep track of."

"The kids'll be here when you get back. Ray and I'll watch the kids."

"Box this ad in, or give it a funky border?"

"Box it in," Marisse said. "Keep it simple."

On Saturday, Tina asked Leonard to take her out.

"Like a date," she said.

"A date?"

"A date. Pick me up in your car with the stereo up loud and take me out to dinner."

"Pick you up in my car?" he asked.

"Come on, Lenny, be *creative*." She fluffed her hair. "God, I'm tired of videos on the weekends—you'd think we were a couple of old married farts."

He picked her up at seven-thirty. He snuck out while she was still putting on her makeup, cruised around listening to the Beatles for a while, and then came back to the house. He cranked up the stereo as he turned the corner. It felt cool. He got a quick pang of sense memory: the feeling he used to have cruising in his customized VW bug through Tina's Long Island neighborhood, the stereo blasting and the breeze coming in the windows. A date with his wife, after nineteen years of marriage. It didn't seem that long. He always thought you were supposed to feel old, or at least middle-aged, by this time.

He left the stereo thumping "Sergeant Pepper" and went up to the door of his house. The screen needed patching. He rang the bell, and then remembered that that was on his list to fix, too. Seth answered his knock.

"Hello, Seth," he said. "Is Tina ready?"

Seth looked at him as if he had just landed in a spaceship.

"Is Tina ready? We've got a date."

"Date?" Seth asked, without moving a muscle on his face.

"A date, junior. As in *going out?*"

"Going out? You mean we're not watching videos?"

"*You* can watch as many videos as you want. Tina, your mother, is tired of videos on Saturday night, and I'm escorting her out."

Seth locked the screen door.

"Wait here, sonny," he said. "Make yourself at home."

Leonard smiled as Seth turned away. The little bastard.

"Mom! There's some friggin' weirdo down here asking for you! Driving a boom box."

Tina came down tightening a red belt around her white jumpsuit. Just like it used to be, Leonard thought. She was never quite ready when he'd arrive, still slipping on her shoes or tying back her hair.

"My date!" she said. "And so punctual!"

She kissed Seth on the forehead. "There's pasta salad in the fridge, sweetie. And I got you two videos: *Terminator 2* and *Beverly Hills Cop.*"

"Have her back by midnight," Seth told Leonard. "Or your ass is grass."

They went to a new place in Peterborough, a converted mill with brick walls and glass tables and black lacquerware. They had salmon mousse and veal *au forestière* and a good Chardonnay. Tina was enjoying herself, and this made Leonard happy, because she had wanted to have a nice evening. A small thing to ask, really: just a nice evening out. No house projects in the way, no emergencies with the kids. To be well-off enough to have a nice evening out and not worry about it. Not bad, he thought, sipping espresso.

After dinner they went over to the little place that played folk music and listened to an Irish trio. Leonard didn't care much for Irish music; it always sounded like a parody of itself. But Tina liked it, and he enjoyed the two brandies he drank there.

When they got into the car for the drive home, Tina scooched over on the seat next to him. "You know what I want to do?" she asked.

"What?"

"Go parking."

"Parking?" he asked. "As in making-out-in-the-backseat parking?"

"Yeah, that kind of parking."

She was serious. She had that expectant look, a kind of anxious smile that begged him not to turn her down.

"Okay, sure," he said. "I may be a little rusty."

"I can refresh your memory," she said, and grabbed him in a way he was not expecting.

"Where to?"

"Go up Pack Monadnock," she said. "I've always wanted to go up there at night."

The mountain was only five minutes away. As they wound up the access road, their headlights picked up tree trunks, rocks, small glowing eyes. At the top, a couple of cars were slewed in front of the picnic tables, with some kids sitting on the fenders, drinking. Leonard pulled around to the far side of the parking lot and backed in under some trees.

"Let's get out," Tina said. "I want to see the view."

The night was beautiful. The sky was a deep, deep blue against the deeper black of the mountains, and in the valleys the lights shone from the small towns. Off to the southeast, Boston glowed bright. Tina hugged up against him, her jumpsuit a white slash in the darkness. She felt good under the jumpsuit, and he was glad they had stayed in shape over the years. He couldn't imagine having become dumpy and unattractive to each other. When he kissed her, he remembered the pleasure of kissing in the night air.

From the mountain road, a truck engine ground and shifted, ground and shifted. It emerged into the lot and pulled over by the kids drinking.

They went back to the car and made love. While they were so engaged—the jumpsuit was a minor inconvenience, but at least over the years he had perfected the technique of removing a brassiere—he was aware of other cars and motorcycles arriving over by the kids.

"Popular spot," he said afterwards, straightening his clothes.

"I can see why."

He squeezed her arm. "God," he said, and exhaled. He rolled down the foggy window. "Mmmm."

The evening air wafted in, bringing the cool smell of spruce. Kids' voices, rowdy. A beer can clattered on the parking lot.

"Leonard?"

"Mmmm."

"Are you happy?"

"Of course I'm happy. Aren't you?"

"Yes, I am," she said, leaning her head on his shoulder. "This was a great date. We need to do this more often."

"Sure. Whenever you want."

"I mean it. I need more than PTA meetings and Little League."

"We've got it pretty damn good, Tina."

"I know we do. I'm not complaining. I just need some excitement now and then. You want to pick a weekend and let's go to New York? Just the two of us?"

"New York?"

"We can see a show, listen to some music."

"Get mugged, bang up the car."

"Oh God, forget it."

"How about Maine? A weekend in an inn? Walks on the beach, breakfast on the porch."

"Sounds exciting. Like I'm going to get a nosebleed any second."

"Look—I hate New York. It's dirty, it's expensive, it's a hassle. It's not what I want to do."

"Forget it."

"Sorry. It's not my thing."

Across the way, someone was revving a motorcycle. Another beer can clattered across the lot, closer this time.

"Time to roll," Leonard said. "The natives are getting restless."

"Mmmm." Chickenshit, she thought.

He started the car and eased out from under the trees. The headlights cut across the gang of kids; many of them turned to look.

"Jesus!" Leonard exclaimed. He aimed the car down the mountain road. "That was Marcie! I'm sure I saw Marcie."

"Oh?"

"Yeah. Didn't you see her? In that blue T-shirt from school?"

"Mmmm, no. I didn't see her," Tina said, but she didn't really register what Leonard was saying. The face she had seen was not Marcie's. It was just a glimpse, but he had turned toward them; she was sure she had seen his ponytail.

Tina finished her workout and looped a towel behind her neck, began vibrating her muscles loose. The afternoon was free. Wednesdays were short days, the paper having been put to bed Tuesday night. After some filing and cleanup in the morning, she had come by the club to exercise. Now the warm afternoon stretched lazily before her: no work, no kids, no husband until six o'clock.

She found Jason doing calf extensions. His gray T-shirt was blotchy with sweat. Strands from his ponytail curled behind his ears.

"Want to go get a beer?" she asked.

He smiled. "Sure," he said. "Let me finish this set."

"Great—meet you down front after your shower."

As she took her own shower, she thought: It's only a beer. It's like having lunch. It's no big deal. But when she brushed her hair, she looked into the mirror to see what she found, and she found she could not hold her own gaze. So she grinned and crinkled up her eyes and pursed her lips for the lipstick. You wanton thing! she reproached herself. Asking a young guy out for a beer! She left the top button of her blouse open, since Jason seemed so interested in necklines.

She drove them to the China Goddess, a dive run by some Chinese who came up from Boston every day in a van. The clientele was bikers and millworkers. The place had no windows, and the giant tiki goddess over the front door was giving up its paint to the weather.

"So *this* is where the hip, trendy, thirtysomething crowd hangs out," said Jason.

"Ha! This is where I can get an egg roll and a Chinese beer," she said, thinking, This is where no one I know will see me.

Inside, the place smelled of fried wonton and disinfectant. It had a gaudy Polynesian decor with toothy statuary and red Naugahyde upholstery. She chose a booth along the far wall. Jason stood aside and waited for her to sit. She smiled: such the young gentleman!

The waiter came over and she ordered a plate of egg rolls and two Tsing-Taos. Jason began telling her about plans for college. He had even driven over to Durham and spoken to a UNH admissions counselor about a film studies program. "I'm too late for the fall semester," he said. "But I can shoot for January."

"That's great," she said. "I can picture you at UNH."

She could, too. She imagined him under the big trees in a leather jacket with a backpack slung over his shoulder, talking to a couple of girls.

"A lot of cute girls over there, Jason."

"I noticed," he said. "I parked out by the tennis courts."

The waiter brought their beers. She raised her glass. "To your college career."

"To those girls in their tennis skirts."

He grinned and held her eye. A muscle worked in his jaw. He had that twenty-year-old bravado, assured that he could approach girls playing tennis, and that they'd stop their game and talk to him.

"Well, I'm glad I'm not *their* mother," she teased.

"Hey, I'm a healthy growing boy. Don't tell me you didn't have a good time in college, Ms. Love Generation."

"I didn't go to college," she said. "I had Marcie."

"Ah," he said, and spread his hands as if he had made a point. His forearms were so taut and smooth, she had an overpowering urge to run her fingers along them. "Speaking of Marcie," he continued, "I was talking with her about her school down South.

Sounds pretty cool."

The egg rolls came. She spread some hot mustard on the plate.

"When did you see Marcie?"

"The other night, up on the Pack."

"You mean you actually deigned to speak to the babe?"

"Hey, cut it out. Marcie's cool."

"I thought she was too much of a little doll. Too much of a glamour puss."

"Come on, you know what I meant. I've never really gotten to know Marcie—she's a lot cooler than I thought. I just never got to talk to her before."

The egg rolls were as coarse as grass, but the spicy mustard went straight to Tina's sinuses. She loved that rush, and she washed it back with the beer. Two motorcycles rumbled up outside. The bikers entered, haw-hawing and slapping themselves off. They gave Tina the eye on their way to a booth in the corner.

"Do bikers have jobs?" she asked in a low voice. "Or do they just ride around all day?"

"They work in the mills," Jason said. "Garages. A lot of them are Vietnam vets."

"Why do they all look like that? So beefy?"

"It's all beer fat. They run on Budweiser."

"That's what we need to do with you," she said, touching his arm. "Work on a beer belly for you. Drink up."

They drained their beers, and she signaled the waiter for two more. This time Jason proposed the toast.

"To Marcie," he said.

"Okay, to Marcie."

She drank and looked into the smiling mouth of the tiki god over the booth. She had an urge to be twenty years old again, to be a pretty girl in tennis whites. But she had never been one of those prissy little things. She had hung out on boardwalks in her bikini, snapping gum and drinking Cokes. She had chosen her boys, taken them onto the beach at night. And she had become a mother at the same age as other girls were going off to college and playing tennis.

Jason's hair was still wet, slicked along his skull and tied tightly back. He was talking about Marcie, rattling on. How do you arrange an affair? she wondered. She couldn't exactly check into the Hurley Motel. She knew Mr. Walmsley, the proprietor. She did his ad every week. Her house was out. And Jason lived with his parents. Drive out on the back roads and do it in the car like a couple of teenagers? God, it seemed so desperate!

"I mean, she's got a crazy streak a mile wide, and she loves to party, but basically she—"

The beer and the mustard were starting to kick in. She drank from the bottle, took a long pull and savored the froth in the back of her throat. As she did, she looked at the grinning tiki god again, and a phrase came into her head: . . . *not laughing at you, laughing with you.* She wondered how Jason would react if she looked him in the eye and said, *Have you ever made love to an older woman?* As if on cue, a loud guffaw erupted from the bikers across the room.

"Assholes."

"Huh?" Jason said.

"Nothing," she said. "How come you're so interested in Marcie all of a sudden?"

"I—well, I just saw her the other night, for one thing. She *is* something we have in common."

She held his eye and reached up to her hair. She did it slowly, brought her elbows together knowing what they did to her blouse, and fluffed her hair. She saw his eyes dart.

"Is that all we have in common?"

He flushed quickly. "Armpits," he said. "We have armpits in common."

She laughed.

"That's kind of a shock," he said. "Seeing your armpits. They look like a private part. They look like a shaved vulva."

"European women don't shave theirs."

"Their armpits or their vulvas?"

"Their armpits. I don't know about the other." *Vulva* was not a word she used. Where did kids come up with these clinical terms? Sex education class, probably.

"Do that again," Jason said, sipping his beer.

"Do what?"

"That thing with your hair. I want to see your armpits again."

"Oh, please, Jason."

"No, really. Please, just do it."

What the hell, she fluffed her hair. She moved exactly the same, even took a deep breath.

"Wow," he said, leaning back. "I like that blouse. I do like that blouse."

Now she leaned back. She had the sudden sensation of being at the beach, standing in deep water and feeling the undertow pull at her. She wished she could take the move back. She wished she had on a sweater. She wished she could control her impulse to provoke men, when she really didn't mean anything by it. She didn't know what to say, so she changed the subject.

"So what's your interest in Marcie?"

"I'm interested in her armpits." He drank his beer.

"I'm serious, Jason. I'm her mother, remember, and I want to know."

His eyes slid away from her. "Look, I'm just getting to know her. I think she's neat. Like I was saying, I think she has this basically inflated vision of herself, like you guys must have just spoiled—"

God, she thought. How little they know about things. She tuned out Jason's words, but his voice washed on, like surf in the background. What was she doing here, drinking beer in a biker bar with a kid her daughter's age? She looked over at the waiter. He stood silent and watchful, his narrow eyes expressing nothing. What was that word they always used for Orientals? Inscrutable? That was it. That was this waiter exactly. He stood quietly in his neat white shirt and short jacket, he brought them food and drink, he cast no judgments. The bikers getting soused, the lady with the kid, it didn't matter. He waited on his clients and attended to his restaurant, and then, late at night, he returned to his wife, to his China goddess, in Boston.

How decent, she thought. How very decent. Through the buzz of the beer and Jason's prattle, she realized she was thinking of Leonard. He had been with her this whole time, a quiet, hovering presence. He was always with her, had always been almost as long as she could remember, from their crazy first years when he was still in school and up at night with a baby in one arm and an engineering text in the other, and from apartment to dingy apartment and then to their first house, a ranch—what a thing, a house of their own!—and then their current farmhouse: what, nine years ago now? ten? and all the work they had put into it, painting and wallpapering, and Leonard balancing himself up on the roof or crawling around in the basement with some dirty old pipes or mucking out the gutters. Throughout it all, throughout all the years, Leonard had been a good man. Had taken seriously his role as father, husband, pal. Loved her and the kids as best he could, which was to say, considerably well. Even now, as she sat across the booth from this prattling boy-man, she could feel him spreading his arms and saying, *Enjoy yourself—I know why you have to do this.*

She looked at the waiter and smiled. He thought she wanted something, so he nodded and came over.

"Oh, thank you," she said. "Just our check, please."

"Jeez," Jason said. "Just when I was starting to lose my inhibitions."

"Save your inhibitions, kid. You'll need them when you get older."

"Huh?"

"Never mind. Listen—" She looked at her watch. "I've got to run Amy to her softball game. I completely forgot."

"Time to turn back into Mother?"

"Something like that. Listen, I'm sorry, really. Can I drop you someplace?"

"No thanks," he said, looking around. "I'll take my Harley."

She left a twenty on the table and thanked the waiter on the way to the door. Behind her, the bikers hooted.

The afternoon sun was bright after the dark interior of the China Goddess. She fumbled with her sunglasses; there was an awkward moment of silence.

"Well, hey," Jason said. "That was fun—we ought to do it more often."

"Um, I don't think so."

"What do you mean?"

"I mean, I don't think it's a good idea for us to get together like this. I think I've given you the wrong message, and I apologize for that."

"What message? That it's okay for two people who find each other interesting to go out for a beer?"

"It's not that simple. It's not so black and white. It gets all complicated with things like open-necked blouses and shaved Volvos or whatever. One of the things you learn as you get older is that there is no black and white. There's only shades of gray."

"You just can't keep from lecturing me, can you?" He got a taunting smirk on his face. "Is that what you do to your husband—flash him a little tit and then lecture him for looking?"

In an earlier time, she thought, a woman might have slapped a man for a crack like that. But she just shook out her keys.

"You sure I can't drop you someplace, Jason?"

"It looks like you just have," he said.

Oh, Christ. Now he was going to sulk.

"Look, Jason, I'm sorry you're taking this this way, but we have to face facts: I'm a married woman, and you're young enough to be my son. I like seeing you at the health club and the video store, but that's going to have to be it."

"Unless I start dating Marcie." The smirk was back. God, she hated it.

"You steer clear of Marcie," she said.

He hoisted his gym bag. "Here's to you, Mrs. Robinson."

She watched him in her rearview as she drove away. He stuck out his thumb at an approaching pickup truck. Although he stood in a tough kind of slouch, he looked young and small by the side of the road.

Marcie's call came at 2:35. Tina shot out of bed and got it. Leonard groaned in his sleep and ducked under the pillow.

"Ma?"

"What's wrong, sweetie?" She could tell from Marcie's voice it was bad.

"Just come get me, Ma?"

"Are you okay? Marcie?"

"I'm okay. But hurry. He's coming back, I know it."

Oh, Christ. Goddamn! Tina beat her stomach.

"Where are you, baby?"

"You know the convenience store across 101 at the foot of Pack Monadnock? I'm in the phone booth there. But it's too bright and I'm going to hide in the woods. I jumped out of his car and ran down one of the hiking trails to get here, but he's already driven through twice—"

"Who's he and where's your car?"

"My car's at the Stone House. I'll explain later. Just hurry, please."

"Are you okay, Marcie?"

"I'm okay, Ma, really, I—"

"Did he—" She did not want to even think the word. "Do you need—"

"Headlights, Ma. Bye."

"I'm on my way. You hide. I love you, sweet—"

The phone clicked dead. She pulled on her sweatsuit. Leonard shifted under his pillow but didn't surface. Before she left the room she paused, knelt by the bed, and put her hand on her husband's back. She felt the ebb and flow of his breathing, the ebb and flow. Then she rose and left to pick up her daughter.

FIVE

The Summer of Driving Naked

The same summer the purple finches nested on the front porch, Ray and Marisse Vann started driving around town naked. It started over dinner one Friday evening. As they spoke of the small events of the day—Ray had gotten a new graphics program for his computer, Marisse had lunched with Tina—Ray told Marisse of something unusual he had seen on his way to work.

"It's just getting light," he said. "Cars still have their lights on, and I'm cruising down Route 3 in the passing lane. Doing about seventy. I see this pair of lights moving up on the right—not too fast, but steady. It's not a cop; the lights are too close together. It gets up next to me—some kind of American compact—and it's a man and a woman, the man driving. But something looks funny. Just something. The guy doesn't have a shirt on. No big deal—it's summer, a lot of guys drive around without shirts. But this is six o'clock in the morning. It's still cool out. Okay, they pull past. The windows are a little steamy. After they passed me, I realized something: the woman didn't have a shirt on either. I thought—it was just a perception—I thought I saw her bare shoulder.

"I tucked in behind them and when I got an opening I passed them. Hiked myself up in my seat, and sure enough, this woman did not have a top on! These two are driving down Route 3 in the middle of the morning commute absolutely naked!"

"Come on," Marisse said. "How did you know they were naked? I mean totally?"

"You can just tell. There's something about the way they were sitting. A little . . . hunched forward, or something, like they were covering themselves up. And the steamy windows."

"Anybody can have steamy windows at that hour of the morning."

"No, it was different. I'm telling you, these people were naked. They saw me looking at them and they both broke out laughing and waved at me. They do this for kicks."

Marisse searched his face for any sign that he was putting her on. "I'm not kidding you. Naked. Right down Route 3."

The next day was Saturday, a day of chores for suburban working couples like Ray and Marisse. Marisse went to the bank and the supermarket and the drugstore. In the afternoon, she locked herself into her studio to work on a painting. Ray went to the dump and the hardware store and then after lunch he cut the grass. The frigging grass, he thought as the red mower spewed clippings and fumes all around him, it's cutting the frigging grass in the summer and raking the frigging leaves in the fall and shoveling the frigging snow in the winter. You own a house and then you're a slave to it. The whole thing needs painting and the bathroom light needs to be fixed and the roof needs to be patched and the chimney is starting to come apart. A storm last winter blew down a brick and it sounded like somebody dropped a bomb on the place.

That evening Ray and Marisse ordered out for Thai food and watched a video. It was a Dennis Hopper film that left them deadened: they didn't feel like watching more TV, didn't feel like reading, like going to bed, like making love; didn't feel like anything, really, so they wandered through their downstairs rooms for a few minutes and then drifted out into the backyard. It was a nice night. They were in light clothes, and the freshly cut grass smelled good, but the mosquitoes found them, and Marisse could not abide mosquitoes. Ray could not abide the thought of going aimlessly back into the house. Why were movies like that so popular? People felt dead enough already, he figured. They needed to feel a little more dead just to feel alive.

Then he remembered the couple in the car.

"I've got an idea," he said to Marisse.

"If it'll get us away from these mosquitoes, I'm for it."

"Let's go for a drive naked."

"I'm not for it."

"No—let's do it."

"Ray, I am not going for a drive naked."

"Just down the street. Look—it's dark, it's late, there's nobody out. We'll just go down to the corner and back. It'll be a kick."

Marisse considered this. Ray was nuts. The very idea of driving past the neighbors' houses—it scared her but also made her smile. She could tell Tina on Monday over coffee, and they'd crack up. And it wasn't as if she had any kids to be respectable for. What the hell. She pulled her T-shirt over her head and threw it at Ray.

"Get naked, big fella. We're going for a spin."

Ray shucked off his shorts and headed for the garage. It was one of the things he loved about Marisse—whatever crazy idea he came up with, sooner or later she'd go along. The concrete garage floor was warm and gritty after the cool grass. Marisse started to bring her T-shirt into the car.

"Uh-uh," Ray said. "You have to be totally naked. Physically and psychically. No chickening out at the first streetlight."

She hung her shirt and shorts on the lawn mower. The velour bucket seat of Ray's Honda felt soft and nice, and she giggled as Ray folded himself in behind the wheel. They sat in the dark a moment. Marisse switched on the radio and found the Boston blues show and adjusted the volume.

Ray backed out and didn't turn on the headlights until the car was in the street. The green-white dashboard illuminated their bodies. They looked at each other. Marisse giggled again. Ray snorted and shifted into second.

Most of the houses were dark: the Rosens', the Bains'. Marisse imagined Cynthia Rosen, the picture of suburban motherhood, asleep in a summer nightgown, a light robe nearby in case she had to get up and tend to one of the girls, and she wondered what Cynthia would think if she knew Marisse was riding past her house without a stitch on. Well! Cynthia would be appalled! Past the Stevenses' and then past the Bartolomeos' on the other side of the street. A light in the Stevenses', but everything else was dark. Under the streetlight they were momentarily illuminated. She looked at Ray: his chest hairs, slight belly, and thighs were all visible. His lap was in shadow. She could see her breasts, white in the light.

"Wow," she said. "Good thing there's only a couple of streetlights."

"The better to see you with, my dear," Ray said, and chucked her under her near breast.

They went round the big curve at the lower end of the street. The houses down here were not as well-kept as the Victorians and four-squares up at her end, and Marisse didn't know anybody down here. She began to feel more comfortable in her nakedness. All the houses were dark, the people asleep. They all seemed so safe in their little dens, snug in their burrows. She, on the other hand, felt a touch of danger, of wildness. An animal of the night, she thought. A night bird.

Ray wore a bemused look. She couldn't tell what he was thinking. She reached over and ran her hand along his thigh. At the
corner, where Monadnock teed into Main Street, Ray began to
swing the car around.

"Go down Main Street," Marisse said. "Just a little ways."

He looked at her like, *You were the one uptight about this.*

"This is fun," she said.

There were more streetlights on Main Street, but also sidewalks,
so the houses sat farther back. A pair of headlights approached and
the car swooshed by, illuminating them only to themselves. What
if the car had sideswiped them? she thought. Or what if a cop
stopped them, a random drunk-driving check? The farther they got
from Monadnock Street, the more exposed she began to feel. There
were laws about public indecency.

"Maybe we ought to go back," she said to Ray.

"Sure," he said. "This was farther than I imagined anyway."

They passed another car on the way back, and then they were
on Monadnock Street, climbing the hill, going around the curve.
Halfway up, they could see a flashlight's jittery beam, and then
their headlights picked up a person walking. An old man, Nicolo
Bartolomeo, out for a late walk. Marisse sank down in her seat, and
then they were past.

"Hey, old Nicko, get a load of this," Ray said to the closed interior of the car. "A naked lady driving past your house."

"Oh, leave old Nicko alone," Marisse said. "Get a load of the
naked lady yourself."

Next morning, Ray put on some jazz and settled in with the Sunday
paper. Marisse went out to water the petunias. She had three pots
of them hanging across the front porch. A pair of purple finches
had made their nest in one, so she was careful as she watered that
pot. The finches had begun building their nest in May, and the
predominant sound since then had been their distinctive "CHEEP!"
The female would sit on the nest while the male stood guard at any
of several posts: the maple tree in front of the house, the birch on

the side, the telephone line across the street. He'd announce his presence: "CHEEP!" It was an assertive statement. "CHEEP!" *I'm here!* "CHEEP!" *I'm here!* It was both a reassurance to his mate and a warning to other birds, marauding cats, and clumsy humans.

The finches' situation was not simple. They had shown both brilliance and shortsightedness in their choice of the petunia pot. Brilliance, because the pot hung from the eaves of the porch, out of the reach of cats and tucked neatly away from the rain, and the leafy canopy of the petunias gave both camouflage and protection from the sun. But it was shortsighted, too: the petunias had to be watered in order to maintain their leafy protection, and the nest could be easily flooded.

Marisse took her watering duties seriously and approached the nest quietly. She kept a stepstool on the porch so she could see exactly where she was pouring. And she poured only enough to sustain the petunias and not soak the nest. As soon as Marisse opened the porch door, the finches flew to one of their various posts and began raining curses upon her: "CHEEP! CHEEP! CHEEP!" When Marisse was done, they'd alight on the pot, inspect the nest, and then settle back into the process of perpetuating their species.

This morning was no different, and the finches took off as Marisse opened the screen. She loved the colors of the male—raspberry, dusty rose—but the female was as drab as a sparrow. Hunker down in the nest and have babies, while the male flits about putting color into the world. If the female finch were human she'd be one of those housebound mothers who did nothing but tend the kids— never put on a party dress, never see her skin under neon light. Never, she thought, remembering last night with a guilty little smile, go for a drive naked.

In the living room, Ray looked up from the Sunday paper and watched Marisse pour the water into the petunias. He felt good from the night before and from the jazz playing, and the sight of his wife performing this simple act filled him with love. She used a blue earthenware crock, and poured with such attention and tenderness that she might be tending her own babies. She'd make a good mother, he thought. Probably she would. She was a kind person and giving of herself. She was attentive to her cats, and that ought to be some indication. But she shared his boredom with things domestic, even though she still wrestled with the notion of having children. Ray had made his decision: he did not want kids. He liked kids well enough, as long as they weren't spoiled brats, and he enjoyed spending time with his nieces and nephews. All his friends who had kids told him he'd make a good dad. But he just did not have any desire to be a parent, and he figured this was reason enough not to do it.

For Marisse it was not so simple. As the woman, she felt the burden of children more heavily, and at thirty-five, she felt the biological sands running. Every month another grain slipped through the hourglass of her uterus.

As she finished watering, she noticed someone walking past the house. Old Nicolo from down the street. He spoke first: "'Nice day."

"Beautiful," Marisse said. "I have a pair of finches living in my petunias."

"Purple finches or house finches?"

"That's the male there." She pointed to the telephone wire, where the bright male was perched.

Nick shaded his eyes. "Purple. Not red like the house finch."

"CHEEP!" said the finch.

"That's him," Nicolo said.

"They make a racket," Marisse said.

"Turn up the music," Nicolo said, nodding toward the front door. "That'll drown 'em out."

Next Saturday night, they went for another drive. It was not impulsive this time; they planned it over breakfast. They set it all up just so: Ray grilled swordfish for dinner and Marisse made a Caesar salad. They split a bottle of wine. They listened to John Coltrane and Sonny Rollins, and nursed their wine until it was late enough.

They joked and mused, and looked forward to their naked drive like a couple of kids anticipating Halloween.

They headed out into the country. This was not hard to do in a town the size of Hurley, and within a few minutes they had left the streetlights behind. Ray opened the Honda's sunroof and plugged in a Thelonious Monk tape. Marisse settled back into the plush velour bucket and looked out the sunroof at the stars. They passed farmhouses with glowing windows, barnyards brittle in sodium illumination, and contemporaries with their beams and soaring glass triangles.

God, it was lovely! Marisse noticed, as they passed under trees, how the headlights illuminated the veins of the leaves. She began to see details: the weft and warp of cedar shakes, the cold etch of a wrought-iron railing. She smelled the sweet earthy dairy and the dank forest mulch. She felt the window with the back of her hand: cool ice. Why had she never noticed these things? She had the sudden desire to paint, to capture with her brush the texture of the night. Above the piano and bass and the rushing air, she heard the drone of peepers. She shifted in the seat and her own scent rose to her. It was wonderful, all your senses turned on as they couldn't possibly be when you were fully dressed and focused on a destination.

Ray pulled up out of the woods and drove along a high ridge in the town of Wilton. The sky opened wide on all sides. Marisse could look back to the right and see the lights of Hurley, and over to the left those of another town—Peterborough, she guessed. Higher up, the blinking red lights of a radio tower. She hiked herself up in the seat and stuck her head out through the sunroof. The wind blasted her ears and whipped her hair. The night! Blasting along naked in the night! She pushed herself higher until she was shoulders and chest out of the car. The night rushed by, all wind and flashing fenceposts and the sting of her hair, and up high, the slowly moving sky. She stood all the way up and held on to the rim of the roof. She shut her eyes. She wished she could be completely out there, legs and arms flailing, the night wind seeking out her hidden corners.

Ray grinned and accelerated. Marisse's knee was right beside his cheek. He loved the little crease her leg made at her hip, and the smooth plane of her stomach. He downshifted into a curve and wailed out the other side. The car was precise, the road smooth; he could run like this all night. Up here on top of the ridge you could see thirty miles in any direction, and off to the southeast was the distant glow of Boston. He wound through another curve, the tachometer needle jumping and the overhead cams making a nice high whine, and Marisse shifting her weight easily to counteract the g-forces. He came out of the curve and upshifted. Marisse's thigh next to his cheek: he leaned over and rubbed against it.

She felt the scratch of his beard; electricity rippled her skin. She returned the nudge and arched her back, giving the electricity a circuit around her buttocks and up her spine. The move rechanneled the wind and it swept down her back and through her legs, and she opened her eyes and there was another curve ahead so she braced herself and felt the pinprick of an insect hitting her chest.

Ray downshifted for the curve, the last on the ridge before heading back down into the woods, and noticed out of the side of his eye, ahead, on a tangent line to the curve and seen between Marisse's thigh and the windshield pillar, a glinting. A jittery reflection a fraction of a second away, and even as he hit the brakes and threw his arm out to brace Marisse, he knew the deer would step into the road. He braked hard but smoothly, holding Marisse, who strained backward to keep from being thrown out, and with some internal sensor modulating the pressure between his brake foot—*not too much, not too much!*— and his arm around Marisse's waist—*hang on, hang on!*—he brought the car to a sliding stop as the deer wobbled stiffly out of the brush and onto the road, eyes rolling, legs ungainly on the pavement. Its fur was patchy on its flanks, its winter coat still shedding. Ray heard the ticking of the Honda's valves, the clicking of the deer's hooves. An adrenaline rush came, fluttering his gut and his nerves right down to the fingers. Marisse slumped back into her seat. The deer flicked its tail and then trotted off into the woods on the far side of the road.

"Wow!" Marisse said, reaching out. Only when she touched him did he realize his tumescence. "Some ride." Her breath was quick.

Ray took it slower going home, winding down through the hills. Marisse turned up the stereo and reclined her seat. The piano notes twinkled out through the roof and into the sky, became stars. By the time they pulled into the garage, Marisse was almost asleep. Ray had to nudge her out of the car and half-carry her into the house.

"I think I want to have a baby," Marisse said. "A little girl."

"Sure. Anything you say."

"Ray, I saw the cutest little girl in the supermarket today. Curly blond hair, wet from the pool. Tan little stick legs, neon sunglasses. I mean, break your heart."

"Sounds pretty cute."

"I think I'd like to have a little girl. Someone to pal around with."

"What if you had a little boy?"

"No. No, I'd have a girl. Like a little sister. Tina's girls wear her clothes, and she theirs. They have a ball together."

"Tina started having kids when she was a teenager. By the time your daughter's old enough to wear your clothes, you'll be in floral housedresses and orthopedic shoes. She'll get a real kick out of your aluminum walker."

"Well, I think I want to."

"Right." They'd had some version of this conversation twenty, thirty times. Marisse would see a cute kid and get to thinking about it again. Ray knew that she needed him to talk her out of it, to reassure her that life would be okay without children. It wasn't hard for him to do this, so he played along until she was pacified.

"You think I'm too old?" she asked.

"You're getting there. Statistically, women over thirty-five are twice as likely to give birth to boys anyway."

"Get out. Where did you hear that?"

"It's common knowledge. Ask anybody who's waited until their thirties to have kids. They're talking boys."

"Well, a little boy wouldn't be bad either."

"Yeah, you could swap clothes. You'd look great as a GI Joe."

"I'm serious, Ray. What about when we're old? We'll have some neat young adults to keep us company."

"Are you kidding? How often do most kids see their parents these days? How often do we?—twice, three times a year, tops. Christmas, and once in the summer, and maybe one other time, if they come to visit us. You want company in your golden years, don't go counting on your own flesh and blood."

"Hmm . . ." she said. "Hmm, yeah. What if they turned out to be jerks? What if I had a boy and he turned out to be a druggie or a 7-Eleven robber or an accountant?"

"You'd better think this through," Ray said. "Kids are your basic big deal."

"Yeah, maybe. I can enjoy other people's kids and not have my own. Your sisters have plenty of kids for the family, and my brother."

"Right. And we don't have to worry about them mooching off us in our old age."

Throughout June and July, the CHEEPing of the finches was as regular a sound as the scraping of the crickets or the drone of a neighborhood lawn mower. When the first little bird hatched, it was bald and wormlike, and at first Marisse thought one of the adult birds had brought back a dead invertebrate as decor. But the little scrap of meat soon showed signs of life, opened its violet eyelids, sprouted some hairlike feathers. And soon it was joined by its siblings, five little birds in all, a quiet rustling in the bottom of the petunia pot.

Marisse was more careful than ever with the watering can, because now she worried about drowning the little finches. They were soon covered with down, and then feathers, and before long, they too began making little peeps. Even in their high-frequency piping you could hear the assertion, the claim to being, that would mature into the cheeping oratory of their parents. Eventually they got big enough that Ray and Marisse could count all five adolescent heads from the living-room window. How would they leave the nest? Marisse wanted to know. Ray answered, without knowing the specific logistics, that they would one day learn to fly. He had watched chubby prepubescent robins fluttering around the backyard, encouraged by their parents, trying their wings and eventually gaining flight. A few short glides at first, terminated by feathery tumbles in the grass, but it wasn't long before they got the hang of it and were easily launching themselves and gliding in for smooth landings. He assured Marisse it would be the same with the finches.

Through July, Ray and Marisse continued their late-night naked drives. Sometimes they went for long blasts out in the country, with music pumping out through the sunroof; sometimes they just tooled around town—through the residential back streets, up and down the commercial strip. On these around-town cruises, Marisse kept her hair pulled over her shoulders. Her nakedness wasn't visible. Nothing looked unusual, really. A man without a shirt on, no big deal. A couple of times they even went through the drive-up window at Dunkin' Donuts. The attendant was a middle-aged woman in thick glasses, and she simply thanked them and smiled as she passed them the bright bags of doughnuts and coffee. Sometimes when they got home they'd make love; other times they'd read or just go to bed.

"It's fun," Marisse told Tina at work. "It's just good, clean fun. We're not bothering anybody."

"But don't you worry about getting caught?"

"At first. Sometimes still. But unless we do something wrong or get into an accident, there's no reason for a cop to stop us. We're not hot-rodders or hell-raisers. We don't look like bad dudes. A middle-class couple in a Honda sedan doesn't exactly make a cop reach for the flashers."

"It sounds kind of crazy. God, you don't take any clothes at all?"

"None. That's what makes it exciting. You're just out there. Just you. It feels kind of liberating."

"Liberating? What do you need liberating from? You've got a good job, a good place to live. Maybe you need a hobby. They give belly-dancing lessons over in Nashua. Maybe you ought to have kids."

"It's just fun," Marisse said. "Actually, it's more than fun. It's kind of therapeutic, like a hot tub to Californians."

"Yeah, well," Tina said, "Leonard would never go for it. I mean, God, he's a Little League coach."

In August, thunderstorms. Mornings were muggy, with haze thickening and blocking the sun. By afternoon the clouds had started rumbling into each other, and the storm would break on Ray's drive home. Sometimes the storms would last into the evenings. Ray would take his coffee onto the front porch and squat against a column and watch the show. Marisse was concerned about the finches during these storms, because the wind would whip the petunia pot around. But the pot never fell, and the birds stayed hunkered down in their nest.

Until one Friday morning, that is, when Marisse went to water the petunias. The day was warm and close, sure to storm later. She was stuffy from the humidity, her sinuses blocked and achy. After Ray left for work, she filled her watering crock and opened the front screen. The two adult birds flitted from the nest. The young finches were a bobbing mob in the base of the petunia pot. They had shouldered aside the petunias and were about to tumble out of the pot, like too many passengers in a lifeboat.

Marisse climbed onto her stepstool. She was so congested her head felt as full as the watering crock. As she raised herself to eye level with the finches and breathed in the damp mustiness of their nest, she felt a tingling in her sinuses, a pressure in her chest, and before she could turn her head, eyeball to beady eyeball with the young birds, she sneezed. The finches exploded from the nest as if expelled from her nasal passages, and in an instantaneous rite of passage, flew off to all corners of the yard.

Marisse was too shocked even to pour the water. The nest was now empty, the finches dispersed. The adult birds, with much cheeping, rounded up their young and gathered in the birch tree. As if by prearranged signal, they all took off and flew directly across the street to the telephone wire. There they sat, the sleek parents and the chubby young, all cheeping and grooming their feathers, and generally acting pleased with themselves. Again as if on signal, they fell silent and then took off for a big swoop above the street and landed in the maple tree. They kept this up for the rest of the day. But slowly they began to drift away. When Marisse came home for lunch, their cheeping was less frequent. And when she got off work she stood in the driveway to watch for them. There was the occasional bright arc across the gathering clouds, a three- or four-bird formation swooping over the telephone wires, but clearly, the finches were leaving.

She felt a pang of sadness. She went up onto the porch, but saw no dark mass at the base of the petunias, heard no comforting peeps. She had raised those finches, damn it, and now they were gone. The phrase "empty nest" came into her head, but she felt it just below her heart.

The thunderstorm started and Ray came home. She told him about the finches. He thought the sneeze was pretty funny, but he didn't pay too much attention to her sadness over their departure. The work week was behind him, an evening of thunderstorms was ahead, and while Marisse cooked dinner he popped open a beer and flipped through the mail. The lights flickered during dinner, and Marisse asked Ray if she ought to draw a tub of water. What for? he asked. She wasn't sure, really; her mother had always filled the tub before thunderstorms.

After dinner, Ray cleaned up the kitchen while Marisse sipped her coffee and read a magazine. Another storm began rolling in, and she figured Ray would take his coffee onto the porch. It would be too lonely for her out there.

Instead, Ray suggested a drive.

"I don't know," she said. "In a thunderstorm?"

"It'll be wild," he said. "Lightning flashing all around. A dark and stormy night. Werewolves." He showed his teeth.

Marisse was apprehensive. "What if something happened?" She imagined their nude bodies being found in their lightning-struck car, the bizarre headlines.

But Ray teased and talked her into it. He wanted to head for high ground, where they could really watch the storm. What the heck, she thought. It beats sitting around feeling blue. On the way to the garage, though, she stopped in the laundry room and grabbed the first two things she found: a pair of Ray's gym shorts and a beach towel. She knew it was cheating, but she stuffed them under the passenger seat before Ray got there.

Ray headed toward Lyndeborough. A lot of ridgetop roads, no cars. As the lightning flashed and thunder rolled, they had the night to themselves. "Wow!" Ray would say after a spectacular lightning bolt, and there would be a moment of reversed afterimage on their eyeballs. At the base of one of the long, high ridges, Ray rounded a curve and in a lightning flash they saw a sight so absurd they both thought it was a hallucination: a kid on an aqua moped, wearing a tropical-print shirt and shorts, buzzing up the mountain road. They were by him in an instant, and his weak headlight barely flickered in Ray's rearview.

"Did you see that?" Ray asked.

"Jesus," Marisse replied. "That's that kid. Christopher something. He hangs around with the Rosen girls. He looked more exposed than we do. He wasn't wearing a helmet."

"Hell, he wasn't even wearing shoes—he had on flip-flops." Ray shook his head. "What's with kids anyway, riding around in weather like this?"

"You think we ought to go back and give him a lift?"

"Right," Ray said, and continued in a falsetto, "So then, officer, these two naked people pulled up and tried to make me ride with them. . . .' "

He had a point, but the kid had looked so vulnerable.

Ray found a turnout with a view of the valley, and he pulled the car off the road and shut off the lights. The rain pelted the roof. Gusts of wind shook the car and sent sticks and leaves past the windows. "Yeah!" Ray said as lightning arced over the valley and thunder boomed overhead. He was enjoying the storm, but Marisse was quiet. She didn't like storms, they frightened her. And she was thinking about the finches. How would they survive a storm like this? Where would they stay? With the wind blowing debris about, they should be in their nest. She pictured the family of birds huddled under a branch of a large tree, the trunk and upper limbs providing shelter, but in her heart she knew that they probably were not together, that the young finches on their day-old wings would be fending for themselves.

"Light show!" Ray said, as lightning flashed across the valley. "Far out!"

From their vantage point, they could see lightning striking the far mountainside, and then, after a big forked bolt splintered into the valley, the lights of a whole village flickered and went out.

"There goes Wilton," Ray said.

And then, farther down the valley, another set of lights shut off, as if a switch had been thrown.

"Lyndeborough Center."

"Do you think it's safe to be out here?" Marisse asked.

"Sure," Ray said. "We're grounded by the tires."

"I don't know, Ray."

"Oh, come on. Enjoy the show."

"What about the finches?"

"The finches? What about them?"

"Do you think they're okay?"

"Sure, they're okay. Nature has this way of taking care of its own."

"They only learned to fly today."

"Hey, don't worry. That sneeze did them more trauma than this storm. They're cooped up someplace nice and cozy."

He reached over for her, but she edged away. Lightning flashed. Ray howled his appreciation, but Marisse couldn't share it. Each lightning flash was like a searchlight, and they seemed to be coming closer. She huddled in the seat as the thunder boomed again. She did not want the lightning to illuminate her. She had an empty nest inside. Where other women had a nest they could fill with eggs and young birds whenever they wanted, she had only an empty straw bowl.

"What if every time the lightning flashes somebody could see us?" she asked. "Would you want them to?"

"Huh?"

"Nothing. Forget it."

"Will you relax? What's with you tonight?"

She slid over against him.

"I'm cold," she said.

He put his arms around her. "You sure are," he said, and switched on the heater. "We'll get you warmed up in a second. Or we can go. I just felt like seeing the storm."

"No big deal."

"No, really," he said. "Is it about the finches?"

"It's nothing, really." She wished he would shut up. She wished she were home.

"They're okay. Don't worry."

Electricity illuminated the car, thunder boomed right overhead, and a lightning fork etched out in front of them. It forked again and—they saw the whole thing—struck a large pine not fifty yards from the car. There was a ball of fire as the tree simply exploded. Several things happened at once, although the strongest image was that of the whole top of the tree falling straight down. It seemed to happen in slow motion, because as the top was falling, the middle of the tree blew to pieces in the fireball and things began hitting the car: first the shock wave and then in rapid succession a peppering of needles, a rain of splinters, and then chunks, branches, and a huge limb that CRACKed into the roof on Marisse's side. She screamed and jumped for Ray, the car shook, and then it was over. In a couple of days they would return—clothed—to see the damage: ten-foot-long splinters driven two feet into the ground, some thrown a hundred yards from the tree, which was seared and split from the jagged stump, the newly exposed flesh black at the edges, and the top of the tree in a heap, the needles still green. But right now, all they saw was the heavy limb across the windshield as the storm still raged.

"Jesus," Ray said. "Are you okay?"

She nodded. "I'm okay." When she heard her voice she realized she was sobbing.

"We'd better get out of here," Ray said.

He shifted into reverse and tried to back out, but the limb made a hideous scraping against the car.

"I'll have to move it," he said, and reached for the handle.

"Here," she said, and produced his gym shorts from under her seat.

"Thanks. Jeez, thanks for thinking of this."

She wrapped herself in the beach towel as she watched her near-naked husband tugging ridiculously at the limb, and when lightning flashed again—not so close—he ducked instinctively by the car. He got up immediately, but she had seen his face. Ray was scared.

Somehow this made her feel good. Enjoy your light show, Ray.

She got out to help him. The limb was long—longer than the car—and wedged between the wheel and the fender. She joined Ray in tugging at it, but it was jammed too tight.

"You go lift the heavy end," she said. "I'll work it free from the wheel."

He hoisted, she shoved from the side. She felt the limb budge, so she braced against the fender. "Pull!" she yelled at Ray, and as he pulled she shoved as hard as she could. The limb popped free of the wheel well, and they dragged it off. The fender was scraped.

"Lucky it didn't blow the tire," Ray said.

He started to back out. Just as he did, though, there was a whoosh and lights behind the car. He hit the brake. A large dump truck rumbled by, too fast. The storm was abating; the lightning was less frequent, the thunder farther away. The rain was steady, and the wiper on Marisse's side was bent.

"Close call," Ray said.

"Close call."

"That limb could have come right through the window."

Halfway down the mountain they rounded a curve and saw headlights. But something was wrong. The beams were tilted at a crazy angle. They weren't moving. Ray thought it was a reflection, or a trick of lightning. But then he saw the dump truck, slid off in the ditch, and the driver in the road, bending over something. Ray braked to a stop. The headlights illuminated the white T-shirt of the truck driver, his baleful look, and, at his feet, a twisted mess of bright aqua metal, a wire-spoked wheel rotating slowly, its red reflector winking at every rotation.

"Oh, God," Marisse said.

Ray got out. There was a dark shape just beyond the moped.

"Is he okay?" he asked the truck driver.

The truck driver didn't respond. Ray saw him blink behind his glasses.

"What the hell happened?" Ray asked, his voice rising. He knelt down. The kid's eyes were open. Blood came from his mouth.

"Are you okay?" Ray asked the kid.

There was no response.

"Are you *okay?*" he yelled.

He passed his hand in front of the kid's eyes. Nothing. He felt for a pulse, got nothing. He dug deeper for a vein in the neck. Put his head to the kid's chest, and heard nothing but a faint gurgle, like water spiraling down a drain.

He looked up. The truck driver was working his mouth as if

chewing, and he was rubbing the side of his head. It was bleeding, just above the cheekbone. His eyes were unfocused.

"Are *you* okay?" Ray asked.

The man made a noise like the bleat of a goat and walked into the middle of the road. He made a kind of circle and came back.

Ray returned to the car.

"It's bad, isn't it?" Marisse asked.

"I think the kid's dead. I can't get a pulse. The other guy's in shock."

"Oh God, Ray. I knew we shouldn't have come out tonight."

"Shut up and let me think."

"Oh God, oh God, oh God," Marisse said. Ray felt a tingling in his fingers, the touch of the kid's throat lingering on his hand. "Oh God, oh God, oh God," Marisse said, and right in time with these two syllables, a flashing yellow light reflected off her face. Oh God, flash-flash, oh God, flash-flash.

It was an electric company truck. It crested the hill and bore down upon them: flash-flash, flash-flash. Ray waved it down. There were two linemen inside.

"There's been an accident," he said. "You got a radio?"

They had. They called the police, and then went to look at the kid. Ray went to sit with Marisse. She was crying. He held her close.

The local police came first, then an ambulance, and finally the state police. They photographed. They tape-measured. They asked questions, they scribbled in pads. They filled the air with the metallic crackle of radios, and with blue flashing lights and red flashing lights and brilliant flares. They carted the body away: a siren split the night. They had Ray describe what he had seen. They went away and talked with the truck driver, and then they came back and had Ray describe again what he had seen. A tow truck arrived, and the local cop left with the truck driver. The state cop came back over to the car.

"Mr. Vann, I'll be writing up a report when I get back to the barracks. I've got just one more question for you. Would you mind telling me what you're doing out here in your present attire?" He passed his flashlight over Marisse, wrapped in her beach towel. "You and your wife."

Ray looked down at himself. He looked ridiculous; it was the first time he had noticed. All he had on was his shorts, and his legs and arms were covered with road grit and pine needles. He felt like just telling the truth, but he held back. He needed to say something, though. The cop looked him right in the eye, and the silence was growing.

"We were swimming," Marisse said.

"Swimming," the cop said.

"Skinny-dipping, actually. Up at the quarry." She jerked her head up the hill. "The storm took us by surprise and we made a run for the car. The truck went down over the hill not a minute before us."

The cop switched the beam back to Ray.

"That the way it happened, Mr. Vann?"

"That's it. We occasionally like to go skinny-dipping in the quarry. Only at night, of course."

"Of course." The cop switched off the beam.

"You folks be careful driving home. We may need to speak to you within the next couple of days."

The rain eased to a light drizzle, and neither of them spoke. The lights of Hurley came into view, and Marisse took quiet comfort from them. Streetlights, stoplights, even the damned McDonald's golden arches—these were the beacons that charted the passage home. As they turned up Monadnock Street, Marisse watched for their house, for the front porch light. She wanted to get inside, wrap up in a quilt, and walk from room to room, touching familiar objects.

SIX

Assault on the For Sale Sign

They moved through the suburban night with the stealth of commandos. Through a patch of woods, across backyards, around gardens. Dressed in black, they moved like shadows. On soles of rubber, they crept like cats.

Real cool, until Leonard Walker stumbled into the Marcoux's badminton net. He was out in front, the point man. When he walked into the net, he shrieked, thrashed at his head, tangled the net, and tumbled to the ground, dragging the support poles with him.

"Jesus," he said, "I thought it was a giant spiderweb!" He slapped at his face, tried to shake the net off.

"Sh-h-h!" hissed Susie Stevens. "You'll wake the whole neighborhood!"

Susie got Leonard untangled, and Ray Vann

and Ed Jacques helped him up. Ahead of them, just beyond
the Marcoux's birch trees, was their target: the floodlit Barr Construction sign announcing the houses for sale in the new development.

Barr Construction
Announces
Monadnock Woodlands.
A Collection of Saltboxes,
Garrisons, and Ranch Houses.
Starting at $189,000.
Call 603-868-6222.

They were going to hit the sign tonight, and hit it hard.

They were a little guerrilla band: Ray, Ed, Leonard, and Susie.
Suburban guerrillas. They had a specific enemy, and, like other
guerrillas, they had a strategy for resistance. But unlike their coun-
terparts in urban trouble spots around the world, their tactics
did not include the use of guns and bombs and hostages. No, Ray
and Ed, Susie and Leonard used whatever weapons they happened
to have in their garages or laundry rooms. After all, this wasn't
Beirut or Belfast or Berlin. This was Hurley, New Hampshire.
And their enemy wasn't a CIA agent or a British soldier or a
western industrialist, it was a particular real estate developer: Bill
Barr.

Tonight the weapons of choice were a can of black paint and a
one-inch sash brush.

Barr's sign gleamed creamy white with green lettering, glowing
in the light of in-ground spotlights. It sat back from Monadnock
Street, a good fifty feet up the new street that Barr had put in and
named after himself: Bill Street. It was the dumbest street name
Ray had ever heard, but it was typical of the developments that
spread all over New Hampshire in the 1980s. The developers

named the streets after themselves or their wives or kids: Jennifer
Court, Justin Lane. It was as if the bastards knew the houses they
were building wouldn't last, so they named the streets after themselves in order to leave *something* permanent behind.

In the spotlights' glare, the sign was as bright as a McDonald's
drive-up menu. Ray checked the street for cars.

"Everybody got the plan?" he asked.

The others murmured their assent.

"Okay—take your positions."

Ed slipped into the woods at the edge of Monadnock Street to
watch for cars. Ray carried the stepladder, Susie the paint and
brush. Ray steadied the ladder for Leonard, whose black nylon
windbreaker zinged with every movement.

"Okay," Leonard said. "Got that paint?"

Susie handed him the paint and the brush.

"Thanks," Leonard said. "Take your position and keep a sharp
eye out."

"Check," Susie said. She gave him a thumbs-up sign and drifted
back into the woods with Ed.

Ray held the ladder as Leonard worked. The black paint came
off the brush shiny and dense, and Leonard formed his letters well.
They'd be easy to read from the street. Leonard was about halfway
through when a low whistle came from Ed: three short notes meant
a car. Leonard came down the ladder, careful not to spill the paint,
and Ray laid the ladder flat. He and Leonard ducked behind the
sign.

The car passed, its tires squishy on the blacktop. Gert Bartolomeo in her big Olds. Ray and Leonard waited until Ed whistled the
all clear: *Bobwhite! Bobwhite!* Then they set up again, and finished
the sign without incident. They signaled Ed and Susie out of the
woods and stepped back to admire the job. Leonard had drawn his
letters in capitals, and the disparity gave a nice hostage-note look
to the sign.

BarF DEstruction
Announces
Monadnock WASTElands.
A collection of SHITboxes,
GARISHsons, and RaUnchY Houses.
A RIP-OFF at $189,000.
Call 603-868-JUNK.

Susie quickly set up her camera and tripod, and with the flood-lights illuminating the sign, made several exposures. They knew that Barr would repaint the sign the next day, but by then Leonard's wife, Tina, would have deposited the photos on the editor's desk at the newspaper.

"Don't forget the letter to the editor, too," Ray said.

"Ten-four," Leonard said.

Next afternoon, Barr had two gofers scraping and scrubbing and repainting. By the time Ray got home from work, the sign had been returned to its original state. But on Wednesday, when the paper came out, there was the photo with the caption "New Marketing Approach for Barr Construction? No, just some area residents expressing their opinion of the new development in their neighborhood. See Letters, page 3."

The editor was sympathetic to their cause—partly because he believed in it and partly because Tina Walker and Marisse Vann worked in the paper's advertising department—and in this issue he ran the letter that Tina submitted with the photo.

To the Editor:

The photo that accompanies this letter will serve as fair warning to rapacious real estate developers, of which we seem to have no shortage in southern New Hampshire: If you develop land irresponsibly, as Barr Construction is doing, you will find a number of obstacles in your path toward a profitable conclusion of the enterprise.

If you destroy the natural beauty of an area, we will destroy your capacity to earn a living from it. If you alter for the worse the character of a neighborhood, we will alter for all time the reputation of your character. If you break promises to the abutters of the land you develop, we will break your resolve to go to work in the morning.

The choice is yours. You can have either a nice For Sale sign in front of your development, or you can have a sign made by us.

Most sincerely,

Cell Four, Residents Against Irresponsible Development (RAID)

Cell Four had gotten started because of the trees. Six weeks after the Hurley planning board shot down the condos, Barr had been back with a new plan—this time for six single-family homes. At the planning board meeting, the neighbors inspected the plan, muttered back and forth. For the most part, they approved. If anything was going to be done with the property out back, this was probably the least disruptive.

Ray was concerned about the trees. Barr's plan did not show any trees being left between the neighbors' property lines and the new houses, and the existing trees seemed like a good natural buffer.

"We'll keep some of our privacy," he said. "And the new owners will appreciate it, too."

"Seems reasonable," John Boylston said, and turned to Barr's engineer. The engineer and the lawyer hovered over the plan.

"Gonna be tight," the lawyer said. "There's not much room on those bordering lots, especially the one behind Mr. Vann. We'll do the best we can, that's about all we can tell you."

But Ray wanted it in writing. He wanted to see the plan redrawn with a buffer of trees—a good thirty-foot buffer.

"Thirty feet is impossible," the lawyer said.

"There's a fifteen-foot setback," Ray countered. "You need to leave that anyway, and if you site a couple of these houses differently, you can easily leave the trees standing. Everybody'll retain their privacy, and your properties will be worth more."

It seemed pretty clear to Ray. But he saw Barr give a slight shake of his head, and the lawyer said, "We're confident that the plan as drawn meets the requirements of the town and the abutters."

The neighbors disagreed loudly, and John Boylston spoke up. "I think Mr. Vann has a point. You've got some nice trees in there now, and you can't build within fifteen feet of the property line, so why not just leave that fifteen feet of trees? Anybody else on the board have anything to say?"

The other members of the board looked at each other, shrugged, consulted their watches, and more or less agreed. The lawyer came over and whispered with Barr for a minute. In the end it was agreed that the plan would be redrawn to show a buffer of trees. Two weeks later everybody was back in the town hall for a look at the new plan, and sure enough, there was the green, feathery band behind the existing stone walls. They all agreed it was a plan they could live with.

So, one morning shortly after this second meeting, the neighbors were appalled to see a gruesome machine in the woods, laying waste to the trees within feet of their property lines. It was a prehistoric-looking thing, a mechanical tyrannosaur with diesel lungs and a carbide-tipped shriek as it grabbed the trunk of a tree with two clawed arms and lopped it off at the ground with a blade the size of a tractor wheel. The operator sat in the air-conditioned cab eight feet off the ground and moved the thing forward on clanking tracks. He could cut through an eighteen-inch oak in seconds, and he just dropped the trees where they fell.

Ray was getting ready to leave for work when he heard the racket in the woods. He walked back. Leonard was already there, behind Susie Stevens's, where the machine was working.

"He's not leaving the buffer," Leonard said.

It was true. The guy was cutting right up against the property line. The machine screeched through another oak.

Susie came out from her solarium. She was in exercise clothes. "What's going on?" she asked. "He's cutting down all the trees!"

"He sure is," Leonard said. "He's violating the plan."

"At the rate he's going, he'll have the woods cleared out in a day," Ray said.

They ran to the back of the yard and tried to flag the guy down.

He was a rawboned, hard-looking man in mirror-lensed sunglasses. He paid no attention. Ray waved his arms. Leonard kept pulling his hand across his throat: "Hold it! Hold it!" The guy was working within five feet of Susie's stone wall, cutting a swath ten feet wide. "Stop!" Susie screamed. The guy kept on cutting. His machine screeched and ground off another tree and tossed it aside.

Leonard picked up a stick and threw it at the machine. It bounced harmlessly off the caterpillar track, and inside the cab, the guy laughed.

Leonard turned and headed for Susie's garage. "You keep your lawn mower in the garage?" he asked, and when she nodded, he said, "I need a bottle, like a Coke bottle!"

Susie met them in the garage with a six-ounce Perrier bottle. "It's all I could find," she said. "I went to recycling yesterday."

"It'll do," Leonard said. "I think I remember how to do this."

He poured some lawn mower gas into the bottle, then looked around. "I need a rag." They couldn't find one, so Leonard unlaced his deck shoe and pulled off a sock. It was a peach-and-cream Lands' End argyle sock, and he stuffed it into the neck of the bottle and soaked it with gas.

"Who's got a light?" he asked. "We'll get that sucker's attention."

"There's some matches in the barbecue pit," Susie said.

They went to the back with the Molotov cocktail, its ridiculous sock hanging out, and Susie lit the fuse while Leonard held it.

"*Viva la revolución!*" Leonard yelled with a big grin, and threw the bottle.

It bounced off the arm of the machine without breaking, but then it hit the spinning blade, burst, and flared into a small fireball in the boughs of a felled pine.

"Whoo!" Susie yelled. "Yankee go home!"

"Burn, baby, burn!"

The guy cut the machine back to an idle and vaulted out of the cab with a fire extinguisher. The little flame was already dying out, but the guy gave it a short blast. Then he turned toward the neighbors. He carried the extinguisher in one hand, like a club, and he tapped it lightly against his thigh, flexing his forearm muscles. He walked up to Leonard.

"What the fuck do you mean, firebombing my fucking machine?" Leonard did not cut an imposing figure, standing there with one bare foot. But the smell of pine blood was thick in the air, and the man responsible was leering at him from behind his mirrored shades. Leonard stepped up to him.

"What the fuck do *you* mean, cutting down our fucking woods?"

"Your woods? Barr's woods, bub. I'm cutting the new street."

"There's supposed to be fifteen feet of trees left. Check the site plan."

The guy produced the site plan. It was not, to Ray's surprise, the one that had been approved in the meeting. It was the first one, with no buffer. Ray pointed this out to the guy, but the guy shook his head.

"This is the plan Barr gave me. This plan tells me to cut all these trees down."

"This is the wrong plan," Ray said. "Barr's trying to pull a fast one."

The guy turned toward his idling machine. "This job is costing Mr. Barr three hundred dollars an hour. I'm not in business to lose people money, and shooting the shit with you ain't my idea of a day's work. You got a problem with this job, take it up with Barr."

"We'll take it up with the police," Susie said.

They went inside to call the police, and they heard the tyrannosaur crank up again. The police told them it was not a criminal issue, and they should call the selectmen's office. The selectmen's administrator told them it was a matter for the building inspector. The building inspector's secretary told them the building inspector was out at a job site, but was expected back after lunch.

"The woods'll be gone by then!" Susie said. "Please contact him if you can and get him up to Monadnock Street."

The tyrannosaur was halfway across Susie's back lot, slicing off the trees and tossing them aside. Even worse than the mechanical gnashing was the noise that the leaves made as the torn-out trees were shoved past the still-standing ones. It was a rushing of leaves that you normally associated with high wind. Ray knew it was the last sound the trees would ever make.

Susie was crying. Her face was as beautiful and composed as ever, but quiet tears ran down her cheeks. Leonard was beside himself with agitation, thrashing his arms and pacing. Ray went back and waved the guy to a stop. He explained that the building inspector would be out after lunch, and would he please hold off until then?

"What the hell," the guy said. "I gotta go pick up some hydraulic fluid anyway. I'll give you till one o'clock, but you keep your buddy the fuck away from my machine or I'll break him in two."

Ray and Leonard called into their offices to say that they'd be late, and then Ray tried calling a few neighbors, but by this time they had all gone to work. He and Leonard and Susie hung around in the solarium, and a couple of times walked out into the backyard, but didn't get too close to the boundary. The guy came back and began tinkering with his machine. Finally at five to one, the building inspector, Jim O'Brien, showed up eating a tuna sub. "What's going on?" he asked.

"He's not leaving the fifteen feet of trees," Ray said, nodding to the downed trees.

"I'm working according to the plan," the guy said.

"The wrong plan."

They looked at the plan again. It was the first of the two plans, and it had been signed by the planning board moderator.

"This plan is in order," O'Brien said. "It's been signed off by the planning board." He jabbed a tuna-smeared finger at the signature.

"It's a mistake," Ray said.

"There's nothing I can do to stop this man from carrying out the details of an approved plan."

Ray had never liked O'Brien. Thought he was lazy. O'Brien attended planning meetings only sporadically, and you'd see him in the diner having breakfast with contractors. Ray had never liked that.

"This is not the plan that was agreed on by the planning board and the abutters," Ray said. "Either it's a mistake, or somebody's been bribed."

O'Brien spat tuna fish. "This is the approved plan. It's got Johnny Boylston's signature on it. You got a problem with that, take it up with Johnny."

"Can you make the guy stop until we talk to John?"

O'Brien consulted with the guy while he finished his sandwich. He came back over. "The guy agreed to take the afternoon off. You've got until tomorrow morning."

John Boylston was not at home. Ray got an answering machine. No one at the town hall knew how to get in touch with him. Ray tried calling his house until late at night, and Leonard even drove over there.

"Place is dark," he said.

Ray found Barr's number in the phone book. Barr answered with a single "Yeah." Ray explained the situation. There was a silence on Barr's end; Ray imagined the toothpick flicking back and forth. Finally, Barr said, "So?"

"So I'm asking you to stop cutting the trees back there until we resolve the site-plan problem."

"I'm not going to stop a goddamned thing," Barr said. "I've got a job to do, and I'm going to do it."

"You're in violation of the legal agreement you made with this town," Ray said. "The town's been notified of it, your equipment operator's been notified of it, and now you've been notified of it. You cut one more tree out there before we get this resolved, we're going to wind up in court."

"Don't threaten me, goddammit," Barr said. "You scumbags up there on Monadnock Street have been trying to stop me from earning a living since the day I started this project—"

"We're not trying to stop anybody from earning a living, Barr. We're trying to protect our property." *Scumbags.* The word hung in the air like a bad odor. "And I take offense at your choice of language."

"I don't give a shit what you take offense at, scumbag. It's my property—I'll do what I want with it."

Barr was a shitkicker. Ray knew a shitkicker when he saw one—he had grown up among them in his little upstate New York hometown, he had worked with them in construction and railroad jobs, indeed, he had almost become one, would have had he not gone off to college and then found good work and gotten some rough edges knocked off. When Ray pictured Barr on the other end of the phone, he remembered the bone-deep depression of waking up in the morning to face another day of meaningless work, knowing that tomorrow would be just like today, that the future would stretch away into a murky, gray haze of uninterrupted labor. He remembered what it was like to arrive at a job site on a cold, damp morning to slog around in the mud and masonry, to mark the passing of the day by its relief from work: coffee break, lunch, smoke break, quitting time, and then the nearest bar. Over beers and shots, the men with whom he had worked would voice their dreams of getting out—by hitting the lottery, by inheriting a bundle, by robbing a bank—and then they would brutally censor those dreams, through drink, through violence upon each other and upon their women.

Ray simply hung up the phone. He was upset all night. He didn't sleep much, and nothing Marisse could say or do would calm him. He felt as he had when he was working construction, arguing with some dumb son of a bitch, and the guy resorting to the only tools he had: verbal abuse, macho bluster, the strength of his anger. He knew that once a guy like that crossed a certain line, he was not equipped to back himself off. Like a bulldozer without a reverse gear, all Barr could do was blunder forward.

On his way to work the next day, Ray left a message on the cab of the machine: *Do not cut any more trees until the site plan is resolved.* Later he tried calling John Boylston again. Still no answer.

When he got home from work that night, the woods had been cut all along the property lines. A thirty-foot swath, right up to the stone walls. Trees lay strewn every which way, their leaves curling and dry. It was sickening, and the whole neighborhood turned out to survey the damage. Neighbors clustered in backyards, shaking their heads. Children played on the tree trunks, laughing and shouting. Later, John Boylston returned Ray's calls. He'd been fishing, he said, and just got home. He'd talked to Jim O'Brien, and it appeared that a mistake had been made, and the wrong copy of the plan signed.

"One of those things," he said.

In the following days, Barr clear-cut the rest of the five acres. Now when Ray and Marisse and the neighbors looked out back, they saw, through their thin hedges, withering leaves, exposed roots, and much more sky than ever before. Over the next few months—through summer and into fall—they watched as Barr's men chipped up all the trees and hauled them off, stumped the five acres, began building the new street. They watched them bulldoze and grade and roll out a skin of blacktop, watched them backhoe cellar holes and haul away topsoil. They watched them pour foundations and frame stud walls and sheathe and roof and side. They listened to the hammers pounding and trucks rumbling and workmen cursing. By and by there appeared a slate-blue cape on lot #1, a tan garrison at #2, a white ranch at #3, and then, in various stages of construction, another cape at lot #4 and two saltboxes at #5 and #6.

When Ray and Ed would break from mowing their lawns or washing their cars, they'd gripe about the development. They were both burned about Barr's cutting all the trees.

"That spiteful son of a bitch," Ed said. "Come in here and ruin it for everybody, just because he didn't get his goddamned condos."

"Ought to be some kind of justice," Ray agreed. But they'd just shake their heads and try not to look at all the destruction out back.

It was Susie Stevens who came up with the idea. She was jogging past the house one Saturday morning when Ray was heading off to the dump.

"I'm taking notes," she said. "When the time is right, I'll use them. They've put some totally warped wall studs into that ranch, and I believe the garrison is actually sitting on the property line of the cape."

Ray had noticed that when they poured the footers for the salt-box in back of his place, the workmen had thrown all kinds of junk into the forms: beer cans, old shingles, even household garbage.

"Those footers have got to be weak," he said.

A sly smile spread across Susie's face. "We could put this information to good use," she said.

They decided to call another meeting. Ed Jacques had mentioned shoddy workmanship, and so had Leonard, so Ray figured they'd be interested. Susie said she'd ask around the neighborhood.

Ray mentioned it to Marisse, but she thought it was just another of his nutty schemes.

"I've got better things to do," she said. "I just want to forget about the whole thing. It's bad enough having to look at that mess without rubbing your face in it all the time."

"We're gonna rub Barr's face in it," Ray said.

"Why bother, Ray? It's done."

The other neighbors apparently agreed with Marisse, for on Monday night it was Ray, Ed, Leonard, and Susie in Susie's solarium. Susie's husband, Bob, popped in to say hello, but then disappeared to work at his computer. Susie broke out the beer and put on some jazz. She had a blue neon light in the solarium, and as they drank beer and pooled their notes—"Shaky front wall at #2," "Wet basement in #6"—Ray had to admit it felt pretty cool to be plotting against Barr in such a setting. Through the blue haze and the alcohol buzz he was taken back to the political rap sessions of his college days. In 1969 and 1970, he and his friends—freaks, they called themselves—met in various dimly lit and incense-choked pads to smoke dope and drink wine and plot the occupation of the administration building or the invasion of ROTC headquarters to protest the war in Vietnam. It had been exciting, and even though he now winced over the rhetoric and the idealism, he believed that that early experience had given his generation a belief in the ability to enact change. They had rallied on campuses; they had stopped the war. Twenty years later, Ray thought with an ironic grin, they stopped the condos.

Sitting in Susie's solarium, Ray got a whiff of the intensity of his earlier life. Everything—the music, the professors' discussions, the evening news, chance encounters on the street—had carried a feeling of importance, as if the country were in full dialogue and speaking through every voice. Ray remembered living like this, with all his senses on, all his receptors working overtime to take in the beat, the words, the images, the new experiences—in short, to grow. Like flowers with a tropism toward light, Ray and his generation grew toward the action of the world, toward change. And now they had more action and change than they could handle—big-time jobs, kids of their own, too much to do and never enough time to do it— and here they were planning further action against this developer.

With the exception of Ed Jacques, who was older and a true rock-ribbed New Hampshire Republican, the others had activism in their pasts, too. Leonard, like Ray, had attended his share of rap sessions and rallies, but while Ray had protested at New Paltz and ridden the buses to Washington, Leonard had stood on the sidelines at Penn and watched. Susie, a little younger, had attended Berkeley for a while and had helped start a center for battered women. She set the tone for the group, with the neon and the jazz, and she was the one who gave them their name: Cell Four. A guerrilla unit, a *cell*, Susie had insisted, because it implied there were other cells like theirs. Susie was a flight attendant and had studied terrorism and guerrilla tactics as part of her training. Cell Four, Residents Against Irresponsible Development. Suburban guerrillas!

They couldn't stop Barr from building, they couldn't even demand that he do good work. But what they could do, they would; they would make him lose money. They would make it so hard to sell those houses that Barr would lose every cent. They began to meet in Susie's solarium once a week. Susie's husband was a marketing guy for Digital and he traveled a lot, and when he was home he was more interested in his stereo equipment or his Porsche than in

Cell Four, so he left them alone. At their second meeting, Susie showed up in a black beret and jumpsuit. She said everybody would take it more seriously if they dressed the part. With her Asian features, shiny black hair, and lovely cheekbones, she looked like a real guerrilla and gave the little suburban gathering an air of the exotic.

They made a pact: each person would plan a mission and the others would help carry it out. Leonard's was the first: the Assault on the For Sale Sign. After the picture and the letter came out in the paper, some of the other neighbors mentioned the sign, speculated on who did it. Ray and the others hadn't let on, had just shaken their heads and smiled. Heck of a thing.

Ray and Leonard began to wear black to the meetings. Ed refused to go this far, showing up in his polo shirt and Bermuda shorts. Ray looked at Susie in her jumpsuit and at his own black jeans and turtleneck. Goofing, he thought. Acting out. When Susie raised her Sam Adams bottle to toast "the new world order," meaning one without developers like Barr, Ray felt embarrassed. Plotting revolution over a designer beer. That they had taken action and stopped the condos was good; this seemed more like playing games.

What the hell, he thought. If they made an example of Barr, maybe they'd prevent another developer from doing the same thing in another neighborhood. Power to the people, and pass the jalapeño dip.

Ray had another beer and listened to the electric guitar on the stereo. Susie began outlining her mission and suggested they reconnoiter the operation. They took flashlights and headed out back. The night was damp and misty, and the blue light from Susie's solarium glowed eerily into the backyard. The electric guitar, fast as blue neon, gave Ray a tingle of excitement as they headed toward the development. *Suburban guerrillas!* It beat sitting at home watching a video. He carried his beer like a hand grenade, and the others fanned out ahead of him. Their black shapes merged with the night. Their shoes squeaked in the wet grass. They spoke in whispers.

SEVEN

A Wreck on Nantucket

The Jeep was overloaded, but that didn't slow Tina down. She brought it over the crest of a dune, front wheels spraying sand, gassed it through the gully, and shot up over the next dune.

"Whoo-eee!" somebody yelled.

"Go, Tina!"

Ray said nothing and hung on to Marisse. They were in the back under the roll bar, and he was glad of it.

They were three couples: Ray and Marisse Vann, Leonard and Tina Walker, Mike and Ann Andrews. In the Jeep they had two coolers—one of food and one of beer. They hadn't broken into the food yet, but they were doing a number on the beer.

They were on Nantucket on business. That

was the story, anyway. Marisse and Tina—both graphic artists—
had this designers' convention, and though there were speakers and
seminars and the usual conventiony things, there was also plenty of
partying. The designers' association did this late every summer.
They picked a cool place to party—a resort in the White Mountains, an inn in Bar Harbor—put together a loose agenda so they
could in good conscience and within the guidelines of the IRS call
it a convention, and then started lining up the food and music.

Marisse and Tina worked together, and this was the third year
the Vanns and the Walkers had been to the convention. Leonard
and Ray got on well. Back home in Hurley, they'd give each other
a hand with house projects. Leonard had helped Ray plumb his
bathroom, and Ray had helped Leonard shingle his barn. When
they went to these designers' conventions, Leonard and Ray would
go fishing and check out the local pubs.

This year they had Mike and Ann along. Mike and Ray worked
together at Gentry Systems, and they were on the convention
agenda as speakers. Well, Mike was. As the sales guy, he was to
give a presentation on the graphics software they produced at Gentry. Ray was the technical guy, so he was just there to make sure
everything worked okay.

The presentation had gone fine, as had the whole convention.
Leonard and Ray had caught some bluefish, and they all had hit
some good restaurants at night. Now it was the last day, warm and
sunny with an offshore fog. After the pressure of the convention,
they felt like cutting loose a bit. They had rented the Jeep for an
afternoon of four-wheeling in the dunes.

"Anybody else want a turn?" Tina asked.

"You bet," Mike replied.

When Mike took the wheel, Tina slid over onto the cooler
between the seats. Leonard was in the passenger seat, Ann, Marisse, and Ray in back.

"Yo, Ray, how about a cold one?" Mike asked.

"Me too," Tina said.

Ray got the beers from the cooler behind the rear seat, and Mike hit the gas. The dunes here were steep, the sand deep. Every time the Jeep got out of the track, it would bog down and Mike had to muscle it back into line. But when he was in the track, Mike drove even harder than Tina had. When they came up over the top of the dunes, the windshield held nothing but clear sky. There had been a few other four-wheel-drives along the way. As Mike flew blindly over each dune, Ray prayed there wasn't another vehicle just on the other side.

Sitting on the cooler, Tina had her arms around both Leonard's and Mike's shoulders. Her arms were bare and tan, her back freckled. She squealed over each dune. Tina was a flirt. With dark Italian good looks, a go-for-it metabolism, and a meet-me-under-the-boardwalk glint in her eye, she attracted men, and she played it up. In the festive mood of the convention, she had hit on most of the guys there. Especially Mike. She would joke with all the guys— "There once was a girl from Nantucket"—but she'd hold Mike's eye just a little longer. Or, when passing the wine bottle over dinner, she'd linger on his hand.

Even now, she held her beer in her right hand. It was off her husband's shoulder as much as on. But she held on to Mike with her left hand, and didn't let go. Mike played it cool. He acted as if he didn't notice. He concentrated on his driving. Mike looked like a professional golfer: blond, beefy, reasonably fit. Being a typical sales guy, Mike was affable, always slapping you on the back, punching you on the shoulder, saying the right thing to the women. He was twenty-six years old making a hundred thou a year. He owned a nice house in Hollis, drove a Corvette. He had no existential problems, and why should he? Life was good for Mike. Sometimes he struck Ray as nothing so much as a human golden retriever. Well-groomed, well-fed, a pleasant disposition. *And so good around children!* Mike bounced happily through life like a golden retriever at a neighborhood barbecue. Sometimes Ray half expected him to roll over to have his belly scratched.

Mike knew Tina was hitting on him. A couple of times during the convention, he had turned to Ray and said, "Man, that Tina is some hot ticket!" and once, when she passed by, "Mmm, nice." But driving the Jeep, with Tina hanging on to him, Mike played it cool. He had to. His wife was sitting right behind him. Ann was never too far away. She tried to keep Mike on a short leash. She knew he was attractive, and they had been married only a couple of years. Mike was on the road frequently, and had the salesman's usual collection of stories. But Ray didn't think Mike could have gotten along without Ann. Whenever Mike traveled, Ann packed his suitcase. She picked out his suits, his ties. She packed his shoes in individual little shoe mittens to protect their shine. She seemed to enjoy mothering him. She seemed to believe that if she could keep him helpless, she could keep him.

Ann was as preppy as Mike, but without his puppy-dog appeal. She spoke in either of two voices: a nasal whine when addressing Mike, and a too-cheerful chirp with anyone else. It was fairly nauseating, and Marisse had confided to Ray that Tina's wish was to "gag her with a Fair Isle sweater."

Mike barreled the Jeep down the face of a dune. Ray's stomach hit bottom.

"Whoooh!"

"Oh, Mike!"

"Why don't you give somebody else a turn, honey?" Ann said. "You had a good tu-u-urn."

"Sure—hey—anybody else? That was great!"

Mike and Leonard started to swap places, but Ann stopped them: "Mi-i-i-ke, maybe Ray wants to sit in front so he can see. You sit back here with me-e-e."

Ray would have been happy to stay tucked in back, but Mike had obediently tilted the seat forward. Ray crawled out. Tina and Marisse exchanged a look that said they'd gladly dump Ann in the nearest dune.

Leonard eased the Jeep down to the hard-packed sand near the water. It wasn't as exciting as the jolting of the dunes, but here Leonard could run fast and flat. It was certainly safer, if you didn't get too close to the water. Back on the rental lot, Ray and Leonard had noticed a Jeep-sized hunk of crumpled metal. The frame was twisted like a corkscrew, the fenders were ripped away like broken wings, the shredded tires pointed in four different directions, all the glass was smashed, and the thing was packed full to the dashboard with sand. Ray had asked the rental agent what had happened.

"Got stuck in the soft sand by the water," the guy said. "Tide got to it before the tow truck did. When that happens, the surf just pounds it and pounds it. Rips it up in ways you could never imagine." He finished writing up the rental agreement, which was on Ray's Gold Card. "Keep it out of the soft stuff, fellas."

Leonard did. He knew how to keep a steady hand, hold the Jeep in the packed sand. He was running about fifty, and it felt comfortable.

Apparently too comfortable for Tina, for after a while she said, "This is boring. Let's stop and eat."

Leonard found a good spot. The beach broadened out, and he pulled up near a large driftwood log. They opened the coolers and spread out the bread, sausages, cheese, and fruit.

Mike announced that he had to "offload some Heineken" and trotted away to the nearest dune.

"Watch out for poison ivy, honey," Ann called after him.

Tina whispered to Marisse, "Shake it well before zipping up, sweetie!"

And Marisse whispered back, "Wash your hands after touching it, pumpkin!"

Leonard got out his fishing knife and cut up some sausage and cheese. Everybody but Ann had another beer.

"You guys go ahead," she chirped. "Somebody ought to stay sober for the drive back. Go ahead, drink up. I bet it's good and cold!"

Up the beach, a couple of surf fishermen were casting into the waves. The offshore fog bank had gotten closer, but the sun was still warm. They all settled into the sand around the log with sandwiches and beers. The sun felt good on their arms and faces, and they just ate and listened to the waves for a while. From somewhere, a foghorn moaned. Marisse and Ray snuggled against each other, drowsing. Everyone else was quiet, too.

After a while Tina got up, stripped off her sweater, and ran down to the water in her bikini. Everyone watched her run. Even after three kids, she was in great shape.

"Can't keep her out of the water," Leonard said.

"I bet it's nice," Mike said.

"Too cold for me," Leonard said.

You could see Mike wanted to go, but he was holding himself back. He was perched forward, like a dog in a point, almost quivering. If anybody else had made a move to the water, he would have bolted forward. But it would have been too obvious, him running after Tina alone. Ann paid no attention, drew little designs in the sand with a stick.

Tina came back dripping, her skin taut with goose bumps. She grabbed a towel out of the Jeep and began drying her hair.

"You guys look like you're ready to fall asleep," she said. She finished drying herself and opened another beer. She surveyed everybody, threw the towel into the Jeep, and then got into the driver's seat. Started the engine.

"I'm going for a little spin," she said. "Anyone else want to come?"

Leonard waved her on. The sight of Tina in her wet bikini was enough to make anybody want to hop into the Jeep with her, so Ray knew what Mike must have been feeling. Mike looked around, thumped his leg twice on the driftwood log—just a moment's hesitation—and then he got up.

"Sure—I could use a little breeze."

He got into the passenger seat, and they took off. They went past the surf fishermen, turned up behind some dunes, and were gone.

The waves splashed. The fog bank moved closer.

Nobody spoke. It was like the aftermath of an accident. At some small moment during the weekend, a swerve had been started. It had been a long, swooping swerve until this afternoon, when it had quickened into a skid and then a collision. Now, after the impact, they quietly took stock. Marisse and Ray exchanged a look that said, *Oh Christ, are they in trouble* and *Thank God this isn't happening to us.* They avoided meeting Ann's or Leonard's eye.

Ann got up with her stick and walked aimlessly down to the water. Leonard lay back in the sand and shut his eyes. Ray realized it was not the first time he had been through this. Leonard was too strong and too steady, poor bastard.

Marisse instinctively snuggled closer, but Ray had to get up. He didn't want to walk down by the water with Ann, so he headed in the opposite direction, away from the sea. There was a low dune about thirty yards behind the log. Ray climbed it and on the other side was an eerie sight: a brackish salt pond completely surrounded by dunes, and on the far side, riding up a solid sand wave, the wreck of a once-elegant sailboat. An Alden, he could tell by the sheer line. A thirty-six footer. The stern was sunk in the pond, the keel was stuck in the sand, and the bow rose right up off the dune and pointed to the sky. The mast and most of the deckboards were stripped away, the planking was torn, and the ribs were cracked. All the wood was bleached silver.

Ray walked around it, touching the warm hull planks here and there. He looked in through the holes; the cabin was awash in sand and vegetation. The galley was wrecked. There was a torn mattress on one of the berths, some beer cans strewn about, and a scrap of blue cloth at a porthole. Somebody's nice boat, once. A lot of work had gone into keeping her trim—scraping and sanding and caulking, sealing and painting and varnishing. She had been beautiful. Ray imagined the owners cruising the familiar island waters every summer, maybe even anchoring off the little beach he was now picnicking on. But then along came a big blow, moved sea and sand and boat, and altered it all forever.

He gave a thunk on the hull, and inside something skittered away. It wasn't sad, this wreck of a sailboat. It was just reality, bleaching in the sun.

He headed back to Marisse. She was sleeping in the lee of the log. He knelt beside her, and she stirred quietly.

Tina and Mike were not gone long; they were gone long enough. After a while, Ray heard the Jeep coming, and Marisse sat up. Tina parked in front of the log. Mike got out first. His face was animated. "Hey, some great dunes down that way! We oughta take a cruise through."

Tina said nothing, looked at nobody. She came over to the log and retrieved her sweater and pulled it on. Leonard didn't move, didn't even open his eyes.

Ann was some distance down the beach, walking towards them. "Hey, Annie!" Mike yelled. "Let's go do some dunes!"

Ann didn't respond.

Mike turned. "Want to go do those dunes? Anybody? Leonard?"

"Shut up, Mike," Tina said.

Leonard sat up slowly. He looked up the beach in the direction they had taken. Then he reached along the log to his fishing knife. He considered the blade, smeared with mayonnaise. Ray looked at Mike. Mike was watching Leonard. Leonard wiped the blade on his jeans and then turned back to the log. The scraps of lunch were still there. Leonard took the remaining length of sausage and slowly and methodically began cutting it into small pieces. He rested the knife blade on the skin of the sausage, and in a quick motion, sliced through. Each slowly oozing piece lay where it was cut.

Tina turned away. Mike looked like he wanted to disappear into the sand.

Leonard cut the sausage down to the last half inch and swept the pieces into a paper bag. He stabbed the knife into the log. Then he headed up the beach in the direction Tina and Mike had taken with the jeep.

Only Ray, the other fisherman, knew what he was doing.

"Time to head back," Ray said. "If that fog sets in, we'll have a tough time getting out."

Tina and Marisse started to pick up the rest of the lunch. Up the beach, Leonard handed the bag to one of the surf fisherman. Good bait, pork.

Ann walked up, got directly into the backseat. Mike followed, and somehow had the sense not to say anything. Ray nodded to Marisse; she got in back with Mike and Ann. Tina threw the rest of the stuff behind the seat and got up front on the cooler. She gave Ray a flat, level look. The last thing Ray did before taking the driver's seat was retrieve Leonard's knife. It was greasy, and he had some trouble pulling it out of the log.

Leonard got in without speaking. The fog bank had now moved in close. It was just a few yards off the beach. Ray knew that if he ran on the packed sand just above the waterline, he could get them out before the fog settled in. He got up to about fifty and held it there.

In the rearview mirror, Ray could see nothing but Tina's face. She looked straight ahead. There were small lines at the corners of her mouth. In the outside mirror, he saw the fisherman cast his bait into a solid bank of fog.

EIGHT

Operation Capitalist Dogs

S usie and Bob Stevens were stereo buffs. They had a whole room in their house—a media room—that looked like a cache of hot electronics: wall racks full of tape decks, receivers, amps, CD players, tuners, mixers. They had a video screen the size of a bay window. The night Cell Four met for Susie's mission, she took everyone into the media room and held up what looked like an armor-clad stereo speaker. "Remote speakers," she said. "We'll hide them near our rear boundaries, and then we'll deliver a little message to Mr. Barr's prospective customers."

She was making a tape, she said with a slight smile. She wouldn't tell them about it—it was a surprise. First they had to install the speakers.

"They're waterproof, shockproof, and completely sealed. They contain a small internal receiver. We'll transmit from here."

They installed the first speaker under the eaves of Ray's garden shed, which sat at the back of his yard. Susie held the flashlight, Ed the speaker, and Ray wired it to the rafter tails. They stuck the second speaker deep into the rhododendrons between Ray's lot and Ed's. The third speaker went inside a long-vacant doghouse at the rear of Leonard's yard, the door opening toward the development.

"Oh, that's wonderful," Susie said. "You'll see why."

Susie had all kinds of mature shrubs in her landscaped backyard, so the remaining speaker went inside a hemlock hedge. All the speakers faced Barr's development.

"There's one more thing we have to install," she said, leaning up against a big pine tree. In her black Lycra tights, black sweatshirt, and black beret, she looked to Ray more like a poet than a real guerrilla, but Ray was happy to keep up the illusion. She wore a roll of duct tape around her wrist like a bracelet, and held up a device that was hard to make out in the dark.

"It's a motion detector," she said. She slapped the trunk of the pine tree and pointed to a branch that hung out over the new street.

"Somebody want to give me a boost?"

Ray, Leonard, and Ed stepped forward as one man. Susie chose Leonard's back to stand on, and when she got up the tree, she ducttaped the device to the branch hanging over the street. Then she pulled a staple gun from under her sweatshirt and stapled the detector's wire to the branch and down the trunk. The high hemlock hedge ran between her property line and Leonard's, so she fed the wire through it and then into an open window of the house.

"The tape will be done by the weekend," Susie said. "But make sure you read the paper tomorrow."

The next day, the editorial page bore Susie's letter, entitled "A Message to the Capitalist Dogs."

To developers who would profit at the expense of local residents:

You will not succeed in your attempt to profit by destroying the neighborhoods we have worked hard to make beautiful. One of your kind in Hurley has chosen to destroy a beautiful woods and to put up cheap little houses and sell them for exorbitant prices. He may try, but he will not succeed. If you'd like to see where his investment will go, take a drive up Bill Street, just off Monadnock Street, this weekend and roll down your windows. Our watchdog committee will be there to greet you, as it will be for any prospective buyers.

Most sincerely,

Cell Four, Residents Against Irresponsible Development (RAID)

They gathered in Susie's backyard early Saturday morning. Ed had made an early run to Dunkin' Donuts, so he broke out the coffee and sweets, and Cell Four dug in behind Susie's hedge. Before too long, the first realtor's car came rolling up the street. As the car passed under the branch of the pine tree, the speaker in Susie's hedge barked. Barked, like a dog.

"Woof! Woof!" the speaker said.

It was answered by the speaker in Ed's rhododendron.

"Arf? Arf?"

"Woof!" Susie's speaker replied.

From way down in Ray's garden shed came a drawn-out howl: "Aaar-ooo-aahhh! Aaa-aaa-roooooooahhh!"

The speaker in Leonard's doghouse yapped like a poodle: "Yap, yap, yap, yap, yap!"

And again from Ray's shed: "Ruff! Rrr-rrruff! Ruff! Ruff!"

It was a magnificent tape. It started out slowly, each dog's voice isolated, and then began to build—a duet, a woofing bass and an arfing trumpet in counterpoint: *Woof! Arf? Woof! Arf? Woof!* Then a ruffing chord progression, *Ruff! Rrr-rrruff! Ruff!*—a trio improvising, noodling around, barking riffs of dog-jazz, and then a snare-drum *yap-yap-yap-yap-yap* and then the full band woofing and arfing and ruffing in up-tempo polyphony for a few minutes, then a staggered, aggressive jam for a few more, then a fierce chorus for five whole minutes to a full-volume crescendo topped off by that long howl, like a wailing saxophone, from Ray's shed: *Aaa-aaa-roooooo-aaahhh!*

A few minutes of silence as the tape rewound. The realtor's car had stopped in front of the white ranch, but the people hadn't even gotten out. *Uh, excuse me—we had something a little quieter in mind.* The car turned around in the driveway, the realtor looking from side to side. *Jeez, never heard those dogs before.*

Everyone congratulated Susie, shook her hand, hugged her. Cell Four had repelled the assault.

"Flee, capitalist dogs!" said Susie.

"Aaa-rooo-aah!" Leonard replied.

Ed was concerned, though. "What about the Bains?" he asked, nodding to the house next door. "And how about the Rosens?"

"Oh, I checked with them," Susie said. "The Bains are in Maine for two weeks, and the Rosens said they'd like to stick it to Barr too, so we should go for it."

With the motion detector in the tree, the tape clicked on every time a car came up the street. It played probably twenty times that first weekend. The response of the prospective buyers was pretty much the same—many drove off without stopping. Those who did stop looked around for the dogs, couldn't find them, went into the house, looked out through the front windows, couldn't spot the dogs, and came outside looking at each of the neighbors' houses like, *How can they live here with that racket? Isn't there a dog ordinance in this town?*

The barking did get pretty hard to take, but since it seemed to be working so well, the neighbors tried to turn a deaf ear. It bothered Marisse, though, and she told Ray so.

"Don't you guys think you're taking this a little too seriously?" she asked. "I mean, the houses are built."

Ray shrugged her off and turned up the stereo. During the week, nobody was home to hear the tape, and the next weekend was even better than the first. Word had gotten around, so now not only realtors and their prospects drove up, but also townspeople and other gawkers as well. The barking was pretty much constant.

By Saturday night, Marisse had had it.

"How long are you going to keep this up?" she asked.

"As long as it takes," Ray said.

"How long is that?"

"Until we drive the price of the houses down so low, the guy loses his shirt."

Marisse gave Ray a look that made him feel about as clever as a yapping dog, and then she called Tina Walker and arranged to go to the beach the next day.

"To the beach?" Ray asked. "It's supposed to rain tomorrow."

"It's nice and quiet in the rain," Marisse said. "We'll find a snug spot and wrap up in blankets."

"Just so long as you don't take any of those extended Jeep rides with Tina," he said.

Marisse laughed. "Hey, we don't know that anything happened," she said. "Besides, another day of that barking and I'll go nuts."

Marisse and Tina were late getting back from the beach. The clouds had lifted late in the day, and the evening was warm and sticky. Around dusk, Ray went out for a walk. Even as he left the house he knew where he was headed. He tried to convince himself to head up the street, in the opposite direction, but once out the back door he cut across the yard to the development. He walked down the new street. With the trees gone, he could see right into the backs of the neighbors' houses, and the vision he carried in his mind was the blue light of Susie's solarium.

There were no pine-tree shadows in the back anymore, just the evening sky and a half-moon beginning to rise. Ray could hear Cynthia Rosen talking to one of her daughters, could see her in the kitchen window as she cleaned up after dinner. The other daughter was practicing the piano. The Bains' place was dark—they were still in Maine. Ray approached Susie's with trepidation, and sure enough, the solarium was glowing blue. The shrubbery around her place was so high he couldn't see much, so he edged down the property line on the Bains' side.

Ray was pointed toward this place by an inner compass needle that aligned on the blue neon light. He had to acknowledge it: Cell Four was stimulating—the blue neon, the jazz, the black guerrilla clothing. Susie, certainly, added a sexual undercurrent to the group. Ray hadn't seen anything overt, but he felt it in their plotting and logistics. If he and Ed and Leonard were doing this alone, they probably wouldn't have kept it up this long. Susie set the tone, struck the pose. She was definitely an attraction. But probably the biggest stimulant was the nighttime foraying into Barr's development—it was like being behind enemy lines. There was a buildup of tension as they planned the mission in the solarium; it stayed with him through his workday and his commute and his dinner conversation with Marisse, always drawing him toward the frayed treeline at the back of his yard. During the mission itself there was a giddiness that made him feel agile and strong, as if the soles of his black Reeboks were spongy, as if the paintbrush or speaker that he carried was not so mundane an object at all, but a pistol or a grenade. And at the end of the mission there was a release, a quick flooding of the nerves followed by a quiet sense of finality. Now that he had gotten involved with Cell Four, he could no more stop thinking about Susie's solarium or their nighttime raids than an alcoholic could refuse a drink, or a junkie a fix.

So tonight, with nothing else to do, Ray was drawn to the blue solarium. He could see two heads on the futon couch; Bob must be home. He felt a little relief at this. He would just stand and watch a bit. It was hard to make out any details; the couch faced away from him, so all he could see was the two heads: they were close, and by turns they would lean forward or back. He could hear the clink of ice cubes against glass. Just another suburban ritual, he thought: a couple having drinks on Saturday night. From behind him came the Rosens' piano; Jenn was practicing her chords. In the still-glowing sky a bat fluttered haphazardly. The ice cubes clinked, and the two heads came together in a quick kiss. Together again—a longer one. The bat swooped low over the solarium, and the heads disappeared behind the couch: another ritual in progress. Saturday night, the pressure and sapped energy of the work week suspended, a day of chores and domestic puttering done, a good dinner and a few drinks, and this is the closest a suburban working couple gets to a perfect moment for lovemaking.

One head popped up. Susie stood and walked across the room and went into the house. She had on a loose white blouse, her legs bare. The bathroom light went on. In its glow, Ray saw the other head appear on the couch, and something registered as both familiar and odd. Familiar, in that he recognized it. Odd, in that he couldn't identify it as Bob's.

The bathroom light shut off. Even as Ray's eyes readjusted to the dim blue light, he saw Susie reappear in the solarium and stand on the threshold a moment. The head on the couch shifted, rose with the body: a man in white running shorts. He crossed the room to embrace Susie. But it was not Bob Stevens's hulking, ex-jock's mass that did this. It was the whippet-lean profile of Leonard Walker.

They kissed, and Ray felt a stab under his heart. Leonard and Susie moved back to the couch. Ray eased along the Bains' hedge and out to the street. He needed to walk. Jesus, Leonard! He and Susie! Sure, Ray felt a little jealous: some part of him, which he kept well suppressed, wished to be a rogue, a rake, a playboy; he had toyed with the idea of making a move on Susie. And he felt disappointment: the part that ruled over the rogue and kept it in check couldn't help but be disappointed that Leonard had acted on it and was at this moment enjoying the results of his action. But Ray had never betrayed Marisse and had no desire to do so. Holding on to this thought, he walked the night streets and began to change his tune. Leonard—how could he risk his marriage to Tina and the comfort of his son and two daughters? Susie was his next-door neighbor, for Christ's sake.

Ray walked down by the railroad pond and watched the moon reflecting on the water. Somewhere across town a hot-rodder squealed his tires, and close by the ducks were muttering as they settled in for the night. Little details began to click: why Susie stood on Leonard's shoulders to get up the tree, how she would automatically sit next to him at the meetings, how Bob was never around when the group met. God, they were so brazen. Tina could have as easily been standing behind the hedge. No, he realized, she wouldn't.

He was feeling pretty righteous as he walked back up Monadnock Street, and he noticed that the lights were on in the front of Susie's house. The Bains' was dark, of course. As he approached his own driveway there was a crunching of gravel, and Leonard stepped out from the shadow of the big maple.

"Evening, Ray," he said.

"Leonard."

"Nice night," Leonard said. "Just taking a little air."

He was wearing the same white shorts Ray had seen a few minutes before.

"Taking a little air?" Ray said. "Or airing out?"

"Hmm . . . how's that?"

"Airing out. Cooling down." Ray thought he should stop, but he couldn't help it. "Composing yourself before you face Tina and the kids."

Ray watched Leonard studying his face, but he knew the street-light was behind him. A shadow of fright or guilt passed over Leonard, and then he chuckled.

"Yeah," Leonard said. "Yeah. So you know."

Ray didn't say anything, just looked up at his house. The lights were on inside; Marisse was home from the beach.

"How did you find out, Ray?"

"I just did. Jesus, Leonard. So close to home."

"So close and yet so far. Listen, let's walk up the street, eh?"

They passed Ray's house. The shades were still open, and Ray could see Marisse at the table, drinking a cup of tea.

"Tina doesn't know?" Ray asked.

"No, God no. I'm at Cell Four, or a Little League meeting, or on my Good Humor route. Out for a run."

"How long's it been going on?"

"A while. It was building up since they cut down the trees. Since that scene Tina pulled on Nantucket. The first time was the night we hit the sign. You and Ed left, and I was all pumped from doing the sign, and—I don't know—Susie and I were out there together. She was pumped, too. You know how she gets. One thing led to another."

They reached the end of the street. The police chief's white spitz barked at them, so they turned around.

"Are things okay with Tina?" Ray asked.

"Okay, yeah. We bring out the best and the worst in each other. This is not one of our best phases."

"It all looks so good from the outside," Ray said. "I mean, you'd never know. It looks like you guys have it pretty nice."

Leonard was quiet a moment. They walked in silence.

"Nice, yeah—it's all so nice," Leonard finally said. "It's all so fucking nice. Look at this." He waved his arms around. "Nice little neighborhood, nice little town."

He stopped in front of a landscaped cape that belonged to a family named McElroy. The bay window flickered with the blue glow of a television. "Watching their Saturday-night video, man. All over town, nice little families watching their videos. It's the entertainment high spot of the week."

They walked on.

"Sometimes when I'm watching a video with Tina," Leonard said, "I don't even see what's going on. You know what I'm thinking about? Ice cream. I'm thinking that come Monday I've got to go off to Digital and develop software, write my code. And I'd rather be selling ice cream. I'd rather open up a little ice cream shop. Drive my truck around and sell treats to kids. But you can't pay for three college educations on ice cream, man. That's what I'm thinking as we're watching our video. I'm going to be writing code for the next fifteen years. Writing code and watching videos. When this thing with Susie came up, I just went with it."

They stopped in front of Ray's house. Marisse had pulled the shades, and the glow from the windows was inviting. Ray wanted to be in there with her.

"I don't want to hurt Tina," Leonard said. "You know what I'm saying?"

"Yeah, I know what you're saying, man."

"Thanks, Ray. Thanks for listening."

"Sure, Leonard," Ray said.

Cell Four heard from the developer that week, in the form of a letter in the paper.

> To the Editor:
>
> It's a sad day when a selfish few can spoil it for the many. The Cell Four people on Monadnock Street are being selfish in their attempt to discourage people from buying homes in their neighborhood.
>
> We are trying to provide affordable homes to folks, and the Cell Four people would try to stop us. There is a shortage of affordable housing and the people of Monadnock Street, instead of being good neighbors, are being narrow-minded and selfish. Slam the door behind you, is their attitude.
>
> Yrs. truly,
> Bill Barr

By the third weekend, the real-estate cars—Caddies, Lincolns, Mercedeses, Volvos—had slowed to a trickle, and it was mainly the sightseers coming around in their station wagons, pickups, and compact Japanese cars.

"Must be pretty bad," Ed Jacques said, "when you go out of your way to hear a bunch of goddamn dogs barking."

It was that weekend when Operation Capitalist Dogs went down the chute. Ray was out back fixing a screen when Leonard whistled at him from his yard. The tape was barking, and Leonard waved Ray over.

"I got a funny feeling about this one," Leonard said, nodding to the cape at #4. In front of the cape was a blue van, and a very fat man eased himself out of the driver's seat.

"He came around with the real estate people last week. Then he was around yesterday. Now he's back."

The fat guy weighted probably four hundred pounds. His stomach just kept curving down into his pants and crotch. His jowls shook as he tottered around the front of the van, his head cocked toward the barking. *Arf? Arf?* He stopped at the passenger's door. Then he did a strange thing. He paused. He closed his eyes and let his head loll back, listening to the tape as if listening to music. *Yap, yap, yap, yap, yap!* The tape was just building toward the crescendo, and he listened for probably a full minute. Then he inhaled a deep breath and smiled a slow smile of . . . appreciation? Peace? *Aaar-ooo-aahhh!* He turned toward the sliding door of the van and whipped it open, and out tumbled three writhing, yelping Irish setters. They jumped around the fat guy, bounced into each other, nipping and yelping, and then in typical pea-brained Irish setter fashion, careened away in different directions. Whether they were being driven crazy by the tape or just acting normally, it was hard to say, but they took off in a haphazard clamber, barking, one running east while his head was pointing due north, two rashing into each other and tumbling, yelping, bouncing up, and zigzagging away, their floppy red coats making them look like the most ungainly creatures on earth. They seemed to be looking for the barking dogs. They clambered this way and that, barking for the other dogs, sniffing around the other houses under construction, breaking through Susie's hedge and then bouncing and flopping trying to get back over. One of them wound up in the Jacques's yard, humping the rear wheel of Ed's garden tractor.

In the midst of it all, the fat guy stood smiling, calm, utterly serene. He was clearly a being in perfect harmony with his surroundings. When the tape stopped, the Irish setters continued to fill the neighborhood with their yelping and barking. The fat guy

walked around to the front yard of the cape, and with a little jig-
gling, pulled up the For Sale sign and put it into his van.

Ray and Leonard looked at each other like, *What have we done?*
Christ! Irish setters! A nutty fat guy!

"Looks like we can tell Susie to unload the tape," Ray said.

"Looks like we oughta start building a fence," Leonard replied.

But they didn't have to. The Big Fat Guy, as he came to be
known by Cell Four, had a fencing crew put up a five-foot chain-
link fence all around his yard. Even the front. Steel-gray and industrial, it was the ugliest structure brought in yet.

"Nice," Marisse said. "The prison-yard motif. When do the
barbed wire and searchlights arrive?"

It was ugly, but it kept the Irish setters in. When they weren't
bouncing around, digging holes, sniffing each other's crotches, and
generally acting like a genetic experiment gone bad, they would
maintain a vigil at the front of the fence, staring at the neighbors'
houses as if waiting for the tape to start again so they could set off
in a frenzy of canine idiocy. Which they did often enough without
prompting. At night it wasn't so bad; Ray thought the Big Fat Guy
kept them in the basement. And during the weekdays most of the
neighbors weren't home. But on Saturdays, when Ray or Leonard
or Ed were working in their yards, or on Sundays when they were
trying to read the paper, the commotion was enervating.

"Nice work, Cell Four," Marisse said, putting on the earphones
of her portable tape player. "Hope we got the price down real low
for the Big Fat Guy."

They had, in fact. Thelma Jacques went down to the town hall
and checked the deed. A hundred and forty-nine thousand. Down
from one eighty-nine. Forty thousand bucks gone to the dogs.

NINE

Seduction of the Good Humor Man

Susie Stevens drove north from Logan thinking about two things: the Good Humor Man
and a fudgesicle. Not necessarily in that
order. Her flight from Denver had been a killer.
One of those that made her want to turn in her
wings and do something else for a living. First
the plane was delayed on the runway for two
hours while they fixed a hydraulic problem, and
then they lost an engine on takeoff and had to
go back and wait another two hours for a new
plane. The crew was bitchy and short, having
gotten only a little sleep the night before, as the
flight *into* Denver had been diverted because of
thunderstorms. She landed in Boston five hours
late, sleep-deprived, and when she finally found
her red Jeep Cherokee in the parking lot, she
had fudgesicle on the brain. She was thinking of

how good it would feel on her throat, after the closed-cabin dryness of the airplane. She was thinking of how sweet it would be on her tongue. She wanted to bite into that cold, sweet fudge and let it melt slowly in her mouth.

She was thinking, she realized, of the Good Humor Man. She looked at herself in the rearview, tucked back a wisp of hair. The digital clock on her dashboard said 5:15. If she stepped on it, she'd catch him just heading out for his evening run.

When Leonard Walker backed his Good Humor truck onto Monadnock Street, he felt as if he were going back in time. The big trees, the turn-of-the-century houses, the occasional stone hitching post. There were even a couple of barns, one of which he owned. Barns, just three blocks from the center of town! Of course, there were anachronisms: a scattering of ranch houses, a street hockey game with kids on neon skates, a boom box blasting out rap music. Even Leonard, the Good Humor Man, was an anachronism—his truck and uniform vintage 1956. He loved the compression of time on this street, where he, looking as if he had just stepped out of Eisenhower's America, could sell ice cream in front of a Victorian-era house to people in the shadow of a satellite dish. Norman Rockwell in a time warp.

He jingled his bell and set in motion a chain reaction that ran up the street. Kids heard the bell and called to their parents, "The ice cream man! The ice cream man!" and a general scurrying ensued: feet thrummed on hardwood floors, screen doors slammed, the street hockey game dissolved into a scramble for spare change. Inside family rooms, on cedar decks, in backyard gardens, Monadnock Street residents heard the bell and almost involuntarily rose from their Barca Loungers or deck chairs, straightened up from weeding tomato plants. They reached for penny jars or coin purses or jeans pockets. Images floated into their minds: orange cremesicles, ice cream sandwiches, cherry pops. There began a general gravitation toward the edges of the street. Barefoot kids in shorts, fathers in T-shirts, mothers in light summer dresses—all aligned before the tinkling white truck like filings around a magnetic field.

He drove to the top of the dead-end street, turned around in the police chief's driveway, and before he began his slow and musical descent, he paused, idling in neutral. He saw before him, in almost precise symmetry, a tunnel view of suburban perfection: the gray street running straight downhill, the colorful flecks—rose and tangerine and aqua—gathering at the sidewalks, the bright green lawns stretching to the white houses, and, framing it all, the deep green of the pine woods. He breathed in the pine and the charred tang of a backyard grill and a hint of his own sweat. Perfect. Just perfect. To the Good Humor Man, this was a moment of perfect anticipation known to only a few others: the jet pilot facing the runway before takeoff, the minister surveying his congregation before the sermon, the farmer eyeing a ripe cornfield.

Perfect, he thought. But just at that moment a bright red Cherokee bobbed into view at the lower end of the street. Oh, man. Not quite perfect.

Three houses down, he stopped for the Bomb-pop family: orange and lemon for the parents—about his age, late thirties—cherry and rainbow for the little boy and girl. The kids always got to step forward to pay, and the little girl did it with such seriousness that when he handed her the bomb-pop and a nickel's change, he doffed his hat and said, "Thank you, ma'am." Always made the parents smile.

Next stop, an older couple in front of a white farmhouse. The Dixie Cups, he called them. White hair and ruddy complexions.

"Nice evening," the old man said.

"Beautiful evening," he replied. "How are you folks tonight?"

"Still living," the old woman said.

He laughed with them, their regular joke. He put his hands to his temples and shut his eyes. "Wait, don't tell me. I'm getting a vision. Two Dixie Cups. One vanilla, one chocolate swirl."

"A real psychic," the old woman said. "Ought to rent you a big tent and give 'em a come-to-Jesus. Make more offa that than you will Dixie Cups."

The old man unwrapped his wooden spoon. "I had a '56 like that one," he said, nodding at the truck. "Never should've traded it."

The street hockey game was next, a bunch of darting, jittering boys, one of whom was his. Seth had to pay just like anybody else, always ordered a Toasted Almond. Leonard was usually at this stop for a good twenty minutes, as the half-dozen houses in mid-street emptied and everyone from the kids on skates to teenage girls to four or five sets of parents—the Jacques, the Rosens, the Bains, all his neighbors—came out to order just about one of everything. And he had a bit of everything, too. Sure, he had the traditional Good Humor fare—cremesicles, fudgesicles, twin-pops. Eskimo Pies, Frozen Milky Ways, Kool-Pops. But he offered more than that: Italian ices, sno-cones, half-pints of Häagen-Dazs and Ben & Jerry's. He had Stonyfield frozen yogurt from over in Wilton and homemade ice cream from Pete's right in Hurley. Heck, he could mix up a shake or a malt, even an egg cream if somebody wanted it. He could make fresh fruit sundaes, banana splits, parfaits. He had something for everybody. His goal was to be the definitive Good Humor Man.

For Leonard believed in the curative properties of ice cream. He believed there was an ice cream dish to match every state of mind, to counter every neurosis, to calm every anxiety. Peaches and cream to brighten the spirit, banana nut fudge to humble the ego, vanilla sherbet to assuage guilt. Sometimes, when people couldn't make up their minds about what to order, he would ask them how they were feeling. If they said tired, he'd suggest a chocolate-dipped sugar cone to restore their vigor. If they said fine, he'd go with a lemon ice to maintain an even keel. Yes, there was a perfect ice cream for everybody; you just had to know human nature and you had to know your ice cream.

He rolled on down the street, got cones for two couples in tennis whites, laughing. He approached his house with trepidation, hoping Tina would not be outside. She had been washing the dinner dishes when he left, so probably she would not come out front when she heard his bell. Even though he and Susie were discreet, he still felt anxious.

Tina did not come out. Just past his place, though, Susie slammed the door of her Cherokee and turned toward him. She wore her crisp airline uniform, navy blue with a white blouse, and her hair was tucked back in a knot. A pair of gold wings above her breast. She waved him to a stop.

"Howdy, neighbor," she said.

"Hey," he said. With her hair pulled back, the striking angles of Susie's face showed: her almond eyes set above her high cheekbones, her delicate jaw. His fingers ached to trace her planes and angles, to feel the soft give of her flesh.

"How was your flight?" he asked.

"Terrible," she said. "Delays, rerouting. Everybody pissed off. I'm dead on my feet."

"Sorry to hear that," he said.

They maintained a distance and decorum when they met in front of their houses: two neighbors greeting each other at the end of a day. Still, Leonard could feel the looming presence of his house, every window an eye that scrutinized him for the slightest untoward sign.

"The only thing that got me through was thinking about ice cream," she said. And then in a lowered voice, "And, of course, the ice cream man."

He allowed her a little smile, and then turned toward the truck.

"So I'm glad I made it in time," she said. "I'll have a fudgesicle, please."

He considered this, but it wasn't right. "No—no, I don't think so."

"Excuse me?"

It would be easier just to give her the fudgesicle and be on his way, but it really wasn't what she needed. "A fudgesicle isn't best for you tonight, after the flight you've had. Chocolate isn't soothing enough."

"Huh?"

"Chocolate is for excitement, to heighten your senses. You need to relax."

"But—"

"No—hang on. I'll fix you up in a second."

"But I've been thinking—I've been *craving* a fudgesicle since like *Buffalo*."

"Trust me."

He mixed her up a strawberry-and-sweet-cream shake, with real strawberries—plump, juicy ones from Hillside Fruit Farm—a spoonful of sour cream, a dash of nutmeg, and a hefty shot of white rum.

"Go sip on this and then take a shower. In an hour you'll be sleeping like a kitten."

She laughed and shook her head. Took a sip.

"Wow!"

She took another sip.

"Um! Wow, this is great."

He nodded and smiled.

"How much?" she asked.

"Two bucks."

She dug into her wallet and paid him. "Thank you. Fudgesicle—what fudgesicle?"

"That's more like it," he said, and started to back away.

She lowered her voice again. "See you tomorrow?"

He couldn't help it, his eyes darted toward his place.

"Sure," he said. "See you then."

She sat on the back steps sipping the shake. It really was delicious. Funny how he just took charge and made it. The last rays of sun were warm on her face, the granite warm under her legs. From up the street, the kids at their hockey game came to her as background chatter, as soothing as birdsong. She sipped her shake and lounged like a cat on the warm steps, screened off behind her hedge from the rest of the world. The tension began to seep out of her shoulders. Her head stopped buzzing.

When the shake was finished, she picked up her overnight bag and camera case. The big house was empty, as she knew it would be. Bob was in—where was it this week, Atlanta? Toronto? His job kept him traveling a lot, and of course her flying schedule kept her coming and going. They still joked about their home life—at the Digital company picnic, Bob told his colleagues he was installing a 900 number at home so they could at least maintain a sex life. But the truth was, Susie was getting tired of the pace, the craziness. They saw each other maybe a week each month. Maybe ten days. And even then they each needed time to recover from their most recent trip. When he was rested and ready for an evening out, she was just getting back from a West Coast layover. Or when she had had a few days at home and wanted to, say, go to the beach, he was preparing a presentation for the Seattle sales group.

It was nuts. She carried her bags upstairs. It was no way to live.

She didn't bother turning on any lights. She liked the in-between feel of the waning day. She dropped her bags in the bedroom and then undressed. Wow, Leonard was right—she was beginning to feel drowsy. She ran the shower hot. The steam filled the darkening bathroom and made it as close and comforting as a womb. She lingered under the hot water, barely awake, the taste of rum on the back of her tongue. When she began to get little dream bursts, she shut off the water and fell into bed with her hair still wet.

He drove home and pulled into the barn, shut off the compressor, and plugged the freezers into the wall circuit. He wiped the condensation off the outside of the truck. With the damp cloth, he rubbed the bugs off the hood and grille.

Leonard had bought the truck about the same time his daughter Marcie went off to college. As last September had approached, Tina had begun to act a little strange. He would catch her at the sink, staring out the window for long moments. Or he'd go upstairs and find her sitting on the bed in the dark. This introspection was unlike Tina. She was not naturally given to it, for one thing, and throughout their marriage they'd just been too busy for it. After

Marcie left, Tina seemed to draw tighter to the other two kids, arranging family hikes and ski trips. But while she was doing this, Leonard couldn't help noticing, Tina began to flirt with other men even more than usual. She'd always been a flirt. She was when they met—just kids, really, both of them eighteen and hanging out on the boardwalk. She was a flirt when they married a year later, and she still was after nineteen years of marriage. Even so, their marriage had been good. She spent as much time flirting with him as with other guys, so it had been fun. And that's what her flirting had always seemed, just fun. Just something she did as a woman to feel like a woman: flirt with a man. It was natural, he assumed. But last year, Tina's flirting at parties or with his colleagues seemed to take on a different edge. Not more serious, necessarily. But definitely more—he grasped for the right word—more *desperate*.

Leonard accepted this trait in his wife, even though he didn't really *flirt* with other women. Kidded around with the female programmers and technicians and secretaries at work, tried to keep things light. But not really coming on to them. Not really saying *I'm available*. When Marcie left for college, Leonard felt the empty space in their home life. Instead of five, there were four. But instead of flirting with other women, Leonard bought the Good Humor truck. He had been toying with the idea of restoring a car—an old Karmann Ghia, maybe, or a VW bus—when he spotted the ad for the truck in *Hemmings Motor News*.

It was a 1956 GMC with 150,000 miles, body in decent shape. The owner had bought it when the Good Humor Company went out of business in 1975, and had stored it since then. The freezers worked, the compressor worked, the fluorescent signs worked—it even came with a Good Humor cap and jacket. The truck became a winter project that stretched well into spring. Every evening when he got home he'd have a quick dinner and then head out to the barn. He'd tune the radio to an oldies station, build a fire in the woodstove, and get to work. At first he planned just to rebuild the engine—a big, sturdy straight six—which he did, taking it completely apart down to the last washer and spring and bearing. He replaced the crank and pistons and rings, sent the block out for remilling, rebuilt the carburetor, and replaced the fuel pump and all of the lines. As long as he had the engine out, he figured he might as well replace the clutch. He noticed a wire wearing thin where it passed through the fender, so it seemed like a good time to replace the wiring. Tracing it through the fenders, he discovered some rust that couldn't be seen from the outside, so he decided to fix that, too. What the hell, you couldn't just patch over one spot—he decided to do the whole body over. He pulled off the fenders and doors and hood, sandblasted everything down to bare metal, cut away the rot and riveted in new sheet metal. He filled and sanded and primed, painted and wet-sanded and painted some more.

He wished you could take a relationship apart as you could a truck. Cut away the rot, pound out the dents, rebuild the very heart of the thing, and put it all back together so that you came up with something shiny and well-machined and . . . not new, of course, but *restored.* Clean and rejuvenated from the wear and stresses of the past, with no signs of the damage incurred along the way. But human machinery retained the dings and dents, the skids and crashes, and once rot started you couldn't cut it out and replace it with something new. Once rot started it was always there. And it was always structural. You couldn't fully trust the structure after that.

But you could live with it. You could even love despite it.

By April he began putting everything back together. The engine first, the smooth milling, the snug fits. Then the body, which he finished painting and then compounded and polished and waxed. He bought a set of chrome wheels and new tires, had the broad bench seat reupholstered. By May he had the whole truck back together, the engine ticking like a pocket watch. One Friday he came home from work, put on his cap and jacket, and backed out of the barn his perfect 1956 Good Humor truck, freezers stocked with ice cream, fluorescent signs glowing, the broad white hood as smooth as a dish of vanilla.

Marcie would be home in a week, and the summer stretched out before him. They'd be together as a family again. They'd get back into a familiar groove. But that was before Nantucket. That was before he sat on a beach and watched his wife drive away in a Jeep with another guy. That was before their long, silent ride home to New Hampshire, before the distant, edgy phase they had entered.

"What happened on the Jeep ride?" he asked Tina, one night in bed.

"Shit happened," Tina answered, and rolled away from him.

And then Susie happened, and he just hadn't known how to stop it.

Leonard had always been a runner. In high school, in college, throughout his working life. It had always been part of his day, as necessary as eating. He wasn't nutso about it, like the macho types in the company locker room, always obsessing about running shoes and accumulated mileage. Running was just something he did. It was not so much an activity as a body part. It was a coil-steel shaft inside his spine. It kept his back straight, his head up, his vision focused on some point down the road. He ran on hot days, cold days, rainy days, snowy days. He ran when he had a headache, and his headache would disappear. He ran when he'd had words with Tina, and afterwards the issue wouldn't seem so important. He ran the night his mother called and told him his father had died, and afterwards it seemed that he had somehow pounded the meaning of his father's life into his own. He ran because he knew he could. Sure, on hot summer afternoons it was tempting to think about sitting on the back porch with a cold beer. But anybody could do that. It took some spine to get out in the ninety-degree heat, with the sun blasting off the tarmac, and start pumping. To give up running would be like giving up his face or his thumbprint: he would become like everybody else. Bland, soft, passive of mind.

He ran at lunchtime during the week, and then on weekends he liked to go for a long, easy lope around the back roads. He had always been light on his feet. To Leonard, running was not the pounding drudgery it was to the less committed; it was an agile springing upon the earth. It was the spring steel coiling and uncoiling, coiling and uncoiling; it was his body machinery in full use. He ran not with destination in mind, or timing, or pace. Rather, he ran without mind. His sense was of muscle and lung and heartbeat in perfect synchronization, carrying him along easily, as though he had wheels.

But lately his weekend runs had not seemed so natural. Destination loomed up and darkened his mind. Purpose settled into his legs and weighed him down. Today was the sixth Sunday he had followed this particular regimen: at two o'clock, pull on his running shorts and socks and shoes, stretch out in the living room or backyard, and then, hearing the Cherokee ease out of the driveway next door, trot out into the street, shaking loose his arms and neck. He would run a mile of back streets and residential neighborhoods, as he did today. He came out onto Main Street for the short block to the entrance to the drive-in movie, and cut in as if to run all the way back through the paved-over cornfields to touch the big screen and then turn around. But just past the ticket booth he sidestepped through a thin spot in the hedge and came out in the rear parking lot of the Hurley Motel. There on the backside of the motel, shielded from Main Street and the eyes of his happily married neighbors, his fellow Little League coaches, his Good Humor customers, sat the red Cherokee like his own personal beacon in front of Room 9. As he drew near, his legs grew weak and his heart pounded. The door opened as if by magic, and there was Susie Stevens wearing red satin panties and a smile, and he knew he had not yet begun to sweat.

Sweat stung his eyes as he ran up Monadnock Street. His legs were always so tired after these encounters in the motel, he was glad that Susie dropped him off just three blocks from home. He veered into his driveway and there was Tina, weeding the tomatoes. She heard him and turned, raising an earth-encrusted hand to shade her eyes. He found the motion touching, the common human need to protect one's vision, his wife's feminine hand covered with the earth from which she put sustenance on their table. He felt a rush of love for her, and had to look away.

"Hi," she said. "Did you have a nice run?"

"Yeah," he said, panting. "Nice run."

He braced his hands on his knees and gulped air.

"Something's been eating my tomatoes," Tina said. "Look at the little teeth marks."

She held up a tomato, and he took it. His sweat turned the dirt from her hand to a gritty little sheen on the taut skin.

"Chipmunk?" he guessed.

"Yeah, or red squirrel."

He loved the way Tina looked when she was gardening. Kneeling among the tomatoes in her halter top and cutoffs, she looked like a supplicant to Mother Earth. Her shoulders were smooth and tan. Streaks of sweat ran down the valley of the small of her back. Her hair was up in a sweatband, and the heavy, dark curls fell this way and that. This was the girl he had married nineteen years ago; this was the woman he had just betrayed for the last hour and a half.

"God, your shirt is soaked," she said. "Why don't you take it off and lie in the sun for a while? Dry yourself out."

"I'll go take a shower," he said. He didn't like the idea of taking off his shirt in front of Tina just now. He was always a little worried about what Susie might have left behind. Sometimes she dug her fingernails into his back so hard that he'd cry out.

He started the shower lukewarm and just let the sweat dissolve. The water ran into his face, and he felt his own salt mingling with Susie's tangy residue. He added hot water, soaped up, began to scrub her off. As he washed his genitals he handled them carefully, tenderly, as a lover would.

A lover. His lover. He had never thought of himself as the kind of man who would have a lover, who would be thought of as a lover by a woman. He had been a husband, a father, a runner, a software engineer, even a Good Humor Man. But a *lover*? He tried to find a way to make the term fit, like trying on a new pair of pants, but no matter how he shifted and adjusted, he couldn't quite get comfortable with it.

He should stop, he knew. He should call it quits. He should get back to his regular weekend running schedule and drive Susie's image out of his head.

Getting her out of his head was one thing. Getting her out of his heart was another. He had not felt this way since he was a young man falling in love with Tina. The sight of Tina coming toward him on the boardwalk in her bikini had been enough to melt him into the sand. It was the same way now with Susie. The sight of her at the open door of the motel made him feel desired and desirable. The way she drifted off to a dreamy, happy doze after making love confirmed it. An exotic, beautiful woman desired him. He was desirable. He was attractive. He was sexual. These were not unimportant things for a thirty-nine-year-old man.

He dried off and slipped into some khaki shorts and a T-shirt from Marcie's college. Downstairs, Tina was washing tomatoes.

"The kids are going to be out tonight," she said.

He knew how he should answer, but instead he said, "Oh?"

"Yes," Tina said. "Marcie's got a date. Amy's going to the movies with the Rosens, and Seth's spending the night with Johnny Marcoux."

He should propose something special, he knew. Take her out for dinner. At least go out for drinks. Instead, he said, "That's nice."

She came over and tugged at his T-shirt. "We can make it even nicer."

"Mmm," he said, and turned toward the refrigerator. "Any iced tea in here?"

On Wednesday nights there were band concerts on the town common. Susie liked to walk down with Bob, when they were both home. There was always a big crowd; the townspeople brought their lawn chairs and coolers and blankets. The police cordoned off traffic so kids could ride their bikes and skateboards in the street, and the residents of the old folks' homes could make their halting way without worry. Throughout the summer there were large orchestras and small, swing bands and blues singers and rock and roll, and at least once, the Air Force Band on a big bus.

Tonight it was a Dixieland band, which Susie liked very much but Bob wasn't really digging. He had run into some friends from Digital, and, as always seemed to happen when employees of the company met in social situations, they began to talk about work. There were two other couples, Dan and Jill Foster and Ron and Karen Genrette, all four of whom worked at Digital. Susie couldn't stand it when they ran into Digits. They spoke in a metalanguage that seemed utterly removed from everyday experience. Indeed, they *were* removed; the band concert was only the backdrop for their own interaction. "Isn't this great?" Jill Foster beamed at her, but then turned to Bob and said, "So, I heard the SDC committee gave you some pushback on the Oz launch." And then they were off on a conversation so filled with buzzwords that they created their own buzzing little hive in the midst of the music and commotion.

Susie couldn't stand it. Leonard worked for Digital, and he didn't speak this way. By now Bob and the others were speaking entirely in acronyms: RAM and ROM and RISC; WORMs and SIMMs and DATs. They'd say these things, and give each other knowing looks. Or somebody would throw in a punchline—"VAXtax!"—and everybody but Susie would laugh. It drove her crazy. She actually expected to look up one day and see speech balloons over their heads, and they'd be beeping at each other in bar codes and cracking up.

She shifted her focus. Here was the populace of a whole town in teeming, rambunctious motion, like a Brueghel painting come to life. In front of her, a mother tried to keep her flock of little blond chicks by her side, while they kept scattering; under one of the big maple trees, some teenagers hung out smoking, too cool for Dixieland; a boy had a girl flattened up against the tree in a tight embrace; a row of elderly women with their aluminum prostheses— walkers and wheelchairs and canes—sat and smiled, enjoying the music. Up on the bandstand the banjo player strummed and the trumpet player tootled along. She kept wanting to hear the music, to allow it to carry her to a different, quainter time, or at least to lift her spirits, but here was her husband and his friends talking about "getting Alpha through phase review," and it was enough to make her feel short of breath.

She kept seeing people pass by with ice cream. She stood on tiptoe to see above the crowd, and sure enough, there on the far side of the common was Leonard's white truck sending out a fluorescent glow. Her heart did a little flutter and she dropped back down off her toes and excused herself, saying she was going to get some ice cream. Bob and the others barely noticed.

She couldn't believe how suddenly nervous she was as she approached his truck, but he saw her coming. He waved and smiled. God, his teeth were nice.

"Hey," he said, reaching out and touching her arm. "I thought you were flying to London."

"Tomorrow. I love to come down here and listen to the music, but Bob ran into some other Digits, and now they're talking shop. I had to get away."

"I see." He eased into a tease. "And I'm your excuse."

"No, no—I really hoped to see you here. I just can't stand it when those guys start talking about work. They take it so seriously, or they get a big kick out of it, and I can't follow along."

"Oh, man, I understand," Leonard said. "Just smile and nod. They'll assume you think they're brilliant."

"I've tried that, but then I worry that they think I'm this dumb Chinese girl who doesn't speak any English. You know, how could Bob marry *her?*"

He laughed and waved his hand. "Don't let it get to you. I listen to that stuff all day, and I don't understand it either. What you need is a nice melon ice to restore your equilibrium. Hang on."

He turned to make the ice, and she felt good seeing him. She felt calmer already just being away from the Digits. She wished she could just hang out here by the truck, listen to Dixieland, and watch Leonard sell ice cream.

"Here you go," he said, handing her the ice. "My treat."

"Thanks," she said. "I like your treats."

Leonard started to say something, but his eye caught on something over her shoulder, and she felt a familiar presence.

"Hey, babe," Bob said. "Thought we'd lost you."

"No such luck," she said, and took a bite of her ice.

"Hey, Leonard," Bob said.

The two men shook hands. "Bob," Leonard said. "Get you some ice cream?"

"No thanks." Bob turned to Susie. "The general consensus is to go over to Stormy Monday and listen to some blues. Get some nachos and beers. Whaddya say?"

"Oh, gee. I don't know. It's nice here."

"Rinky-dink, babe," Bob said, and took Susie by the arm and began to ease her toward the common. She twisted away from him.

"I like it here," she said. "I don't care if it's rinky-dink. I cannot, repeat cannot, sit through an evening of nachos and beers and cigarette smoke and listen to you guys talk about work."

"We won't," Bob said. "I promise. We'll talk about whatever you want."

"I don't want to talk. I don't want to drink beer. I don't want to listen to blues. I want to eat this ice cream and listen to the old-time jazz and then walk home."

Bob turned to Leonard. "Leonard, make her be reasonable."

Leonard raised his eyebrows and nodded to the band. They were playing a rag. "Sure you don't want some ice cream, man?"

Susie tugged at Bob's arm, shoved him toward the common. "Go ahead," she said. "You guys go and do your thing. I'll listen to the music for a while and then head home. I've got to fly in the morning."

Bob gave her a look like, *Okay, but you're forcing me to do this.*

"Go, go!" she said.

He bent and kissed her. "See you around, Leonard," he called over his shoulder.

When Bob had disappeared into the crowd, she turned to Leonard and licked her ice. "I'll listen to the music another twenty minutes or so, and then start hoofing it." She winked at him. "Don't want to stay out too late if I'm flying."

He was two blocks from the common when he spotted her, walking along in her loose cotton pants and chambray shirt tied at the waist. He eased up behind her and rang the Good Humor bell.

"Ride, little girl?" he called out the passenger window.

She hopped in quickly. "Hit it," she said.

He did. They passed the intersection with Monadnock Street, and he glanced up the hill. No cars. Just some kids on bikes and skateboards.

"Where to?"

"Anywhere," she said. "As long as it's private and we don't have to talk about CD-ROM drives."

He switched off the fluorescents over the freezers. "It'd better be pretty damn private," he said. "We're about as inconspicuous as Leonard Nimoy at a Trekkie convention."

He drove towards Brookline, and when they got to the old sawmill he swung in, nosed past the dilapidated buildings, and eased up behind a big, sodden sawdust pile. The cut-wood smell of the sawdust floated in through the windows. The truck's engine ticked as it cooled down. He reached over and touched Susie's shirt where it was tied at her midriff.

"What kind of a Boy Scout does it take to untie this knot?" he asked.

She took his hand and held it to the flat of her tummy. She looked out the window.

"An Explorer, maybe?" he said, and walked his fingers around to her navel.

She squirmed. "That tickles."

"That's what it's supposed to do."

"I don't feel like being tickled."

"What do you feel like being?"

She didn't answer. She breathed deep and let it out, lightly fogging the windshield.

"It smells nice here," she said.

"I only ever bring my girlfriends to nice-smelling places."

"Is that what I am? A girlfriend?"

He could see a mood catching up to her fast. "Oh, hey, it's just a phrase."

"Maybe that's what I am—a phrase. Or maybe just a phase."

"Oh, come on," he said. "What's with you tonight?"

She sighed again, and again the windshield went light blue. "He just got in from his trip yesterday and I fly to London tomorrow. It's the only night we've had together in a week, and he's out with his friends. I leave early in the morning. Sometimes I do feel like a girl friend. Two words."

He put his arm around her. I'm sorry, he wanted to say. The Good Humor Man, who wanted to make everybody feel good, wanted to make her feel better. If you were my wife, he thought, I'd treat you better.

But Leonard's own voice answered the Good Humor Man: Right, pal. You've got a wife, remember? And how are you treating her?

Well, not that great, I admit. But look at the situation we're in. She hasn't been treating me so hot lately, either.

So what? You're a big boy. You can handle it.

It's no fun, seeing her attracted to other guys.

That's part of your problem, expecting life to be fun. Expecting that you can solve everything with a bowl of ice cream. She's not really attracted to other guys. She's just not sure she's attracted to herself. She uses them as mirrors.

And plays me for a sap.

You play yourself for a sap. This thing with Susie is getting you nowhere. It's not essential. It's not, as Bob might say, on your critical path.

No, but it feels good.

No it doesn't. It feels bad.

"You want to just go for a little walk?" she asked.

"Sure," he said.

The sun was almost gone and dusk settled in around the old buildings. A shard of plastic waved idly at an empty window.

"What was this place?" she asked.

"A sawmill and lumberyard. Rough-cut lumber. Went out of business when construction fell off."

"I'd like to shoot it."

"Shoot it?"

"With my camera. I'd like to shoot some black-and-white out here."

"Kind of a lonely place," he said. "But private." He put his arm around her.

"It looks like it's waiting for better times." She eased out from under his arm. "You know what I think about doing sometimes? Just taking all my camera gear and moving back to San Francisco. Opening up a little studio, or working for somebody if I had to. But packing it in here, definitely."

He picked up a rock and chucked it at a pile of logs. "It's an option."

"Hey, I'm sorry," she said. "This isn't exactly a fun date, is it?"

She took his arm, and he escorted her around the rusting mill machinery, the rotting piles of scrap. She spoke about her family in San Francisco, about her plans for a photography career. He kept a pleasant little smile on for her, said "Oh?" and "Yeah" at the right places, but his mind was elsewhere. An image had come into his head, a photo he had taken, oh, ten years ago now, of his family on vacation at the Jersey shore: slightly overexposed and fuzzy, the kids spread out on the beach, Marcie and Amy prancing in the waves, Seth hip-deep in wet sand, and Tina slightly turned toward the camera with a hand shading her eyes. She was smiling at him, a private, shared moment of watching their kids. They had just bought their house in Hurley, he had just gotten the Digital job, and the kids were fine and healthy. Tina's smile held all that. They felt lucky then, blessed. Life was a day at the beach. Now, skirting the piles of scrap lumber with this woman he knew only fleetingly, how very far away that all seemed.

He dropped Susie at the foot of Monadnock Street and wished her a good flight. When he pulled into his driveway, the lights glowed from his living room, the blue flicker of the TV strobed out against the twilight. He pressed the remote control for the garage door in the barn, and waited as it rose. He looked at the remote control, turned it over and examined it as if seeing it for the first time. When had he started using one of these things? He'd always resisted the conveniences of suburban life, considering them too soft, too easy. He used to figure it would be all over the day he refused to get out of the car to open his own garage door, but two winters ago Tina had lobbied hard for an automatic garage-door opener so she wouldn't ruin her leather boots, and now he pushed a button like everybody else. They had an automatic coffeemaker, too. He used to enjoy grinding the beans by hand and then brewing a pot of coffee for just the two of them. Now the coffeemaker turned itself on at seven every morning, and everybody, even young Seth, gulped a cup before taking off. They had a remote-controlled television and stereo so they wouldn't have to get out of their chairs, they had a microwave so they could make a meal in two minutes, they had an answering machine so they wouldn't have to talk to people. They had all the essentials.

He pulled the truck inside and plugged in the freezers. At least nothing had happened tonight. Not really. He could face Tina and the kids without looking guilty.

Marcie's car was gone, so she was out. Amy and Seth were watching TV. Tina was in the kitchen, straightening up. She turned to him, brushing back her hair, and he was struck once again at how attracted he was to her.

"How was the concert?" she asked.

"Oh, fine," he said. "Dixieland band."

"Business?"

"Decent. I haven't totaled out yet." He held up his cash bag and started to walk through the kitchen. Tina stepped in front of him.

"And how about after the concert?" She had this look on her face, the same one she got when she caught the kids at something. "Seth was out skateboarding earlier. He said you drove by the end of the street."

"Oh, I just went out on my usual route, around town a bit."

Tina closed the door to the living room, shutting out the kids and the TV.

"He said it looked like you had someone else in the truck."

When they finally took off from Heathrow, Susie was buzzy and anxious. She looked up the rows and rows of heads—most hair is some shade of brown, she always noticed—and she felt as if she weren't all there. She hated these transatlantic turnarounds. Her body never adjusted to the changes in light and time. Now, on the way back to Boston, she felt as if she had been moving so fast that she had left some essential piece of herself behind. Her head buzzed and felt detached from her body. She felt slightly sick from all the coffee she had drunk at the airport.

There had been a three-hour security delay. After the plane was loaded and ready to go, security had unloaded all the baggage and spread it out on the runway. She didn't mind. Occasionally in midflight—usually on flights out of Heathrow—she'd get an image of the dark baggage compartment, where, nestled deep inside a soft nylon bag, perhaps within a shaving kit, quietly ticking, was a clock mechanism, some wiring, the plastique. She'd push this image aside. If it was to happen, there was nothing she could do about it. But she never minded when flights were delayed so that those who could do something about it tried.

The thing she disliked most about this flight was the crew. Or specifically, the senior flight attendant, Carmen. They had all hung out together in the lounge during the delay, and Carmen had to be the center of attention. She was a hard-edged blonde who wore too much blue eye shadow. She spoke in a brassy, sarcastic voice to the other flight attendants, but then got all gooey and girly with the pilot and copilot. And what Susie hated most was Carmen's ill-concealed racism toward her. Carmen called her "Suzi Chopsticks," as if they were such intimates that Carmen could joke about Susie's ethnicity. Carmen left notes taped to the galley during flight, so the other crew members would see: "Suzi Chopsticks: Japanese businessman in first class seeks geisha for companionship in London." Or: "Suzi Chopsticks: Stir-fry demonstration right after movie." But the rest of the crew didn't go along, and Susie knew there was no warmth in Carmen's humor. She knew the senior flight attendant to be mean-spirited toward women and mercenary with men.

As they came out of the climb and the captain turned off the seat belts sign, she told herself, Just six more hours. Just get through the next six hours, and you'll be home. She held on to a vision: driving up green, shady Monadnock Street, going into her safe, comfortable house, changing into something loose and cotton, and having a quiet meal with her husband. A buzzing head, a nauseous stomach, an airplane full of cranky passengers—she could deal with it all if she just kept this vision of home in her mind.

This sustained her for a few minutes, until the guy in 14A started having a heart attack. She had noticed since takeoff that he was uncomfortable. He fidgeted in his seat, bothered his wife. They were a sixtyish British couple, middle-class. At first she thought Mr. Roberts was just not used to flying, and like everybody else, was bothered by the delay. But he kept shifting, and Mrs. Roberts began to get concerned, leaning over him and fussing. Susie asked if she could get them blankets and pillows. Next time she passed, Mr. Roberts was sitting with his eyes closed, breathing short breaths, but Mrs. was clearly worried. She caught Susie's eye.

"He's having chest pains," she said.

"Oh, now," Mr. Roberts rasped.

Susie felt his forehead. Cold and clammy.

"Have you eaten anything that may have upset you?" she asked.

"Aaah," he said. Mrs. Roberts shook her head.

"Is he taking any medication?

"No, miss."

"Is he used to flying?"

"He did a bit of it in his job," Mrs. Roberts said. "But not so much anymore."

Mr. Roberts gasped and was racked with a spasm that twisted him sideways.

"Oh!" Mrs. Roberts said. "Harry!"

Susie felt for his pulse. Mr. Roberts exhaled and slumped against his wife.

"Harry!" Mrs. Roberts said.

Susie went quickly to the first-class galley, where Carmen was preparing snacks. Carmen gave her an annoyed look, as if Susie had personally caused Mr. Roberts to disrupt the service schedule, but she moved fast and introduced herself to Mrs. Roberts in a polite, professional voice.

"Did he eat anything that might have caused indigestion?"

"Nothing, miss," Mrs. Roberts said. "He didn't feel like eating."

"Any medications?"

"I've already been through this," Susie said.

Carmen ignored her. "I'm just going to take your pulse," she said in her phony, little-girl voice to Mr. Roberts.

Another spasm twisted the man.

"Harry!"

"First-aid kit!" Carmen ordered.

Susie got the kit from the locker. The red locker handle seemed too bright. Passengers began standing in their seats and craning their necks to look at 14A. "Out of the way, please," she said, but the whole scene had a surreal quality, as if she had just walked onto a movie set.

Mr. Roberts's breath was shallow.

"Oxygen," Carmen said. No little-girl squeak now.

Susie began unwrapping the oxygen bottle. The straps were twisted. She fumbled with them. Carmen unrolled the mask, rubber-banded it to the tube, and grabbed the oxygen bottle. "Forget the straps!" she snapped. She twisted the valve, placed the mask to Mr. Roberts's face, and passed the bottle to Mrs. Roberts.

"If you'll just hold that bottle," she said, "we'll get him a little breath of air."

Carmen took his pulse, and Mr. Roberts lay back with his eyes closed. He drew weakly on the oxygen. Mrs. Roberts held the bottle, her eyes darting between her husband's face and Carmen's. Carmen got the oxygen mask's straps untangled and strapped the mask to Mr. Roberts's head. She turned to Susie. "Take his blood pressure, and get the nitroglycerine from the kit. I'll be right back."

She was off to notify the cockpit, Susie knew. Carmen was as efficient as a machine, and as she left she asked the passengers across the aisle to move to new seats so she could have room to work. Susie rolled up Mr. Roberts's shirt, Velcroed the blood-pressure sleeve in place, and squeezed the pump.

Carmen's voice came over the intercom: "If there is a medical doctor or registered nurse on the flight, will you please report to row fourteen on the left side of the aircraft." Her voice was as smooth and polished as a machine part, delivered with the authority of someone used to being in charge.

"Once again, if there is a medical doctor . . ."

The doctor wore a sweater and running shoes. How comfortable doctors on vacation always looked, Susie thought. He conferred with Carmen; Mrs. Roberts watched their faces. The doctor bent to Mr. Roberts, and as he did, Mr. Roberts seemed to wilt: his eyes fluttered, his face sagged, he went limp.

"Help me get him to the floor," the doctor said.

Carmen elbowed Susie aside, and she and the doctor laid Mr. Roberts out.

"Count for me."

Carmen counted while the doctor pumped on Mr. Roberts's chest. From where she was kneeling, Susie could see Mr. Roberts's feet shudder with every compression. He wore brown penny loafers.

Mrs. Roberts began crying quietly.

Susie took her hand, squeezed it for strength.

"He'll be okay, won't he?" Mrs. Roberts asked. "He's a healthy man. Walks every morning and evening."

"He'll be okay," Susie said. She wished she believed it, as his penny loafers shook with the doctor's attempt to keep his life within him.

"It's our first trip to the States," Mrs. Roberts said. A woman across the aisle handed her a tissue. "Thank you. We're going to visit our daughter in Connecticut." She addressed not only Susie but the other passengers as well. "She's got a new baby, so we're going to see him. Our first grandson."

The other passengers spoke to Mrs. Roberts about her daughter and the baby, to keep her occupied. The doctor stopped his chest compressions, and Mr. Roberts was now breathing oxygen. His eyelids fluttered open from time to time, and his wife held his hand. Carmen went up to the cockpit and then came back, and she and the doctor put their heads together.

"I think it would be best," the doctor said.

Carmen turned to Mrs. Roberts. "Your husband seems to be coming out of the danger zone," she said, "but we believe he had a heart attack. The doctor thinks it best that he get proper medical attention right away. I've notified the cockpit, and the captain's recommendation is to turn around and put down at Shannon, Ireland. They'll take you both to the hospital there."

Mrs. Roberts nodded and squeezed her husband's hand. Carmen put her hand to his throat and made a big silly face. "His pulse is stronger than mine!" she said in a loud, phony voice. And as the plane descended over the green and misty Irish landscape, Carmen turned toward Mrs. Roberts and sang, in a bad brogue, "When Ir-r-rish eyes ar-r-re smiling!"

God, Susie thought. She couldn't imagine what poor Mrs. Roberts must be thinking, with her husband lying on the floor and Carmen trying to be bubbly.

The air that came into the cabin was damp, and the Irish doctor was young and cute. His build was lean and his suit slightly large for his frame. Susie fell for him instantly, and wished they could just go off to a pub together and get drunk. He was accompanied by a stout, redheaded nurse, who smiled at everyone and then, with the help of a burly young man obviously her son, loaded Mr. Roberts onto a gurney and wheeled him up the aisle.

Mrs. Roberts collected her things—her coat, her husband's hat, a small tweed bag—and apologized to everyone for the delay. Everyone shushed her, wished her luck, pressed their hands onto hers. Mrs. Roberts thanked her and Carmen—"I don't know what I'd have done without you"—and broke into tears again. Susie hugged her and then watched her move up the aisle, a small woman whose first flight to America had been cut short by an explosion in her husband's chest. Susie thought of Bob, quickly calculated time zones, imagined him performing his Saturday-morning chores. Perhaps he was food shopping, planning a good meal for this evening. At that moment she wanted more than anything to be home, curled in her husband's arms, listening to the steady ticking behind his shirt. She tidied up the seats in row 14, and then went to the rest room to wash her face.

It was a hot Saturday afternoon in Hurley. Leonard had been to the dump in the morning, and had washed the cars, and his body was gearing up for the run. His legs were starting to tighten; they needed the release of the slow seven-mile circuit of town. His weekend run. Or, he thought guiltily, what used to be his weekend run.

He went out to the barn and got the hedge clippers, made a few halfhearted swipes at the hedge. Shards of the showdown with Tina cut into his thoughts. *Who was she? Who was she? Who was she, goddammit?* He really didn't care about trimming the hedge when *You don't just drive off in your ice cream truck with another woman and then refuse to tell*—who really fucking gave a shit about a stupid fucking hedge, about keeping up an image for the neighbors when *Right, right, it's exactly the same only I didn't do it in front of our son, I didn't drive off with someone else with my own children looking on!* The neighbors' driveway was empty and would stay that way until later. It was too early for her to be home from London, and when she did get back *It's payback. That's what it is, I know.* He could take her crying, had seen it enough over the years. But what he couldn't take was her talking through the tears, her voice ragged through the sobs, owning up *I know I started it! I know I have to take what's coming*—because he hadn't cried since he was a teenager and he couldn't imagine the strength it took to speak while *I know what I'm like, I know!* or the risk, the vulnerability, the showing of the throat *I know what I've put you through! But it doesn't make it hurt any less*—And in the end he had felt like a heel, a cad, a man who had failed to be a good husband to his wife. In the end he had simply held her as she cried, and he had tried, had genuinely tried, to cry with her, but he could not do it. He held her, and they fell asleep, and sometime in the night he woke and pulled the sheet over them.

Today he felt wasted, washed out. The heat sapped him. He couldn't do the run. He could barely clip the hedge. He tossed the clippers into the barn, went inside the house, and popped open a beer. At least the back porch was cool, and no one was around to bug him.

When she finally got home and inside her kitchen, she found, instead of Bob and a nice dinner, a note on the refrigerator:

"Susie: Had to go to Seattle unexpectedly. Part of the Boeing deal. Sorry—will call U tonite. xoxox Bob."

She had known as soon as she entered the house, had even had an inkling while she was driving up from the airport: *What if he's not there?* A series of images came to her, all laid out in her mind as if on a black-and-white proof sheet: the kitchen table, empty save for the wooden pepper mill; the dishes, stacked neatly in the china closet; the living-room couch shaded by the drawn curtains; the stereo, cold and dark. The house would be still, void of human stirring, as neat as she had left it. She, like many of the flight attendants she knew, always straightened up the house before a trip.

What if he never came back?

She got another black-and-white image: a small envelope propped on the pillow of the bed, her name scrawled across the front.

She took his note off the refrigerator and crumpled it. The Boeing deal. The AT&T account. The frigging Department of the Interior installation. There was always some goddamned computer operation somewhere that would draw her husband away from her. So instead of holding her in his arms, he was sitting on an airplane somewhere, or in a terminal or a cab, his briefcase on his knees, jotting down notes of a meeting or writing up a trip report.

She thought of Mr. and Mrs. Roberts on the plane, what kind of life they must have had. A decent sort of life, she imagined. Mrs. kept house and raised the kids, had tea with her friends. Mr. got up early for his morning walk, came home at six o'clock for an evening with his family. A decent life, where a wife and husband are happy together—happy *and* together. Where they're good friends and companions, live a long life together, are with each other when they grow old and begin to fail.

She uncrumpled Bob's note, tried to smooth it out on the table. The edges kept curling back up, like the petals of a wrinkled flower. *Will call U tonite. xoxox.*

They would have to talk. They would definitely have to talk.

On Sunday afternoon, Leonard asked Tina to come on his Good Humor route with him. They were being tender with each other, drawing closer, like the skin of a wound growing back together.

"You're not going for your run?" she asked.

"Naaah. Let's go sell some ice cream," he said. "You've never been. You'll get a kick out of it."

"Okay," she said. "Sure. You've never asked me to go before."

"You can ring my bell," he said, and gave her a tentative hug.

When they pulled out, he noticed Susie's Cherokee in her driveway. Just registered it. His neighbor was back from London. He wound down through the streets of town, showed Tina how to ring the bell. They stopped at a Little League game, and she handled the money while he got the ice cream. She had fun making change from his belt changer. Then they headed out of town, to Mont Vernon and then to New Boston and Francestown, stopping here and there to sell ice cream. Tina slid over on the seat to sit beside him, and he put his arm around her, and they rode as they used to when they were dating. The sun began to go down somewhere out beyond Dublin, and they pulled off the road at a picnic area beside a lake. They stretched and admired the view: the last sunrays slanting between the mountains to the west, the lake glowing copper before them. A kingfisher dropped from a pine tree and dove into the water. The air was cool and mulchy, with a scent of autumn.

"This is a nice place," Tina said, and sat cross-legged on top of the picnic table.

"Yes," he said. "It is."

"Will you make me some ice cream?"

He paused before the freezer, and then he knew what it would be. A simple dish of strawberry. He joined Tina at the table, and they passed the ice cream back and forth. The frozen strawberries were sliced in half, like hearts split in two. They fed each other, this man and woman. They nestled together, feeling the last warmth of the sun on their faces, murmuring as warm, contented animals do at the end of the day.

TEN

Truth from Above

E d Jacques's mission was called Truth from Above. Ed's son Ernie built and flew remote-controlled airplanes as a hobby. Ed and Ernie did not usually fly them in the neighborhood, preferring the open spaces of the high school football field or the A&P parking lot. Ernie had three planes: a P-51 Mustang, a Spad, and the one Ed chose for Truth from Above, a Cessna. It had the right nonmilitary surveillance look, Ed said.

Ed took the Cell Four list of all they knew to be shoddy or problematic with the remaining houses for sale: "Cracked foundation on gray cape," "Unfinished soffits in garrison," "Warped joists in saltbox." The Saturday he launched the mission, Ed called everybody over to his backyard. There sat the Cessna in royal blue, and beside it was a small pile of what looked to Ray like toy army men. They were in fact parachutists. On the back of each parachutist, attached by fishing line, was a carefully folded handkerchief.

The first real estate agent rolled into the neighborhood around ten o'clock, getting a small rise out of the Irish setters. He pulled his dark blue Lincoln in front of the garrison two doors down, and spoke with the people in the closed car until the dogs quieted. Finally the doors opened and a young couple got out. The guy eyeballed the house and spoke with the real estate agent, while the wife looked around the neighborhood. Ray and the others lay hidden behind Ed's rhododendrons, so the woman's gaze drifted past. The couple walked up the unfinished front sidewalk to the door, the agent swinging his arms wide. *Look at this yard! Sure beats being cooped up in an apartment, eh?*

After they went inside, Ed turned to his pile of parachutists and selected one. He fitted it to a tension spring on the underside of the Cessna's fuselage.

"Give 'em a chance to cozy up to the place," he said. "Let the real estate tell 'em what a nice quiet neighborhood it is."

Ed had rigged up a plywood runway in his yard. When he started the Cessna, it sounded like a nest of mad hornets. Aiming his remote control and revving up the little engine, he ran the Cessna down the plywood and into the air. It buzzed up over the rhododendrons and into the sky above Bill Street. Ed took it way up, a good hundred feet anyway, so that its fierce hornet buzz faded to a drone, and then he brought it down in a long dive over the Big Fat Guy's cape. The Cessna swooped over the cape at rooftop level, flattened out, and *zzzooomed!* past the second-story windows of the garrison. The Big Fat Guy's Irish setters, positive that Something Was Going On, abandoned their vigil at the fence and started doing their Irish setter thing: arfing and bouncing into each other and crashing against the chain link. Ed took the Cessna up for another long dive, and this time the Irish setters heard it coming. With the Cessna in its screaming descent, they whipped into a frenzy of yapping and howling. The Cessna buzzed the setters; they tumbled over each other, nipping and yelping to get out of the way.

"Oughta put a dent in the nice-quiet-neighborhood theory," Ed said.

He buzzed the garrison a few times and then took the Cessna up into another long climb. The people came outside, and the first living beings they saw were the three mad dogs thrashing each other next door. Then they heard the plane, located it inside their own airspace and screeching down upon their heads, and—the woman actually ducked—turned as it buzzed by at mailbox level. They watched as it climbed again and came back over, slower this time, slower, floating over their would-be front yard, the guy pointing at it, and then, as Ed pressed the release button, they saw something disengage from the fuselage and then the handkerchief popped open and the little parachutist floated gently towards them. They seemed to enjoy this, pointing and smiling as if to mark its descent, the Cessna quietly leaving the scene as Ed eased along the side of his house to land it out on Monadnock Street, how cute, this little parachutist floating into their front yard—*you see, folks, it's a great neighborhood*—and as it landed just to the side of the walk, the woman stepped forward to retrieve it and, right on cue, held up the handkerchief and read what was written on it: "Ask the real estate agent how much water runs into the cellar after a hard rain."

She showed it to her husband, who passed it to the real estate agent, who shot a murderous look around the neighborhood. But he saw no living thing except for the Irish setters settling down, emitting the random yip and yelp. The agent gestured toward the house, tried to guide the couple back inside—*Well, let's just go have us a look at that basement. You know what they say about water in New Hampshire, folks—too much in the cellar and not enough in the well!*—but they had seen enough. The woman was already climbing into the agent's car. The agent gave a last look around, but Ray and the others were all huddled under the rhododendron bushes.

Leonard and Susie left after that first go-round, Leonard saying he needed to get to his Good Humor route. Ray felt a pull toward his Saturday duties—go to the dump, change the oil in his Honda, mow the lawn one last time—but then another real estate car pulled up Bill Street—"Hssst! Ray!" Ed said—and Ray dropped to the grass behind Ed's rhododendrons.

Ed waited to see which house they went to, selected his parachutist, and sent the Cessna skyward. As before, Ed buzzed the Irish setters and the house, and as before, the people came out of the house with the real estate agent. This time, though, instead of being amused, Ray noticed the real estate woman's face. She was middle-aged, nicely dressed and going a bit plump, with her hair tied up in a bun. She looked up at the buzzing Cessna as it made its descent, and an expression of real annoyance came across her face. And more than annoyance—apology, as she looked at the people standing next to her. She looked like a mother apologizing to a neighbor for her kid's handiwork with, say, a baseball bat. Ray's heart went out to her, and he wanted more than anything to just walk away from the rhododendron bush, away from the whole Cell Four thing. But Ed was cutting loose the parachutist, and there it was, floating down toward the little crowd across the street. The real estate woman regarded it like some kind of mistrusted spore, and when it landed in the grass, she guided the people past it to the car.

Ray went home to mow his lawn, but he couldn't get the face of the real estate woman out of his mind. As the mower droned and spat grass clippings, a question floated, as if borne by a little parachutist, into his mind: *Are you doing all you can with your life?* Pow! Just like that, and then another one, floating in: *Have you accomplished everything you wanted to?* It was like a little parachute settling over his brain and shrouding him from thinking about anything else, as he followed his lawn mower up and down. He took stock. He would turn forty next week, and he had lived a good, if uneventful, life. He had married young, and well. His marriage had prevailed over the trials and temptations of the early years. He and Marisse were humming along the smooth, well-defined groove they had created and now appreciated: they loved and sustained each other intellectually, emotionally, sexually. They were each other's best and oldest friends. So he could say that he had "accomplished" a good marriage.

On the career front, he wasn't so sure. He had done something that he had always wanted to: he had helped start up a company and, over the last five years, seen it become successful. But his business card bore a title—Product Manager—that fifteen years ago would have confused him, and twenty years ago made him sneer. Now it was what he did: managed the life cycle of graphics software, from creation to engineering to manufacturing, and on to marketing, sales, revision, and finally retirement. His product was very successful in the publishing community, and had secured him a solid position within Gentry Systems. It still had a good four or five years of life, and if he was vigilant and mildly innovative, he could expect to ride its success with a minimum of effort.

That, he felt, was a problem. You can't keep on accomplishing unless you keep moving forward, like a shark.

He got to the deep grass at the back of the yard, and the mower bogged down. He gave it some gas, and another little parachute came drifting into his mind: *Have you traveled enough? Experienced a variety of things?* Well, enough . . . of course, you can never travel too much. He'd been to New York and Chicago and San Francisco. New Orleans and Las Vegas and L.A. All the convention cities. He and Marisse had taken vacations to St. Thomas and Paris and Cancún. But had he *experienced* these places? He had seen them as a conventioneer or a tourist, but he hadn't actually spent as much time in the local economies as he would have liked to, although he *had* seen, when walking a side street in Paris, an accelerating motorcycle slam into a stopped BMW so directly that it seemed deliberate, and so hard that the motorcyclist went through the rear passenger window helmet first. The BMW driver had paid no attention to the motorcyclist in the backseat, but had dragged the twisted bike away from his car and, hands on his hips, inspected his rear door for damage. It seemed like such a Parisian thing to do.

Ray finished up the yard and scraped out the mower, but he heard Ed's Cessna buzz into the air, and another parachute-question floated over his head. *Have you learned a musical instrument? A foreign language? You always said you'd do these things.*

Mon Dieu! Incoming! He tried to duck the questions by throwing the week's trash into the back of Marisse's Subaru and driving off to the dump, but the parachutes kept blooming.

Is it a mistake not to have children? To live so far from your aging parents?

Shouldn't you live in a city, where you have some culture? Or off in the country, where it's peaceful?

Shouldn't you get more exercise?

Somehow Ray's office found out about his birthday. He figured it must have been Judy, in personnel, with access to his birthdate, although he wouldn't have put it past Marisse to place a phone call. He began to suspect something was up when he passed a yellow sticky note with the number 40 on it, posted outside his door. When he logged onto his Macintosh, he discovered that somebody had configured it to flash 40 at him from all over the screen. He began to get electronic mail messages like the one from the system manager, Ellen Beasley: "Ray: I'm taking inventory on our storage capacities. What size drive do you have on your Mac? 40 megabytes?" And from one of the tech writers: "Ray: What version of Microsoft Word are you running? 4.0?" When he went up front to get a cup of coffee, three or four engineers were hanging around the coffee machine. Mike Edmonds elbowed Ron Lymon and said, "You hear the weather forecast? Temperature's supposed to drop like crazy tonight—down to about forty."

Ray put up with this sort of thing all day. They had cake and coffee for him in the afternoon, as well as the usual gag presents: a bottle of Geritol, some Grecian Formula for his hair, a package of Ex-Lax. He took it all in good humor, and Jeannie, the sales secretary, came by and said, "Don't let them kid you, Ray—you look great for forty," which made him feel good. But still, it began to gnaw at him. He'd never thought about birthdays much, before all this hullabaloo.

That evening, Marisse took him out to dinner. She picked him up at work and they drove into Boston. She had made reservations at a little Italian place in the North End, and she toasted him with their first glass of wine. "Here's to my good-lookin' husband," she said. "How does forty feel?"

"It probably would have felt a lot like thirty-nine," he said, "if everybody hadn't made such a big deal about it."

"Oh, hey—it's just because they like you and know you can take it. It's all in fun."

"Oh, I know," he said. "It is fun. But it makes you think."

It did feel as if a corner had been turned. In your twenties, you still have a lifetime of possibilities ahead; you can do anything. In your thirties, you begin to focus more, begin to lock in. By forty, it seemed, you should be comfortable with your life's work, settled into a career and a home life that will take you solidly into your fifties and sixties and set you up for your seventies. By forty, you should be paying down your mortgage principal, your kids should be well along in school, your college funds should be growing. You should be staring at fifty, looking forward to a vacation home and a Mercedes. Yikes! It made Ray want to duck under the red-checkered tablecloth and hide, to grasp Marisse by the legs and just hold on. Another parachute came floating in: *How do you see yourself in ten years? Five?* Hell, he had no idea. He still felt like a kid. Somehow, he had fooled everybody into thinking he was an adult.

On the weekend of the Pumpkin Festival, Ray and Marisse walked downtown to select their jack-o'-lantern. It was a perfect fall day: the sky clear blue and the leaves at their peak color. The fragrance of woodsmoke in the air. The common was bright with orange pumpkins and fluttering banners and stands selling hot mulled cider and chili. Townspeople in fisherman's sweaters and down vests milled around, visited with each other, toted pumpkins off to their cars. Ray and Marisse checked out the Great Pumpkin contest, where the bloated, misshapen mandarins sat with their weights scrawled on their flanks in felt marker. The winner was over three hundred pounds.

Marisse picked up a couple of small sugar pumpkins for pie, and they were headed for a pile of kickball-sized pumpkins for the jack-o'-lantern when Ray spotted Bill Barr on the other side of the pile with his wife and three boys. Barr wore a corduroy jacket and jeans, and although he was probably only four or five years older than Ray, his hair was going gray at the sideburns. Ray hadn't noticed this before. Even Barr's mustache was gray. But the guy was in good shape, Ray had to give him that. He was lean and wiry, deeply tanned from his outdoor work. His hawklike features seemed softer as he helped his sons pick out pumpkins. Barr's wife, on the other hand, was a hard-edged little woman in a tight denim jumpsuit and high boots. She stood aside, smoking, while the others sorted pumpkins. The boys ranged from knee-high to pimples, and they went through the pumpkin pile like Barr's machine through the woods in back of Ray's house. Barr bent and helped them evaluate pumpkins, and the littlest kid, in a cowboy hat and six-guns, darted this way and that, trying to pick up pumpkins nearly as big as he was.

The kid ran around back of Ray, and Ray suddenly had a vision of what he might have become had his life gone in another direction. Had he continued in construction rather than moved on, had he married one of the hometown farmers' daughters rather than Marisse, had he settled for the status quo rather than pushing on to—to what? he asked himself, and he had no answer, other than to what he was—had he done these things, he might very well be looking at a picture of himself in five years.

Ray suddenly didn't want Barr to see him. He wanted to get his pumpkin and go. He picked up a squat, fat pumpkin and began to turn away, but as he did, Barr's littlest kid came careening around the pile with a pumpkin half his size. The kid wore a pair of too-big, hand-me-down cowboy boots. He ran in front of Ray, hollering, and he cut off Ray's turn so Ray had to catch himself up short. Ray juggled his own pumpkin, then caught it and tucked it to him as if catching a basketball. The kid, though, just one step past Ray, tripped in his headlong rush and went down. His pumpkin hit the ground and split into two ragged pieces. The kid bounced up with typical knee-high-kid resilience, and Ray instinctively bent to help, but when the kid saw the broken pumpkin his face drew down tight and he burst into tears. Since Ray was holding his shoulder, the kid jerked away, howled, looked at Ray and then at the broken pumpkin, and then howled again.

Barr's wife rushed over to gather up her son, and Ray noticed that from across the pumpkin pile Barr had spotted him and was staring. Barr's sharp features were back, as was his flat, level stare. His jaw was working, as if he was contemplating coming across the pile and kicking Ray's butt.

Ray's first instinct was to say, *Hey, he was running and he tripped,* but he realized that even to say this would be some admission of guilt, so he turned and continued making his way to the checkout table next to the pumpkin pile. Barr's kid was wailing at the top of his lungs. Just as Ray got to the counter, Barr stepped in front of him and handed the checkout girl a twenty-dollar bill.

"Take out for the kid's punkin," he said.

The girl looked over at the split pumpkin. "That looks like about a seven-pounder," she said. "Let's call it two-fifty, unless you want to weigh the pieces."

"Just take out for it."

"You want to put it on the tab for the other pumpkins?"

Barr looked at his wife, who was trying to shake the kid quiet. "No," she said. "We'll stop at Wal-Mart on the way home and get some plastic ones."

The kid heard this and realized he was going to have to leave the Pumpkin Festival empty-handed, and he started in with "No! No! Wanna puk-kin! Puk-kin!" The other two boys quickly grabbed a pumpkin each and headed toward the counter.

"Just take out for the broke one," Barr said. He cut short his other two sons with a look. "You two put those punkins down. We'll get you some plastic ones, so nobody can break 'em on you." The cashier counted out Barr's change, and Barr turned his back and walked away with his family, the littlest one still hollering and looking over his shoulder at the pumpkin pile. Ray imagined their ride home, the older boys disappointed and paying no attention to their plastic pumpkins, the littlest one warming up to his. Barr would be silent and grim as he sat at the traffic lights on 101. His wife would smoke cigarettes and watch the malls pass by her passenger window.

Truth from Above ended that weekend. When Ray finished carving his jack-o'-lantern and set it out on the front porch, Ed saw him and came over. Ed told it this way: "The real estate pulls up with this middle-aged couple, no kids, guy looks like a regular guy. The Cessna does its thing, a barrel roll or two over the Irish setters just to get them psyched, and right from the start the guy's outside, watching the plane. Cessna does an outside loop over the roof, and the guy's eyes bug. A touch-and-go off the street, and the guy cheers. Cheers, by God! Applauds, jumps up and down! Pop the chute and the guy catches it and reads it out loud and then says, 'I don't give a good goddamn if the foundation does leak—honey, we've got another RC nut in the neighborhood. Hot damn, we're home!'"

Within a month, they'd moved in. The guy had a gin-blossomed face and a collection of airplanes that made Ed and Ernie look like Cub Scouts. The Red Baron, they called him. The Red Baron had scale-model Cessnas and Pipers and Bonanzas. He had warplanes and cargo planes, antique biplanes and experimental flying wings. He had a whole frigging airport on his driveway every weekend morning, and plane by plane he took them up and buzzed them around. The constant droning drove the neighbors nuts—they'd be raking leaves or setting out bulbs and a P-40 would buzz over; they'd stop working to look across backyards at each other, and hold their hands to their ears or shake their fists at the sky.

And it wasn't just the airplanes they had to put up with. The planes got the Irish setters going, so on weekends there was pretty much a constant din from back in the new development. Ed tried speaking to the Red Baron, tried to persuade him to use the football field or the A&P lot, but the Red Baron said he'd always wanted a place where he could line up his planes right outside the door and fly them whenever he felt like it. At the crack of dawn. During commercials. Settle back into the lawn chair with a gin-and-tonic and the remote control. The rest of Cell Four tried speaking to him, too. They went as a group, in guerrilla black. The Red Baron just pointed to his New Hampshire license plate—*Live Free or Die*—and took to the air with a Jap Zero.

So Truth from Above was not an unqualified success. A few of the neighbors knew who to blame, Ray could tell. Mrs. Bain had stopped waving when she drove past. Old Nicolo Bartolomeo, on his walks up and down the street, passed the house without acknowledging him or Marisse, and Ed said Nicolo and the Bains were cool even to him. But Ed's wife, Thelma, reported back from the town hall that the garrison had sold for one thirty-four: a fifty-five-grand nosedive for Barr.

ELEVEN

The Spite Fence

The saltbox directly in back of Ray and Marisse was the last house to be built. A few trees stood at the rear of the Vanns' lot, plus their garden shed, but it wasn't enough to screen off anything. As the new house went up, they were appalled at how close it seemed. They were used to looking out the back door and seeing woods. Instead, during construction, they saw a raw wall of studs and particleboard and swarms of workmen. Even after the saltbox was finished and stained gray, it still loomed over the garden and most of the backyard. And like the other Barr houses, it was of the cheapest construction: particleboard for sheathing and subfloors— even for clapboards, which began to warp after the first few rains. The basement, like all the others, leaked, and the rear wall of the house was so out of plumb that Ray could see it from his dining room.

Weekends, Ray and Marisse liked to sit at the dining table or in the back sunporch and read the papers. Every time Ray glanced out the window he'd see the house. That out-of-plumb wall gnawed at him. From the foundation to the roof it slanted outward a good six inches, and it gave the impression that the house was going to topple over backwards. He had been taught to build on the square, plumb, and level; the angle of that back wall offended his sense of geometry. Barr, he thought, you sleazy bastard. You ruined a perfectly beautiful woods to throw up a depressingly bad house. The more times Ray glanced up from the paper and saw that wall, the more he knew he could not live with it in his vision.

He decided to build a fence. A nice tall stockade fence would do.

He was at the dining-room table sketching it when Marisse came down from her studio. She was wearing her paint-spattered overalls.

"I'm pregnant," she said.

"Mmm-hmm," Ray said. He was used to this. Marisse got pregnant on the average of once a month. At least, that's how often her period was late.

"My period's late."

"Mmm-hmm." Well, she knew her body.

"I'm serious, Ray. I know my body. It's different this time. A woman can tell."

"Mmm," Ray said. "Boy or girl?"

"How should I—Oh, fuck you. Shut up! Go play your fucking games." She stalked out of the dining room and went upstairs. He heard her shut the bedroom door.

Ray wasn't too worried. In a little while her emotions would crest, she would go into the bathroom, and then she'd come down, apologize, and announce that she'd gotten her period.

Or so he thought.

After a while, he heard her place a phone call. Then he heard her rummaging around in her closet. He went upstairs. She was getting dressed to go out.

"Dr. Kennerly can take me this afternoon," she said. "I'm going over for a test."

It had never gone this far before.

"Are you sure?" Ray said. "You don't want to give it a day or so?"

"I've given it a day or so, Ray. It's over two weeks late."

"C'mon, Marisse. You always figure it wrong. It's probably like four or five days."

"See you later, Ray."

She'd never actually gone for a test. Either her preoccupation had reached a new level, or she really was pregnant. Ray didn't know which he dreaded more.

When Marisse pulled into the driveway, he met her at the back door. She was smiling.

"Hi, Dad," she said.

"Oh, man." Ray noticed two things: a sudden weight on his heart, and a kind of glow about Marisse. She was slightly flushed, and she couldn't stop smiling.

"Can you believe it?" she asked. "I'm pregnant. Heavy with child."

"Oh, man," he said. He hugged her. A fine dew spread across her nose and cheeks.

"I can't help it," she said. "I feel giddy."

"I think we have to talk," he said.

"I'll make some tea."

"Make mine a beer."

They settled in on the couch—Marisse with her fragrant tea, Ray with a Bass ale. She dipped a cookie into the tea; he took a big frothy swill. One of the cats sauntered in and jumped onto his lap.

"It feels strange," she said. "You try so long to avoid it, and then when it happens you feel kind of . . . special."

It settled in on him, gaining weight. "Did you talk to Dr. Kennerly about what to do?"

"What to do?"

"About the pregnancy."

"Ray, he's an OB-GYN. His office is full of stuffed animals and coloring books."

"Well, what are we going to do?"

Marisse dipped her cookie again. "What would you think about having it?"

"Having it?"

"Having a baby."

Ray choked off a swallow of beer. "C'mon, Marisse. You know how I feel about it. I thought you felt the same way."

"So did I. That was before I got pregnant."

"We've always known that we might have to face this situation, and we both know how we feel about it."

"I know," Marisse said. "It's just not that easy, now that it's real. I mean, it's living in there. It's a life."

"But it's not much of a life," Ray said. "It can't see or hear or think. It's like an amoeba, maybe, or a paramecium. It's not as much of a life as a mosquito, and we swat mosquitoes. It's not as much of a life as an earthworm, and we use them for bait."

"Please," Marisse said, and set her cookie aside. "It's the potential. It could be an artist or a singer. A scientist or a doctor. Or just a good person. These days, that's an accomplishment."

Ray looked around the old house with its white walls and minimal furnishings. He liked the spareness, the simplicity of their life. Many of their friends, upon first entering their house, would say, "Why don't you guys buy some furniture?" But he couldn't see cluttering up the place just because there was room to.

"Are you sure you're ready for the kid aesthetic?" he asked. "Our friends who have small kids, their houses look like the aftermath of a toy storm."

"Right," Marisse said. "But somehow I think this decision should be based on more than aesthetics."

"I don't know. You are your aesthetic. I've just never seen kids in our picture."

"I haven't either," Marisse said. "Well, maybe sometimes. I'll see a little girl and think, God, she's so cute—wouldn't it be fun to have a cute little girl to dress up and pal around with? But those are just flashes. Mostly I go for long stretches not really thinking about it. That's not like a lot of women. Most women I know—Tina, Cynthia Rosen, women at work—have this maternal longing. Ever notice how easily they hug children to them—even kids they don't know? They have this natural ability to be mothers, to live through their wombs and breasts."

"Sounds fairly mammalian," Ray said, and reached to stroke her.

Marisse pulled back. "They're going to fill with milk. They're already getting larger. Can you believe it?"

No, he couldn't. He couldn't picture Marisse, with her taut, high breasts, suckling a child. It just didn't fit. Since Marisse was out of reach, he stroked the cat. The cat purred and flexed its claws against his knee.

"I live more through my eyes and hands," Marisse went on. "I feel the need to sketch more than I do to hold a baby. I feel the need to create textures on a surface, to mush paint around. I can feel these things in my hands and arms. Sometimes when I see a cute kid, my hands move. But it's not to hug him to my breast, it's to sketch out the wisps of his hair, or to catch the way the light comes through his ear."

Ray nodded, sipped his beer. At least Marisse related to kids in some way. He sometimes wondered if he did at all. Oh, he got on well enough with kids. He got a kick out of his nieces and nephews, whom he saw at Christmas and in the summer at family reunions. But mostly he didn't think about kids. He had never had the desire to be a father. He had never wanted to reexperience childhood through children. Whenever he thought of his own childhood he felt a minor sadness, the same emotion he had felt back then: a kind of longing, a hollowness as he had apprehended the world and knew not what to make of it. He had been able to keep it at bay with games and playmates and the usual childhood obsessions. When he was twelve and obsessed with baseball, he could pitch a ball at the wall of the barn for hours. But it didn't intersect with the rest of his life, and as soon as he stopped pitching the ball, the hollowness would return. He tried getting his father to play catch with him, but the old man would be tired from work. The old man would make himself a highball and set a lawn chair in the shade of the house, and play "catch," gloveless, from a sitting position. When Ray had Little League games, usually it was his mother who attended. She smoked, and on the rides home from games or practice, Ray would ride in the backseat with his nose out the window, like a dog.

He had always assumed, throughout the confusion of adolescence, that one day the strangeness of the world would clear up and the hollow feeling would disappear. He'd understand the way the world worked: the mysteries of love and sex, of career and society. And to some degree that had happened. He had become an adult. He had found a woman he loved; he had found love. He had learned to make love, to earn a living, to file taxes, to make car payments, and in general to function in society. He had been happy. Somewhere along the way the hollowness had been filled up or squeezed out. Or hardened over, he thought. A tree could grow a burl around a hollow spot and then live on. You could look at the familiar surfaces in your life—the quiet pulse of your street, the reassuring chatter of your neighbors in their garden—and take satisfaction in their familiarity. By these illusions we get through the day. He ran his hand across the leather arm of the couch, felt the prickly little scars from the cats' claws, the wrinkles in the hide from the tanning process or perhaps from the flexing of the animal itself. He looked around the living room—the old house with its wide moldings and spalled plaster—and he marveled at a century's footsteps echoed in the cupped stair treads, a hundred summers' sunshine falling on exactly the same burnished patch of maple floor. He and Marisse had been happy here. They had grown into their adulthood within these walls. They had avoided encumbrances. They had traveled light.

"I want to leave a small wake," he said to Marisse. "I want to experience as much as I can, but I want to do it without leaving ripples behind, without creating monuments—" But he stopped himself, because the monuments he meant included the kind that Marisse made when she painted paintings, and it included other monuments that people create: businesses that bear their names, books that carry their vision, manifestations of the self that live on past one's natural life. He especially did not want to create a living monument, a family that bore not only his name but also his genetics, his facial expressions, his hair coloring, his tendency towards health or disease. Ray did not even want the most common monument of all, the gravestone. When he passed on, he wanted to be buried in a plain pine box with no marker of any kind. Probably they wouldn't let you do that, he figured. Probably even your death was regulated, and the sons of bitches would mandate what you could and couldn't do with your own carcass.

"No kids," he said.

Marisse set down her tea and settled her hands across her stomach.

"I guess I have to say it," she said. "I'd rather make art than kids. Maybe that's selfish, but that's the way I feel. Why should I do something I don't want to, just because everybody else says it's the thing to do?"

"Right," Ray said. He eased the cat off his lap and drew Marisse close. "It's agreed, then."

Portsmouth was an hour's drive from Hurley. In front of the clinic, a small knot of protesters huddled together in the rain.

"Drive on past, Ray," Marisse said.

"But this is the place," he said.

"Just drive around the block, please."

Marisse looked at the protesters and then turned back to Ray. "The woman on the phone warned me about them. She said to just walk past. They can't block our way unless they want to be arrested."

"Okay," Ray said.

Marisse sighed. "They freak me out a little."

"Don't you worry," Ray said. "I'll take care of them." He said this in a calm voice, but inside he felt heavy, laden.

The only parking space was in clear view of the clinic. One man, gaunt and wet, watched them get out, and he must have alerted the others, because as Ray took Marisse's arm and headed toward the clinic, five other faces turned their way. Ray held Marisse tightly and faced the protesters head on. They were a sorry lot, soaking wet from the rain, two men and four women. Working-class, they looked like. Fanatics, he thought. Just let them try something. They stood on the sidewalk in two rows, forcing Ray to guide Marisse between them. The first woman held out a photograph of a bloody fetus, shoved it into Marisse's face.

"If you're using this clinic," she said, "you're both murderers."

"Murderers," somebody else said.

Marisse kept her face down. Ray kept them moving. "Baby killers!" another woman hissed.

One of the men held out a galvanized pail. He held it open towards them, so they couldn't miss the bloody scrap of meat in the bottom.

"This is how you'll kill your baby," he said. "Leave it to die in a bucket."

Ray pushed past them. Marisse had a vise grip on his arm. At the front door of the clinic, a policeman stopped them. "You have an appointment?" he asked.

"Yes," Ray said.

"Name?"

Ray told him, and the officer checked a clipboard. "Right, Mr. and Mrs. Vann. Come on in. We check everybody coming in, just to make sure."

There were several other people in the waiting room, almost all women. The oldest was about Marisse's age; the youngest looked to be about thirteen. She wore a denim jacket and kept sniffling. She was with her mother, who chain-smoked and read magazines. Ray was surprised they'd allow smoking in a medical facility, but then he remembered that this was no ordinary medical facility. People didn't come here with respiratory ailments or chest pains. From time to time a door would open and a nurse would step out and call a woman's name. The woman would get up and follow the nurse. One woman, about twenty, was with her boyfriend. When he tried to follow her, the nurse made him sit back down.

"Mr. and Mrs. Vann?"

A woman stood at a different door and motioned them into a small conference room. She introduced herself as Denise St. John and explained that she would be their counselor. She was about forty-five. She wore her hair and clothes loose, and she had friendly wrinkles at the corners of her eyes. As she explained their options—"carry the baby to term and put it up for adoption, or terminate the pregnancy"—she spoke in a matter-of-fact way that Ray found comforting. The heaviness lifted a little. He could tell by the way Marisse nodded brightly that she felt the same way. Denise St. John looked at them each in turn as she explained the risks of the procedure: "perforation of the uterus, or the possibility that all the content is not removed, which could result in an infection of the blood." Her eyes were direct but friendly and there was an implied *Don't worry—I have to tell you all this but you'll be okay* in her manner.

"When was your last period due?" Denise St. John asked.

"Two and a half weeks ago," Marisse said.

"Okay, we'll get you on the schedule." Denise St. John scribbled into a calendar and went on to explain the procedure: general anesthesia, dilation of the cervix, evacuation of the uterus. Ray cringed at the phrase "vacuum out the contents," as if this were just a little Saturday-morning cleanup job. The heaviness resettled around his heart.

"Can I answer any questions for you?" Denise St. John asked.

"How long will it take?" Marisse asked.

"The actual procedure takes only a couple of minutes. You'll be under for seven or eight. But you should plan a half day for the whole thing, between preparation and recovery. You'll be driving, Mr. Vann?"

Ray nodded.

"Do we have to face those people again?" Marisse asked, nodding toward the front of the building.

"I'll let you out the back way," Denise St. John said. "You don't need to feel any worse than you already do."

Marisse held back the tears until she was in the car. She cried for a while, and Ray comforted her as best he could.

"Oh, God," she said. "You know what it felt like, being in there? In that waiting room? Like, I don't know, Auschwitz. Like a concentration camp. When that nurse kept coming out for those women, it was like they were being called into the death chamber."

On the way home, Ray thought about the protesters. How ugly they had been. Ugly, but effective. Intimidating, even. They could stop a less committed couple, or a more vulnerable woman. And who wouldn't feel vulnerable, going there in the first place? He felt bad that Marisse had to go through this, and he rested his hand on her leg as they drove.

Something else about the protesters stayed with him, in the shadow of his thoughts, and it wasn't until he had drifted back to his fence plans that he remembered what it was. Their eyes. When he had first locked eyes with the gaunt protester, the man's eyes had been as empty as Barr's in the planning board meetings. But when the man held up the bloody bucket, his eyes snapped with hate. These were dangerous people. You could put them into any situation, tell them what to do, and they'd do as they were told. Maybe Marisse's concentration-camp image wasn't so far off the mark.

The eyes of the protester stayed with Ray, and he thought about his fence again, and then he began to get an idea.

When Ray told Cell Four about his fence, they agreed on two things: it would be the riskiest mission yet in terms of public opinion, but it would also be the most successful in achieving their aims.

"Barr'll never sell that house," Leonard said.

"Everybody's going to think you're nuts," Susie said. "I mean sick, sick, sick."

Ed was quiet, looking down at his big hands.

"Ed?" Ray asked.

"You'll have to go before the planning board," Ed said. "Show 'em the plan for the fence, but leave out the rest." Then he got up. "I'm going to sit this one out. It's out of my league."

Ray drew up a plan and submitted it to the planning board. It called for a six-foot stockade fence across the back of his lot. The planning board sent a letter to the abutters notifying them that this would be discussed at the next meeting, and that if any abutter wished to participate in the discussion, he or she should attend.

Neither the Rosens nor Ed, his abutters on either side, came to the meeting. But Barr came in at the last minute. His eyes flickered around the room. There were a few other people—a guy wanting to build a deck off his house, approved; a couple wanting to convert their garage into an apartment, deferred to the building inspector. When Ray's plan was called, John Boylston read the specifics to the rest of the board, and then asked for discussion. One of the board members, an older woman with bifocals, asked, "What is your intent in building this fence?"

"Privacy," Ray said. "As you know, a subdivision was recently built in back of our houses on Monadnock Street, and I'm seeking to regain some of the privacy I formerly had."

"Seems reasonable," one board member said, and the others grumbled their agreement.

"Any abutters have anything to say?" John Boylston asked.

Barr looked around and then stood up. "I'm Bill Barr, the abutter to the rear. If this fence is put up in good faith, fine. But to tell you the truth, I smell a rat."

"What do you mean by that?" John Boylston asked.

"The abutters to my property up there have done everything they could to prevent me from doing business. They vandalized my sign, they harassed real estate agents. I want it to stop."

"It looks like a pretty straightforward fence to me," said John Boylston. He turned to Ray. "Is it your intention to build a fence for privacy?"

"Privacy. Absolutely," Ray agreed. "I'd ask the board to bear in mind that if Mr. Barr had abided by the site plan approved by the board, and left the agreed-on fifteen feet of trees as a buffer, I would have no need to put up a fence."

In response, the board all managed to have their eyes aimed some other direction. Barr spoke up, though.

"Wasn't enough room to leave fifteen feet," he said. "We found that out during site prep, so we had to cut some trees down."

"He cut them all down," Ray said. "Go out and see for yourselves. There's not a single tree on the lot."

"Look," Barr said. "I'm trying to provide affordable housing to people that are having a tough time in this inflated market, and this guy—"

"Excuse me?" Ray said. "Are you making an accusation here?"

"You're goddamned right I'm making an accusation. You scumbags up there have played dirty ever—"

John Boylston cut him off and pounded the table for order.

"Settle down, or I'll by God throw you both out!" he said, glaring.

The board put their heads together, and then John Boylston broke the huddle and spoke. "I realize—we realize—that the whole development up there on Monadnock Street has caused strong emotions on both sides. But it's there, and that's that. Mr. Barr, we ask that you be more considerate of your neighbors—they were there before you were, and they don't appreciate some of the language you use. Rightly so, I might add. Mr. Vann, go build your fence. But understand that antagonizing Mr. Barr has got to stop."

"Thank you for approving the fence," Ray said.

That weekend Ray and Leonard dug the postholes and set the posts. The weekend after that they hung the stockade panels—six feet high and a solid wall at the back of the yard. It blocked out the first story of the leaning saltbox, but it sure made the lot seem shorter.

"You going through with the rest of it?" Leonard asked.

"If Barr doesn't have to abide by his plan, why should I?"

The next morning Ray went down to Toyland and bought two dozen dolls. Not Barbies, not Raggedy Anns, but baby dolls, the kind that look like real babies. Tiny Tears, Baby Sparkles, Rub-A-Dub Dollies. Then he went to the hardware store and bought a half pound of 16-penny nails, a can of red Rust-Oleum, and a handful of small paintbrushes.

That evening toward dusk, Cell Four—minus Ed—gathered back by the fence. They divided up the dolls, and this is what they did: They nailed the dolls to Barr's side of the fence, drove the spikes through their heads, their stomachs. In putting up a Lull-A-Baby, Leonard hit the voice-box, and the thing gave out a plastic "Waaah!"

"Jesus!" Leonard said, jumping back. "This gives me the creeps!"

It gave them all the creeps. But also, in some way, it drew them in. As the dolls hung there with their wide-open, innocent faces, the hammer blows became harder, more urgent. They'd drive the spikes through, and then deliver a couple of extra blows, smashing a face or opening an abdomen. When they finished nailing and smashing the dolls, they splashed paint over the faces, arms, and legs, dripping the red paint down the fence. And then they stood back, panting and sweating, and beheld a wall of carnage.

They looked at each other in silence, as if seeing new people, and then, in the gathering darkness, they parted ways.

Marisse went out in the morning, and came in pretty upset. "You've gone too far," she said.

"It's only temporary," Ray replied.

"I have to live in this town. You don't. You commute off to Massachusetts every day, and sleep here at night, and putter around on the weekends. But I work right downtown. I see the people of this town in my job, at lunch, in the supermarket. You don't have to face them, but I do. I can't believe you've done this, Ray." She clutched her hands over her stomach protectively. "Especially now."

Ray tried to calm her, told her it wouldn't be up long, that it was just there to send Barr's blood pressure off the chart, and that nobody'd make much of it. But he knew and she knew that it was there for however long it took. This was no quick strike, no run-and-gun. This was a siege. And they both knew that something would be made of it.

It started almost immediately. Ray got a call from a real estate agent the first night. "What is that in your backyard?" she asked.

"In my backyard?" Ray asked. "I have a clothesline, a deck, a few shrubs—"

"The fence," she said.

"Yes, a fence, too. It provides me some of the privacy I lost when Barr violated his building plan and cut down all the trees."

"I brought some clients out there today, a very nice couple. They would have made nice neighbors. You know what happened when they saw your fence?"

"What's that?"

"The woman got sick. She bent over and retched before she even made it back to my car. Needless to say, they didn't make an offer on the house."

"You sure she didn't just get a glimpse of Barr's construction?"

"Listen, I can't bring clients out with that thing there. Are you going to leave it up?"

"Ma'am," Ray said, "if Barr is free to blast the earth down to bare dirt and throw up a house that's ready to keel over, I'm free to paint my fence as I want to. If his house or my fence is bad for your business, I guess you'll just have to take your business elsewhere."

"I guess I will. I don't have any choice. But I want to tell you this, Mr. Vann. You're a sick man. You ought to seek help."

Over the next couple of days, Ray got more calls from real estate agents, with about the same message: he was sick, he was an abomination, he ought to be shot. Because the fence was high, he couldn't see people's reactions when they saw it. But on Saturday morning, as he was going from his garage to the back door, he noticed a man in the upstairs window of the saltbox, looking at him. The man turned and spoke, and his wife joined him at the window. They looked at Ray until he had to turn away.

The heaviness was still with Ray on the ride home from Portsmouth. It hung in the air between him and Marisse, connecting them like a palpable cord. It had been worse on the way over to the clinic and had weighed him down during the four hours in the waiting room. And now, though it was still there, he felt the worst was over. Marisse was mostly silent. She wept from time to time and she was clearly in pain, but mostly she stayed quiet and tried to sleep. When they had finally allowed Ray to see her, he had been shocked to see how pale she was.

"There was so much blood," she told him. "When they had me change this diaper, it was everywhere."

Her voice was weak, and she reclined the seat back and closed her eyes.

"I'm not so wet now," she said. "But the cramping is bad."

He wished he could do something to help, wished he could take some of her pain onto himself. It seemed so unfair, that she had to bear all of it, that *her* body had to be so violated for this accident of love. He could cry himself, at the thought of them going into her body, that beautiful body he so enjoyed unveiling during love-making, or so admired as she emerged from the shower. It tore him up to think of her enduring it all for something he had helped create—it weighed on him so heavily that his own abdomen cramped.

At home he made her a bed on the couch and wrapped her in a quilt and brought her tea. She slept and he read, and when she had to go to the bathroom to change her pad, he walked with her.

Once, she woke up crying.

"What is it?" he asked, and took her hand.

"I dreamed I had a little sister," she said. "We were swinging on the swings in the park."

He stroked her hair.

"God, Ray. I feel so empty."

He knew. But there was nothing to be done about it. In his way, he was empty, too, and only with the passing of time would they grow a burl around this particular void.

Ray took the next week off work to be with Marisse. On Monday, Barr came out to look at the fence. Ray saw the truck pull up behind the Rosens', so he went out to the fence with a hammer.

Barr was standing by the slanty wall of his saltbox, hands on his hips. His eyes were narrowed to slits, and the toothpick flickered at the corner of his mouth. Flick. Flick.

Ray gave a couple of whacks on the corner post and then stepped around.

"Well hello, neighbor," he greeted Barr.

"You asshole," Barr said.

"Like my motif? A bit apocalyptic, I'll admit, but in keeping with the new neighborhood."

"Asshole. Fucking asshole."

"If you have an aesthetic statement to make, make it, I always say. Kind of like your no-square-corners architecture."

The toothpick flicked again.

"I'll rip all that shit down," Barr said. "I'll send a bulldozer out and take the whole fucking fence down."

Ray grinned at him and raised his hammer.

"You touch my fence, Barr, and I'll have your head up here with these dolls."

Barr turned and walked away to his truck. Burned the tires.

Came back with a police cruiser. A young town cop got out, affixed his hat to his head, and walked over with Barr. Ray was still pretending to be working on the fence. The cop and Barr stood by the house, talking quietly. Then the officer came over.

"You Mr. Vann? Mr. Ray Vann?"

"Yeah."

"I've got a complaint from Mr. Barr that you threatened him with violence."

"He threatened to tear down my fence. I merely suggested he not attempt that."

"Mr. Vann, you are hereby notified that a complaint has been filed that you threatened Mr. Barr with violence. Should any violence come to Mr. Barr, you will be among the first parties questioned."

"If he doesn't touch my property, I'll refrain from committing violence to his person."

"What about the fence, officer?" Barr asked.

"Outside my jurisdiction," the cop said. "Talk to the building inspector."

Later that day, Barr came back with Jim O'Brien. Ray had been waiting for this, so he went out.

"Hello, Jim," he said. "Haven't seen you out here in a while."

"Jesus," O'Brien said. "Don't you people ever give up? This is the most disgusting thing I've ever seen."

"Disgusting?"

"You're in violation of your building permit, Ray. This was never approved."

"You probably wouldn't know what was approved, Jim. You weren't at the meeting."

"I've reviewed the plan. You were given approval to build a six-foot stockade fence. Period."

"Nobody said I couldn't paint it as I want to."

"We're not talking about the color of the paint. You've built a spite fence. There's a town statute against that. You can't build a spite fence in this town," O'Brien said. "This garbage is disgusting—I wouldn't want my wife and kids to walk back here and see this."

Ray merely nodded. He wouldn't want them to, either.

Barr piped up, "If he's violating his plan, what's the town's recourse?"

They had obviously worked this part out. O'Brien turned to Ray.

"It's my job to ask you to take those dolls down and paint the fence regular. If you don't do it, the town will probably take legal action against you. You may be forced to tear the whole thing down."

He delivered this in his most officious small-town manner. Barr smirked around his toothpick.

"If the town wants to sue me, fine," Ray said. "But let me remind you of a few things. First, I don't know that you could win a suit like that. I'm free to decorate my property any way I want to. Second, let me remind you that Barr is in violation of *his* site plan—he didn't leave the fifteen feet of trees between my boundary and his house. As a matter of fact, his house sits exactly fifteen feet off my stone wall. So if the town is going to start enforcing the plans it approves, let it start by forcing Barr to move his house back ten feet and to replant all the big oaks and pines that were here.

"And third, Jim, since you brought it up, is this matter of you doing your job. If you approved that finished house," Ray said, nodding toward the saltbox, "I'd like to know how you approved that back wall. It's out of plumb a good six inches top to bottom, and that can't be considered structurally sound."

O'Brien and Barr turned around to look. O'Brien backed off a little to get the view. He was seeing it for the first time. Barr glanced at it and then looked off into the subdivision, as if he had better things to consider.

"So think about it, Jim," Ray went on. "Because you weren't doing your job, this house got built out of plan. Any lawsuit against the town would be a direct result of your negligence. It would be expensive to resolve. And because you approved a house with an out-of-kilter supporting wall, you may be endangering people's lives. If you want to make an issue out of my paint job, go ahead. But I assure you, I'll have my say too."

O'Brien pretended to be studying the slanty wall. Barr pretended to be studying his other houses. Finally O'Brien turned to Barr.

"Well, Bill, you want to pursue this?"

Barr looked at the fence, at Ray. He spat his toothpick onto the ground.

"Fuck the cocksucker," he said. "Fuck him and his fucking fence."

The following week three letters appeared in the paper describing Ray and his fence as "sick," "twisted," "a blight on the community." This brought out a wave of gawkers, driving in and out of the street, tramping all over Barr's lot. At times there were four or five cars in front of the saltbox, and not one of the parties had come to see the house.

Before long, the neighbors had had it with Ray and his fence. Those who were already cool to him after the Red Baron moved in—the Bains, the Bartolomeos—now completely shut him off. They ignored him when he drove past, even when he waved. The Rosens next door were still civil, but Ray could sense the distance. If Cynthia was in her yard when Ray stepped out, she'd turn away or go inside. Even Ed Jacques backed off some.

"You really raised some hell with that fence," Ed said. "Thelma says she's surprised you've let it go this long."

The next week there were more letters in the paper. Only now there were as many supporting the fence as opposing it. "Bravo, Mr. Vann!" one read. "You've done what we all wished we could do: take control over our own neighborhoods, instead of being overrun."

During this time, Marisse got back on her feet. She went to work, had lunch with her friends. She functioned normally, but Ray could tell she was depressed. Denise St. John had said this would happen, that it was the same postpartum hormonal shift that birth mothers feel. Ray and Marisse accepted it as normal, but still, it was there. Once, when they were out to dinner and there was a young family in the next booth, the kids telling their parents about dinosaurs, Marisse had gotten so upset they had to leave. "I'm sorry," she said. "I can't look at a child or a pregnant woman without wanting to cry."

Days passed, and the fence stood between them. Marisse wanted him to take the dolls down.

"I can't take much more of it, Ray," she said. "All I hear anymore is your fence this, or those dolls that. I've stopped going to the diner for coffee. I want to go back to the way we were before any of this happened."

"Things change. We've just got to see it through."

"I don't know," she said. "I don't know if I like the looks of what we're going to be on the other end. What are we doing here, anyway?"

"Doing here? Like, Hurley?"

"Yes, Hurley. This street. This house. Look, we're not the average suburban types. We're not going to put any kids into the neighborhood on bikes or skates. We're not into having the neighbors over for barbecues. You commute an hour towards Boston, and whenever we want to go out, that's where we go. That's where our interests are. I could get a good job in an agency down there, or on a magazine. I don't see what we're doing out here, is all."

"Living our lives is what we're doing."

"Right. I draw up ads for the latest, greatest janitorial service or hair stylist, and you chase around in the dark after some poor bastard contractor. Some lives we're living. A couple of real world-beaters, Ray."

By late November the fence furor died back, and the real estate news concerned itself with the general downturn in housing starts. By Christmas the housing market was in decline throughout southern New Hampshire. Nothing was moving. Barr did not even bother plowing out his unsold houses. Ray tramped through the snow one weekend to have a look at the fence, and there were all the dolls doing their duty, little tufts of snow on their heads and shoulders, the red paint fading a bit. They looked so cold and brittle.

With the fence no longer in the public eye, Marisse calmed down and settled into her winter routine of work and evenings in her studio. The backyard was snowed in, so they didn't spend any time back there. They practically forgot about the other side of the fence. Ray joined the health club and played racquetball after work instead of walking in the woods. By February, his pants began to feel looser at the waist. He started running around the indoor track, even lifting some weights. He took Marisse out to dinner in Boston, and they fantasized about living in the city.

By April, spring began to show: robins flitted about the yard, motorcycles disturbed the peace, real estate activity increased. As Ray removed the storm windows, raked up winter-dropped limbs, and mowed the backyard, he heard cars coming and going from Barr's. Doors slammed. Voices carried. One day Leonard came over with news. The saltbox had sold. Thelma Jacques had seen the paperwork down at the office.

"Ninety-nine thousand bucks," Leonard said.

Ray whistled. Ninety grand less than the original asking price.

"Way to go, Cell Four."

They walked back. Sure enough, the For Sale sign was gone. Somebody had planted daffodils along the driveway.

"Neighbors," Leonard said. "Death, taxes, and neighbors."

"Facts of life," Ray said.

"Susie and Bob Stevens are splitting up," Leonard said. "Susie quit the airlines. She's going back to San Francisco. Going to give it a shot as a photographer."

Along the driveway, the daffodils flared like a bright yellow path.

"Susie and I called it quits a while ago," Leonard went on. "She had a bad flight back from London—guy had a heart attack on the plane. It got her thinking about things, I guess. A change of heart at thirty thousand feet."

Leonard paused. There didn't seem to be anything for Ray to say.

"I'm glad it's over, in a way. I got tired of the pressure, the guilt. It got to be too heavy a load. I got tired, period. I got to where I just wanted to come home and have dinner, read the paper, do something with Amy or Seth, and not be making excuses to sneak out every few nights."

Later, Ray told Marisse about the house out back.

"Now that it's sold," she said, "would you please take down those goddamn dolls?"

That week Marisse pointed out a small item in the paper. It was a foreclosure notice on Monadnock Woodlands. The unsold properties would be offered at bank auction. Barr was among the first of many New England developers to be foreclosed during the early nineties; the boom always comes to a bust.

Ray put the paper aside and tried to derive some satisfaction from this, but he could not. It was a sad affair, the whole thing. Everybody lost.

Next Saturday morning, he took his claw hammer and wheelbarrow out back. A battered pickup was parked in front of the saltbox, its bed bearing household goods: a pine bureau, a box of kitchen utensils, a bed in pieces. A local move. Somebody moving from an apartment. With the claw hammer he began ripping down the dolls. Many of them simply popped off; others he had to work at. He loaded them all into the wheelbarrow. When he was about done, he looked up and saw a woman and two little girls by the pickup.

Ray strolled over to introduce himself. The woman was young and thin. When she saw Ray, she instinctively drew her girls in close.

"Hi," he said, waving his hammer. "Welcome to the neighborhood!"

The woman held the girls closely. She didn't speak.

"I'm Ray Vann. From the gray house there."

She nodded as if she knew.

"Oh, hey—don't mind all those dolls. A dispute with the developer—nothing to do with you folks."

The girls looked in the direction of the wheelbarrow, but their mother shook them straight. She just stared at Ray. She had dark hollows under her eyes. Her look was wary. Ray realized that no man had appeared from the house; she and the girls had been unloading the truck by themselves.

"Hey," he said. "You need a hand unpacking your truck? I can go get my wife and—"

"We don't need any help," the woman said.

"It's no big deal—"

"No, thank you."

The woman stared at him.

"Okay," Ray said. "If there's anything—"

"We don't need any help, Mr. Vann."

Okay. Okay. He backed off, waved his hammer. He wheeled the load of dolls across his backyard, and noticed how clear and blue the sky was over his rooftop. Higher up, a daytime moon, pale as a thumbnail, etched against the sky. He looked down at the dolls. Looked again. He was sure he glimpsed, in their vacant blue eyes, a reflection of the man he was becoming, here in suburbia.

TWELVE

Floating Heart

ay left early on Monday to beat the traffic. He liked to be the first person in the office. He'd unlock the front door, disable the security alarm, go around and turn on equipment. He loved these early-morning moments alone, when he could experience the office coming to life: the first, tentative chirps of the fax machine, the reassuring warble of a modem, the startled whir of the copy machine powering up. He made a pot of coffee and settled in at his desk. Cars would pull into the parking lot. Colleagues would stop by. A familiar routine, one that pleased him.

He sipped his coffee and gazed over the parking lot. A family of crows lived in the trees around the industrial park and hung out by the Dumpsters while the day was still quiet. Ray enjoyed their sleek black wings and their sociability, and he envied their easy flight.

He had seen something beautiful this morning. He had driven to work a slightly different way, meandered the back roads to get onto Route 3 in Merrimack. Just before the entry ramp, he passed the Anheuser Busch brewery. He looked, as always, for the Clydesdales, and sure enough, two were out grazing. Farther back toward the river, in the mists, were two other shapes, more slender. A pair of deer, grazing with the big draft horses. Ray pulled over and shut off the engine. It wasn't often that you saw deer in such a developed area. He got out slowly. There was no other traffic. A smell came to him from the barn: horses. A rich, earthy smell that he'd always loved. He tried to close the door quietly, but it thunked and all four animals looked up. One Clydesdale returned immediately to grazing, but the other one looked right at him. So did the deer. The Clydesdale's ears cocked, his tail swept. The deer shifted for a better look, twitched their ears. One raised a hoof and set it down gently. The Clydesdale's eyes locked onto Ray, soft, liquid, powerful. It was an unsettling feeling, and in a movement that felt both goofy and inappropriate, he waved. The three animals turned as if strung to the same nervous system, the deer bounding nimbly and waving their flags. The Clydesdale pounded after them, raising a muscular thunder off the river flats. As the Clydesdale built momentum he gained on the deer, and within fifty yards he was just on their tails. The deer looked surprised, veered sideways. The Clydesdale followed, more agile than Ray would have thought possible, and then, bursting forward and keeping pace for one brief moment, the big horse ran shoulder to shoulder with the bounding deer.

The sight had left him stirred and slightly exhilarated, and now, as a car pulled into the parking lot and the crows flapped off to the pine trees, he felt a craving for mobility, an urge to flee the familiar stasis of his desk. He sipped his coffee and waited for the feeling to pass.

He got busy with his work, and his edginess faded; a pleasant

tedium took over. By the end of the day he had forgotten the
Clydesdales entirely, except for one brief moment on his ride home,
when he found some running room and accelerated into the left
lane. He had a quick vision of the running horse, and then he had
to slow down for clogged traffic.

In his driveway, Ray smelled garlic and curry.

"Chicken stir-fry," Marisse said when he came in. "With a pea-
nut sauce."

Ray kissed her cheek; she said, "Mmm," but didn't look up. She
rapped the wok on the edge of the stove and kept stirring.

She was quiet over dinner, even though Ray tried to engage her
with his story about the horse and the deer. She fiddled with her
spoon, tapped it against the table like a telegraph key.

"I finished a painting today," she said.

Ray raised his glass to her. "Great," he said. "Congratulations."

"Do you want to see it?"

He did. She brought it down from her studio and said from the
stairs, "Close your eyes until I tell you."

Ray heard her fussing in the living room and turning up the halo-
gen lights.

"Okay," she said finally.

It was a good painting. Stronger, bolder than her previous paintings. Marisse was an abstractionist, and she painted on heavy paper
with oil and wax, created textures with sand, scraped away layers
with knives, and built up her image in a physical, interactive way.
Where her paintings just a couple of months ago had been peaceful
and serene, blues and grays, this one was darker and more violent,
with deep red edges protruding out of layers of black and blue.

"Wow," Ray said. "Spooky. Good. Really good, Marisse."

"Do you like it?"

"I like it a lot. It's your strongest painting. I like that mysterious
floating shape."

He pointed to the lower right side of the painting, where a dark
plum hung suspended between a deep blue background and a web
of unsettling red shards.

"What's its title?" Ray asked.

"I don't have one yet. You have to help me title it."

"Oh, boy. How about the ever-popular *Untitled?*"

"Come on, Ray. I mean it."

"Still Life with Train Wreck?"

She got up from the table and began clearing the plates away.

"I'm sorry," Ray said. "I'll have to give it some thought, okay?"

"Okay," she said, but she wouldn't meet his eye.

On Wednesday, Ray decided to surprise Marisse with a cookout. He picked up some lamb on his way home, and then he soaked it in a marinade of olive oil, garlic, and mint leaves from the herb garden. He threaded the dripping chunks onto skewers along with brilliant cherry tomatoes, cool green peppers, and pearlescent quartered onions. When the coals were glowing hot, he put the kabobs on the grill. The meat sizzled. A haze of seared lamb spread across the backyard.

He squatted on his heels by the charcoal pit. Marisse drifted from herb garden to flower bed, from juniper bush to red maple, inspecting leaves, snapping away dead twigs. She paused in front of the fence, not looking directly at it but at the dirt clods that eddied around the base of each fencepost, and then she came over to Ray.

"I hate that fence," she said. "It's such a scar."

"It's pretty gross," Ray admitted.

"We should plant some bushes in front of it. Something to make it fit into the yard a little better. Rhododendrons would work."

"Arborvitae, maybe. Blue spruce."

"Anything to cover it up."

She drifted off again, to the lilac bushes along the Jacques's property line. There was still a little distance between them, Ray thought. A little barrier that hadn't fully come down since the time of the dolls and what they referred to as Marisse's surgery. Ray turned the kabobs and basted them with the marinade. Flames shot up at the fresh oil. Smoke hung in the trees.

They ate on the deck, with the cool evening air rising from the grass. Twilight deepened around them. Fireflies blinked.

"Have you got a name yet?" Marisse asked.

"Hmmm?"

"A name for my painting?"

"Oh. Not yet. Still thinking about it, though."

"Mmm," she said. "Great kabobs."

Ray lit a citronella candle. A bat tumbled through the purple sky.

"Want to go to Boston this weekend?" Marisse asked.

"Maybe," Ray said. "Let's see."

"Let's go in on Saturday, Ray. We could do some bookstores and galleries in the afternoon and then go out to eat."

"Maybe. I drive down that way almost every day, remember?"

"I know, but I feel like getting out of Dodge, pardner. Like cutting loose a little."

Ray let it drop. He didn't want it to turn into anything. He plucked a long strand of grass from between the floorboards of the deck and used it as a toothpick. Fireflies blink to each other in code, bats find insects with sonar, and he couldn't talk to his own wife. He felt the night settle in, and he floated with the last wisps of smoke from the coals.

Friday afternoon, and Ray was glad to leave the office behind. He had just spent two hours in a meeting during which the usual egos clashed, the usual politics were played, and very little was actually accomplished. The air outside was balmy. Ray breathed deep, opened his sunroof, and accelerated out of the parking lot. He anticipated a fast blast up Route 3, but when he got to the highway he faced a sea of brake lights. Typical Friday-afternoon traffic—everybody headed for the White Mountains or Lake Winnipesaukee—and nobody moving faster than ten miles an hour.

If he were to live in Boston and commute out, he'd always be going opposite the traffic. It would be easier. Now he always seemed to be stuck in traffic—getting to work, getting home. It shouldn't be such a hassle. He thought of his evening ahead: dinner with

Marisse—burgers and beers at the Stone House, no doubt. Their usual Friday-night thing. Later, a video, a couple more beers, until the work week was a mindless buzz behind him and the weekend was an empty set ahead. Well, not entirely empty. He had to mow at least the front yard, edge the driveway where the snowplow had gouged it, and maybe paint the porch trim. A van in front of him stopped short; Ray slammed on the brakes. Was that all he had to himself, really—a couple of days, and then back into the sea of taillights on Monday morning? And those two days weren't really his: the yard and the front porch were for the neighbors. And of course there was Marisse, who wanted to go to Boston. If it were up to him, he'd let the lawn go to hell and the paint flake from the railings. He'd spend the weekend reading or listening to music, and maybe then, if he felt relaxed enough, he'd take Marisse into Boston for dinner.

Traffic surged forward and Ray surged with it, only to back off and then stop fifty yards on. What's the rush? he thought. Why the hurry to get home and do the same thing you did last Friday and will probably do next Friday? The same thing week after week: fight the same traffic to get home for the same burgers and the same beers. Only the videos changed.

On his left, a white Mustang convertible signaled to come over. A blond woman in red sunglasses. Hair tied back. Nice. Ray braked and waved her over. Nice package. And polite—she didn't just cut him off as most people did. As the shiny white Mustang eased across his bow, the woman turned and looked directly at him: she smiled and waved thanks.

She left her turn signal on. Spacy, Ray thought. He'd have to sit behind this blinking turn signal—how long? Still a mile below Route 495, where he might bail out and take a back way home. At this rate, it would be twenty minutes to the exit. Twenty minutes behind that blinking taillight. On the shoulder, cars were zipping by in anticipation of 495. Illegal, but if everybody was doing it, no cop was sitting in the grass up by the exit.

He tried to catch the blonde's eye in her rearview mirror, but she was all red plastic and dark lenses. He had always felt an affinity toward women driving alone. Following or passing them, he always imagined catching their eye and establishing the merest of relationships: contact, acknowledgment. The turn signal winked at him, but the blonde gave no indication. She looked so carefree in the open air. Off for the weekend. The lakes. No, the Maine coast. Off to meet her boyfriend. No—her lover. Her husband was away on business, and she was off to meet her lover. On his sailboat. Ray pictured her neat little duffel bag in the trunk. A white cotton sweater. Deck shoes.

The lane-cheaters whizzed by on the right, and then the Mustang eased out there. The blonde whipped a quick look around, her ponytail flashing, and she cut onto the shoulder and hit the gas. Gravel flew and she screeched away. Through her dust cloud, Ray saw the turn signal stop blinking. He gave a quick glance to his sideview mirror and cut over, accelerating after the receding white tail of the Mustang. What the hell, he thought. Go up 495 a ways and cut over above Lowell.

Chasing the Mustang, he felt unshackled, like a dog off its leash. See you around, suckers, he said to the other drivers, and suppressed the urge to give them all the finger. He would catch up to the blonde, pull up next to her on the highway. Meet her eye, smile.

But at the ramp to 495, she took the loop down into Lowell. Just another working stiff on her way home. A better profile than everybody else, that's all. Ray accelerated onto the highway, got up to cruising speed: sixty-five, seventy, seventy-five. The speed and the wind howling over the sunroof made him feel giddy. He couldn't imagine sitting back there in that traffic, crawling all the way to the state line. For what?

He switched the radio from NPR news to a rock station and then another. He hit all the presets, but nothing caught his ear. Hit scan and still came up empty, so he rummaged in the console and picked a tape. Plugged in some Miles and settled back as the quintet started cooking.

More like it.

The wind from the sunroof took his hair a little, and that felt good. He looked up at the sky and breathed deep. This was more like it, man. Blasting along in the breeze with Miles Davis and John Coltrane.

His exit came up and he watched the sign grow larger. He reached for the turn signal, but somehow couldn't manage to throw the switch. Not yet. Part of his brain said, *It's your exit, man—turn! Turn right!* and the other part said, *Gas her on out!* His fingers hovered near the signal, his foot quivered on the gas pedal, his brain did a quick toggle—*Turn! No, gas it!* and at the last moment he simply dropped his hand to his lap, stuck his foot in deep, and sped past the exit. At this moment he should have been slowing to country-road speed, winding down to a pleasant drive toward home and wife. Instead he was heading in the opposite direction at eighty per.

He throttled back to an even seventy and held it there. He knew what he was doing. Driving.

Just driving, man.

He had done this when he was a kid and needed to think things through: what to do about a girl, about parents, about the rest of his life. Just got in the car and drove all night. Wound up in Buffalo or Pittsburgh or, once, Wheeling, West Virginia. Pulled into town at dawn just as the miners were rolling out of the bars with beers in their hands. Just to drive was the thing: get in motion and stay in motion. Drive all night and whether or not he knew where he was going, whether or not he had a map, whether he thought his problem through, or whether he just tumbled along in existential free fall, he always wound up home the next day and he always felt better. Washed clean, somehow. Scrubbed by the miles and the rushing air.

But now, even though he drove without destination, he felt a tug toward home. Marisse was waiting for him. She'd be dressed to go out: a light spring jacket and loose pants. She'd go to the front window and look up the street.

He glanced at the clock. No, too early. She wouldn't expect him for another half hour.

He thought, as he often did when he needed to divert his mind to something that would make him feel good, of the woods in back of his home, of being in the woods and the late-afternoon sunlight filtering through the trees, dappling the forest. His thoughts shifted again and the sunlight fell on water, on ocean water as the waves rolled under the light and cast bottle-green reflections on his mind's eye.

Sunlight on the ocean. The ocean on an afternoon with the promise of summer in the air.

The road hummed under his tires, and he passed a sign: Portsmouth 40. Forty miles to the ocean. What the hell.

He saw Marisse at the window again, and he apologized to her. She let the curtain fall and turned away. Picked up a magazine and went to the front porch to wait.

On the northern end of 495, traffic thinned out and he could hold a solid seventy without getting jammed up. As he passed the exit for Amesbury, he noticed a car beginning to overtake him. A red Audi, coming fast and flat in the left lane. A woman driving. He gave it some gas, an attempt to keep up, but he was too late. She had the momentum and blew by him easily. In the second that she was abreast of him, he looked over: blunt-cut hair, business suit. A telephone. She was talking on the car phone, blowing by him at ninety. She had glanced at him, he thought. He was sure he saw her check him out.

What did he look like to a woman like that?

He regarded himself in the rearview. Okay. Not bad. The wind ruffling his hair a little. Crow's feet at the corners of his eyes. But-toned-down and neat. Not bad.

Or maybe, in his Honda sedan, she saw him as stodgy. Just a guy—less successful than she—on his way home.

Or maybe she didn't see him at all. She was by this time a pair of taillights half a mile ahead.

He passed through the toll booths on I-95. The sun was lower in the sky, the air cooler and salty. As the signs for Portsmouth came up, the emotions of his last visit here returned, and he suddenly missed Marisse. She would enjoy being with him right now, heading for the water and a walk along the waves, and then maybe find a little clam shack for some steamers. He hoped she wasn't worried. By this time she would have put down her magazine and gone inside, assuming he got stuck late at the office.

He drove up Route 1A to a pulloff overlooking a rocky beach. The lowering sun cast long shadows across the boulders. Here and there couples nestled in patches of the remaining light. Farther out, the sea was quiet. Low tide, a gentle rising and falling. He picked his way among the rocks and tide pools, feeling out of place in his office slacks and loafers. He sat on a smooth, flat rock and leaned back on one elbow. The tide pools shimmered in the long, golden light. His brain began to detune, adjusting downward from the frequency of the road and picking up the smaller signals around him. The easy drone of the waves, the viscous suck of tide against rock. He leaned over and looked into the nearest pool. A waterbug flitted, and he made himself feel the twitch in his own nerves. The seaweed fluttered, and it tickled the back of his throat. Antennae wriggled. Moss hissed. Bubbles rose to join the greater air.

A hermit crab struggled from shell to shell, making painfully slow progress. Up one side of a rock, down the other. Up again. He came to a brown-speckled shell, reached out with his pincers and pulled it toward him, stuck his head inside for a quick inspection. Dropped it and moved on. Nearby, a swarm of gnats hovered like a cloud. Out on the waves, a pair of gulls bobbed. So much life! So much wonder in the world! And underneath it all the steady surge of the sea, a breathing organism itself. Ray studied the shifting, aimless patterns of the waves, the deepening of the colors farther out. Shapes formed, disappeared. Almost formed, didn't. So much randomness. He looked at the couples nestled among the rocks.

How, with all the chance and uncertainty in the world, did two complementary beings find each other? How did they recognize each other and how did they make the impossible thousands of connections needed in order to pair up and mate? The initial eye contact, the first smile? The multitude of small acts necessary to bind them together? The myriad more to keep them that way?

He looked back at the hermit crab, picking its slow way. The odds are against us. The universe tends toward entropy. But somehow crabs find new shells. They even find other crabs. Men and women find each other, their hearts floating on a cryptic sea until the right shape is formed.

Ray lay back. He slept a little, or thought he did. As he surfaced into consciousness, he held on his lips the name of Marisse's painting. He crossed the rocky beach delicately, for the light had drained from the sky. By the time he found a phone booth, night was fully upon him. Dialing, he sent his love to Marisse like a message written in water. He listened to the phone ring and ring, anticipating the rare moment of her voice.

THIRTEEN

Moving Day

The house was just about empty. Footsteps on the bare floors rang louder than they ever had, and when Ray called to Marisse from another room, his voice echoed lightly off the naked walls. There were only a few boxes left— the fragile or valuable things they were carrying in the car. The two cats, too, who wandered from room to empty room looking mistrustful and confused, certain that their favorite sleeping chair or scratching hassock had been *just over there* for as long as they could remember.

All the other stuff had already gone. It was the first time Ray had ever used a real moving company, and it had been odd to see strangers carrying out the stuff that he and Marisse had always moved from apartment to apartment. But living in this big old house, they had accumulated things that would no longer fit in a friend's van or a U-Haul truck. They had moved so often in their early days, their constant motion had prevented material goods from catching up to them. Heck, a futon bed, a couple of overstuffed chairs, some crates and boards for shelves, and they had been able to move from married-student housing to summer cottage to young-professional apartment with one trip in a borrowed pickup. But now that they'd been in the same place for seven years, the paraphernalia of sedentary, stable life seemed to attach to them like barnacles on a moored boat: washing machine, dryer, refrigerator, big-screen color TV, king-size bed, leather couch and armchair, a real dining-room table with leaves and six chairs that matched—it was more than they could handle by themselves. So yesterday a long, low-bilged moving van had docked at the end of their driveway, two burly stevedores had lowered a plank, and, as steadily as an outgoing tide, the house had been emptied of its contents.

Marisse was a little blue about leaving. She stood pensively at the French doors looking out to the back yard.

"All the parties we were going to have," she said. "We had your friends from work over that one time, and my pals from the newspaper, but other than that, nothing. Do you realize we never had the neighbors over for a cookout once?" She nodded across the fence to the Jacques's backyard. "I mean, Ed and Thelma have never even set foot inside this house."

"Oh, well," Ray said. "Good fences make good neighbors."

"And the garden I was going to plant. Right." Marisse turned back into the kitchen. "A lot of work we did on this place, though. The wainscoting, the replastering."

"New roof," Ray said, remembering how his soles had stuck to the shingles as they warmed in the sun. "New plumbing in the bathroom. Refinished the floors."

"Painted the whole place," Marisse said. In the living room, she ran her fingertips across the white walls and moldings. "The new people will probably repaint it—or *gak!* put up some frou-frou wallpaper."

"Hey—it's their place. They can do what they want."

"Almost seems a shame after all that work," Marisse said. "Ray, I hope we're doing the right thing."

Oh, Jesus. If there was one thing Ray couldn't stand, it was indecision. He liked to make up his mind and move forward. Provided you were honest with yourself when you made the decision, the result was the right thing to do. If you went forward believing that, you'd be okay. If you waffled and constantly questioned yourself, you'd always feel insecure.

"Well," he said, "it's too late now if we're wrong. As of tomorrow morning, this place belongs to somebody else, and we sleep in our condo in Boston."

Boy, that sounded strange. It would take him a while to get used to that. He couldn't believe he was going to live in a condo. And for all his impatience with self-doubt, he couldn't help but wonder if he'd like urban life. If they could afford it. If they would miss the fresh scent of the lilacs just outside the window, the chirping of the birds when they woke up. The condo was in a nice building in the Back Bay, but he wondered how they would set up their basic life-support network. Where would they shop for groceries? There didn't seem to be any supermarkets nearby. Where would he change his oil? What would his new commute be like, driving out from Boston to Route 128? He had a lot of questions, and the rock in his stomach told him he didn't have the answers. But to reassure Marisse, he said, "We're doing the right thing. It's time to move, that's all."

"I know," she said. "I know it's time to move on."

For the last year, Hurley had begun to feel constraining—too tight around the neck and waist. All the restaurants had become too familiar, walks around town or drives in the country too uninspiring, and Ray could not stand going to a mall in order to see a movie. Marisse had outgrown her design job at the newspaper, and Ray had felt too closed in by the shopping plazas and drive-thrus.

So why move to the city? he asked himself. Surely if he felt hemmed in here, he'd feel it even more there. But no, he countered. The nature of the city had already been established. You knew what you were getting. In the suburbs you were subject to the bad taste of any developer with an eye for a fast buck and a friend on the planning board. If you wanted physical space, you moved to the country. If you wanted cultural space, the city. He wasn't sure which of these *he* needed, but Marisse needed the latter and he just needed to move.

Ray picked up his box of old 78-rpm swing records and turned to Marisse. "This is about it," he said. "The crystal and the pottery's already in the backseat. I'll put these records in the trunk, and then I'm going to say goodbye to Ed."

"Okay," she said. "Give him my best. I'll round up the cats."

The garage was empty except for the bright red Service Star lawn mower. Ray had always liked this machine. It looked so goofy and awkward sitting there in the middle of the floor, but Ray liked it because it was an honest machine: it did exactly what it was designed to do—no more, no less. It had always started on the second pull, always got the lawn mowed. He had cleaned it faithfully after each mowing, changed the oil and air filter at the beginning of every season. Although he and Marisse had offered at their yard sale every item for which they would have no use in Boston—and those that hadn't sold had gone to the Still-Good Shed at the dump—he just couldn't bring himself to sell the mower. He had no use for it in Boston, of course, but he had spent too many pleasant Saturdays with it to turn it over to some stranger who wouldn't care for it, or worse, would butcher it for its parts.

He had known all along what he would do with the mower, and now the time had come. He wheeled it down his driveway, into the street, and then up the Jacques's driveway.

Ed was in his garage, painting a door stretched across two saw-horses. "Hey, Ray!" he said, and waved his paintbrush.

"Hey, Ed."

"Beautiful day," Ed said. "Just painting the door to my poolhouse. Sun raises hell with it every year."

Ray nodded. It was one of Ed's perennial chores, like putting out tomato plants and resealing his driveway.

"You 'bout getting her in shape over there?" Ed asked.

"Just about," Ray said. "Down to the fine hairs."

"Place ain't going to be the same without you," Ed said.

Ray knew Ed meant this. Even though Ed had seen his share of next-door neighbors over the years, Ray knew the older man genuinely liked him. And he would miss Ed. Ed had been a steady, good neighbor. Always there to give him a hand with this project or that, or offer advice on the best place to buy heating oil or to get his car serviced. When Ray had told Ed he was moving, disappointment had flickered across Ed's wide, open face. And when Ray told him it was Boston, Ed had yelped as if pinched. "Why in the name of God are you moving down to that hellhole?" he'd asked. Ed drove trucks all over New England and had often cited his distaste for driving in and around Boston, the poor manners of the drivers, the congestion, the twisty routes. "Jesus H. Christ, Ray! It's all rush, rush, rush! It's nuts, kid."

But after Ed's initial shock he had calmed down and helped Ray spruce up his yard for the day when the house would go on the market: they edged the driveway, trimmed the hemlocks out front. And just two nights ago Ed and Thelma had had Ray and Marisse over for dinner, since all the Vanns' stuff had been in boxes.

Ray stubbed his toe against the rear wheel of the lawn mower. "I'm not going to have much use for the old Service Star down in Boston, Ed," he said. "Thought you might give it a good home."

Ed set down his paintbrush.

"Well thanks, Ray," Ed said. He squatted beside the mower and rested a big beefy hand on top of the pull-cord housing. He patted the thing like a dog. "It's in good shape."

"It's done okay by me," Ray said.

There was a lot Ray would like to say to Ed, about how much he appreciated living next door for the last seven years, about what a good neighbor Ed had been, what a good example he had set. But it was not in their relationship to say much about these things, so they stood in silence looking down at the mower.

"These little Briggs and Stratton engines run forever," Ed said.

"Always starts up," Ray said.

Ed stood up and turned toward the old refrigerator he kept in the rear of his garage. "You got time for a last beer with me, Ray?"

"Sure. That'd be great."

Ed cracked open two Buds and eased Ray out the front door of the garage. They stood in the sunshine sipping the beer and looking out at Ed's magnificent view of the Monadnocks. Ray had always enjoyed walking over to Ed's clearing in the evenings, watching the sun go down. Or in the afternoons, when a thunderstorm was brewing in the west, he could watch the drama of the sky and the mountains.

"I'll miss this place," he said. He held his bottle out toward the Monadnocks. "Not likely I'll have a view like this in Boston."

Ed snorted. "Not likely," he said. "I still think you're nuts."

Ray laughed. "Yeah, probably am." He knew how Ed felt about this place. It was his home. Ray thought it must be a good feeling to know where that place was and to be able to live there. So many people he knew, people of his own age and circumstances, lived wherever their work took them. They didn't live in a place they cared about, didn't live among people they cared about, didn't even work a job they cared all that much about—except as it provided a living. What Ray couldn't figure out was, what did you become after a lifetime of living that way?

Ed seemed to sense Ray's mood, and nodded toward the street. "Let's go sit a minute."

They sat on Ed's granite bench across the street, stretched their legs out toward the valley. The sun was warm on their shoulders. Ed tapped his knuckles against the granite slab.

"Hauled my share of this stuff," he said. "After I got back from Korea."

"Yeah?" Ray sensed that Ed wanted to tell him something, that he was working up to it somehow.

"Yeah. Worked for Putnam's and a couple others. Quarries were still some business in those days." Ed took a long pull at his beer. "My dad worked in the quarries. Crane operator. All his brothers and their father before them worked in granite, somehow. It was just what you did, here. I figured that's what I'd do."

Ray nodded.

"I never finished school," Ed continued. "I've told you that. When my dad died I had to quit school and support the family. Worked in the quarries, did anything I could. Delivered groceries, picked up trash. Then Korea came along and I didn't have any great skills to trade on, so I figured it was a good time to join the army. I was kinda scared, kid from Hurley going off into the world like that. But I figured what the hell, even the army beat picking up trash. I didn't do too bad in basic training, and toward the end the sergeant came through hand-picking guys. Special team, he said. Special team, *maybe*. You had to qualify. Even if you were on the hand-picked list you had to qualify.

"Well, I wound up on the list. They ran us through some special paratroop drills and rappelling and such. Wasn't that big a deal. I mean, by that time I was in pretty good shape, and I'd been crawling up and down quarries since I was five."

Ed paused and drank. He picked at the edge of the Budweiser label with his thumb. "There was this one drill, though. These bridges. They took us off to the rat's-ass far corner of the camp, where a creek cut between two hills. And across the little valley they had strung these bridges. Not regular bridges, of course. Emergency bridges. Get-your-ass-from-here-to-there bridges. Which is what we had to do: get from one side of the valley to the other. In a reasonable time, of course. You couldn't take all day. You'd start out across these bridges, and sergeant or somebody'd start firing a weapon and yelling and whatever else they could do to get you moving. Well, the first bridge wasn't bad. Three ropes—one for each hand and one for your feet. Even had a few little connecting ropes in between so you could pretty much walk across as long as you kept your footing. It wasn't bad, but I'll tell you, that little valley got a lot bigger once you were out in the middle of it and looking *down* on the treetops. I just kept putting one foot in front of the other and kept my eye on the far hillside. I didn't set any speed records, but I made it.

"The second bridge was two ropes, just one over the other about five feet apart. Of course, when you stepped on the lower one it stretched out the distance between the two, and you had to figure some way of keeping them together enough to traverse. At the same time, that top rope had no stability to it, so if you leaned your balance toward it, you could keep right on going face-first, or if you leaned away you'd go over backwards. Either way, you'd lose footing on the bottom rope and it was God's own bitch getting straightened out. Some guys didn't make it. They flopped around like a dragonfly in a spiderweb, used up all their strength, and never got their balance back. I was no lightweight, and I made that bottom rope sink halfway to the treetops and my arms stretched all the way out to the top rope. But I figured out how to get my lead foot under that bottom rope and draw some tension into it, and then scoot myself along with my hind foot. It worked as long as I kept my balance.

"The third bridge was the killer. One rope. Some guys hand-over-handed it like friggin' chimpanzys, whoopin' right on across. Other guys wrapped their legs over the rope and pulled themselves along with their hands. Some of those guys could get out and go like mother hanging out the wash. Others couldn't seem to budge. Well, I hugged myself to that rope and of course it sunk right away and I just slid out over the treetops halfway across, all I could do to just hang on. Then I don't know what happened. There I was at the bottom of this long V, hanging upside down over the valley like a goddamn possum, and I don't know, I just lost all my strength. I tried to pull myself up the long slope of the rope, but I couldn't hardly move. I just seemed to weigh too much to traverse a valley on one rope. I looked across to the far hillside and I began to think I wasn't going to make it. I tried again but it was like my legs was too much resistance and I wasn't going to be able to haul them all the way up that inclined rope to the other side. I thought about those guys doing the hand-over-hand and how they'd made it look easy. Probably *was* easier, I thought, with your legs dangling in space instead of working against you on that rope. So I unhooked 'em and as soon as I swung down onto my arms I knew it was a big mistake. I never felt so heavy! That rope just stretched and boinged like a rubber band, and my feet bouncing just above the treetops and sergeant screaming bloody murder and firing a carbine into the air, and I knew that if I was going to do it I'd better get moving, so I tried setting one hand in front of the other. But soon's I released my grip and felt all my weight on one hand, I had to grab back ahold. I couldn't hang on with just one hand! The other guys were hollering at me and I just didn't know what to do. I thought about those chimpanzy guys and how they'd made it look so easy, and I realized they were about half my size.

"Well, I began to consider the treetops. They weren't that far away. 'Course, these were full-grown beeches and oaks, so there was probably a good fifty, sixty feet below them, but I began to figure I could grab hold of something on the way down and maybe slow things up a bit.

"Then I heard the sergeant just a-boomin' out over the valley: 'You can let go, Jakes,' he hollers. 'There's a net.'

"I looked for a net but didn't see one.

" 'Let go, Jakes,' sergeant hollers. Jakes, that's what they called me in the army. Three years and nobody ever pronounced it right. 'Let go, Jakes! Rest of the team's drawing fire while you dilly-dally!'

"Well, I didn't have much choice. I couldn't go forward, couldn't go back, and was losing my grip anyway. So I just figured I'd take my chances with the trees. I didn't believe there was any net down there."

Ed took a long pull at his beer and gave a little snort. He looked at Ray and shook his head.

"I think the hardest thing I ever did was let go of that rope. But what happened was this: just as I was trying to let go, I got this picture in my mind of being back here in Hurley. I pictured myself sitting up on the cliffs at Tamarack Quarry with Thelma—we used to picnic out there when we was going together. It was summertime and I had my shirt off and we had just eaten sandwiches she'd made. We were looking out over the quarry so still and peaceful and the big trees all around and the Monadnocks in the distance, just like you can see them now, and I got it in my mind to do a nice long swan dive into the quarry, just all that still countryside around and me cutting through it like a jackknife. So I got up and edged out to the lip of the cliff, where there was a little breeze coming up the face of it, and behind me I heard Thelma take in a little breath, you know, and I teetered once and heard her speak my name. 'Ed,' she said. Just like that. 'Ed.' Matter-of-fact like, not afraid, not asking me to back down, just calm and steady, like she was with me, and I heard that in her voice and I felt so good and, I don't know . . . *complete,* that I just kicked on out into thin air, come what may. It felt like as good a time as any, what with Thelma there and the sun and all that beautiful countryside. That's what I thought of up there on that rope, and I held that picture in my mind and the sound of Thelma's voice, and I just let go.

"I went through those upper branches like a mortar shell. God, what a noise—crashing and snapping off timber. I grabbed for what I could. I took a pretty good-size limb in the rib cage and it knocked the wind out of me so I couldn't grab on to it, but it slowed me down some. Then I hit another with both legs and it spun me around and I couldn't hold that one either and dropped on down like a watermelon off a truck, not even close to a trunk or anything substantial, and I thought how there wasn't any quarryful of water at the bottom of this drop, and then you know what? There *was* a net. A ratty, torn-up, shitty kind of affair the sons of bitches had strung up through the trees, and a pretty poor excuse for a net it was, but it stopped me. I hit that thing and slung right down to about five feet off the ground, and after I stopped bouncing I just stepped out. I was pretty banged and bruised, but nothing serious was broken. Ribs cracked from the first hit, that's all. I took a pretty good razzin' from the guys. Cannonball Jakes, they called me after that.

"I didn't make the special team. I don't know whatever happened to those guys, but I wound up in the motor pool. Wound up driving trucks and repairing them, and you know what? It was the best thing that ever happened to me. I learned a skill. I drove trucks in Korea, and when I got back I started out driving for Putnam's, hauling granite from the quarry to the mill. Did some more of it for the other quarries, then some long-distance. Eventually I signed on with the paper mill, and trucks has been good to me ever since."

Ed looked out across the valley.

"Sometimes I wonder what would've happened if I hadn't let go that rope."

Ray nodded, finished his beer. He followed Ed's gaze out at the mountains. They shimmered green in the sun. A glint of reflected sunlight caught his eye: the lookout tower on Pack Monadnock. At night, from up there, you could see the lights of Boston, sixty miles to the southeast.

"I'll miss this place," Ray said. "It's been the best place Marisse and I have lived."

He stood up. So did Ed.

"You've been a good neighbor, Ed." Ray extended his hand.

Ed shook his hand, met his eye. "You too, Ray. You and Marisse have been good neighbors. Damn good neighbors."

They stepped into the street, took one more look across the valley. Ray began to ease away toward his place.

"You take care, Ed. All the best to Thelma. Tell her Marisse says so long."

"Good luck, kid. You know where we are."

Ray cut across Ed's front yard and thought how good the grass felt under his feet, how thick and solid. A good neighbor. He'd been a good neighbor. There were worse ways to be remembered.

Marisse was just bringing out the cats in their travel box. "That's it," she said.

"I'll take one sweep through," Ray said, although he knew everything was out. He walked through the empty rooms, treading lightly to keep the echo down. Stripped bare, the house looked like a different house—older, a little shabby, a repository of segments of many lives, to which his own and Marisse's were now added.

He got into the car and slammed the door. A box of pottery rattled in the backseat. One of the cats meowed.

"Bye, house," Marisse said, and gave a little wave.

Ray pulled out onto Monadnock Street, that thin strand of asphalt leading from their old life to their new one. He shifted gears slowly, gently, so as not to break anything.

HUMCA   FREDA

FREDA, JOSEPH
    SUBURBAN GUERRILLAS

Author In
Fiction Catalog
15th Edition

12.8.04   HUMCA   FREDA

HOUSTON PUBLIC LIBRARY
CENTRAL LIBRARY

DEC 95